I0653136

Unknown Country

Book 2

Light Of An Alien Sun

Sequel to

Light From A Distant Star

By

Gregory J. Saunders

Unknown Country, LLC

Original Artwork by Andres Rodriguez
Cover Design by Gregory James Saunders

First Printing

Library of Congress:

LCCN: 2008928887

ISBN: 978-0-6152-0756-8
PUBLISHED BY UNKNOWN COUNTRY, LLC
www.gregoryjsaunders.com

Printed in the United States of America

A Novel answer to a short question.

This one is for John Grace who asked, "My God, what happened on Earth?" after he'd read Light From A Distant Star. This is my interpretation of what an event of that magnitude would do to our little world and the people in it. Some would go crazy, some would cower in fear, and some would step-up!

Books By

Gregory J. Saunders

Unknown Country

Book 1
Light From A Distant Star

Book 2
Light Of An Alien Sun

Book 3
Light Of The Home World

Zahir
A Novella

Visit
www.gregoryjsaunders.com

Characters in Order of Appearance

Vi-t-ry (The artificial intelligence onboard an Alien Spaceship)

Lt. Colonel James Macintosh "Mac" Crowe (Commander of the Atlantis)
Captain Samuel Phillip "Buck" Rodgers (Astronaut)
Captain Cameron "Cam" Mitchell (Pilot of the Atlantis)
Lt. Colonel John "Cal" Sanderson (Astronaut)
Payload Specialist Susan "Sue" Rael (Astronaut on the Atlantis)
Payload Specialist Tyler Porter (Astronaut on the Atlantis)

Amad Al Zarie A.K.A. Taner Sagir (Terrorist)

Andy Michaels, Special Assistant to the Director (SPB Special Projects Bureau, A Black Operation that reports directly to the President)

Director Sean Evans (SPB)
Commander Silvio Sanchez (SPB, Counter Terrorism Unit)
Communications Specialist, Jerry Smalls, Recon (Korea)

Samin Ali Kasir (Terrorist)

Miles Johnson, Chief of the FCOD (Flight Crew Operation Directorate, NASA)
Deputy, Sam Marconi (FCOD)

Judith Kinsey, Resident of Aspen Colorado

President of the United States, Jon Talbot

Major Tim Givens, Special Forces Recon (Russia)
Captain Sam Winston, Special Forces Recon (Russia)

Specialist Lloyd Sylvan, Astronaut (Discovery)
Marx (Mystery Man of the SPB and Commander of the Enterprise)

Chief Scientist Dr. Jack Gordon (Space Station Unity)
Dr. Rebecca Carver, British Scientist (Unity)
Dr. Demitri Karkov, Russian Scientist (Unity)
Dr. Raymond Sammons, American Scientist (Unity)
Dr. Joshua Yakura, Japanese Scientist (Unity)

Commander Jules "Mad Dog" Sorenson (SPB and Astronaut on the Enterprise)
Colonel Sergei Kirkelev, Russian Air Force and Cosmonaut (Russian Contingent, Enterprise)
Li Tsinlung, of the Chinese National Space Agency (PRC Contingent, Enterprise)
Commander Robert Selkirk, Montana State Police
General Franklin Knight, Army of Christ (Militia)

Prologue

On the planet Mith Sul-Anroth
(Five Months Earlier)

Mid of night. That single point in time signaling the death of the old day and the birth of the new. On earth a bell would toll or clock chime. On Sul-Anroth it was marked by the shadows of a moon, or the turn of stars in the northern sky. That is if it was marked at all. Most of this world rarely witnessed the mid of night. Fast asleep after the cook fires had died away. Slumber the reward for the days toil, each new dawn a gift from the gods.

One of those gods watched over them as they slept. The Great Moon. The living moon. Deminal or SA-cee he was named, or a hundred others depending on the race of the believer or the sect he belonged to. That the moon held a living god none disputed, for only the Great Moon pulsed with life. The two other moons with which he shared the sky, wandered far and never changed. Grey and desolate. Dead things chasing each other on never ending paths. Not so with the Great Moon. He was constant. Always above them, no matter day or night. It was said by the elders that there was a time, far in the past, when the Great Moon had been truly dead. Had not pulsed with the inner fire. None truly believed this to be true because god was constant and never changing. They would simply believe the god had rested during those times, as he rested now. It had been half a season since the blue fire last covered his face. Then, in recent days the Great Moon had been very active, flickering in the sky, his face covered in bale-fire. The blue lightening making the shadows dance. Silent but comforting to those below. Now he rested again, whatever great task a god could be about was done.

Mano'luk was one of the few wisdom seekers of the race known to the clans and the People as Aranu. A being that rarely slept. One who could foretell great things by the wiggle of a hoary-moth as it flew about the fire before plunging to its death. How many circles did it make, how many false passes before the heat finally consumed it. Almost any item, be it animated as a migrating bird or still as an ancient moss bearded tree. Whether it lived with a heart which pumped the heated blood of life, or lay long dead and desiccated in the grave. Whether the stone of the earth or the clouds in the sky, they each told him things that were unknowable to other mortals.

Thus it was Mano'luk who stared at the sky as midnight approached. He sat cross-legged on a terrace of stone, chiseled into a high cliff before the small cave like entrance of the warren. The wide world lay before him and the vault of heaven above. Huge eyes, seemingly lit by an inner light of their own, looked out from underneath the partially cured furs of some hapless beast. Mano'luk was encased in the smelly covering, not bothered by the reek at all. As a statue he sat, watching the heavens for an event foretold, a change of worlds. He had no idea in what form that change would manifest, only knew that the earth had spoken and it would come to pass. His mind had wandered as it chased the possibilities. Earthquake or storm, enemies like a flood. Little did he know that it would be *all* those and more.

A flickering light caught his eye as the Great Moon suddenly sprang to life. Unconcerned he watched, thinking the god awaited the change as well. Then, just as suddenly, the blue light intensified, covering the moon entire in a display far more vibrant than ever before. The moon seemed to writhe in pain and the glow became unbearable to his night adjusted eye, the brightness penetrating the cave entrance and bringing forth two guards in curiosity. The flickering became a pulse of neon blue that seemed to rotate in great waves from pole to pole. Faster and faster came each beat until they matched the hammering heart in the Aranu seeker's chest. He stood, his hide coverings falling forgotten about his feet, his thin shriveled body bathed in the glow beating down from heaven as if their god had become a new and alien sun. Then the beating stopped and the moon became an intense blue wonder that flashed even brighter before being snuffed out.

His guards gasped as the world went completely black. Mano'luk blinked away his tears, eyes squinted until once again he could see. Then the gasp he heard was his own. Where once a god had stood, now only empty space remained. The night was much dimmer with the loss of such a major source of light, and perhaps that doomed Mano'luk. He stepped forward, arms reaching for something that was no longer there. Maybe the world spoke to him, maybe the winds carried a message. If such could be so, the words were lost forever. Mano'luk took one step too many. Without a cry he was gone, plunging from the precipice to the jagged rocks below. Gone was the Great Moon, gone was Deminal or SA-cee, and gone was Mano'luk, wisdom seeker of warren Kilkeep of the once great nation known as Aranu.

Dawn three days later.

A seeker of wisdom from a far different race watched the coming dawn, drawn there by a need far more base than searching for a god. His need was due to an overfull bladder that screamed its displeasure. Still, as relief flooded his body, Niloc-al-teal pondered once more the loss of the moon. What it meant for the world and what it meant for the clans. As Mano'luk had waited for great change, so did Niloc. He had the first budding awareness that events long awaited were now unfolding. A legend or a prophesy or simply a false hope. Which it would be would not be revealed until much later, and as he stood there, his feet firmly planted on the ground, above him the herald of a new age streaked across the heavens.

The twentieth and twenty-first centuries had witnessed many shuttle reentries, all but one under control and all beautiful to behold. But this was not earth and this reentry was far more spectacular. Atlantis had been thrown from orbit by forces even twenty-first century man could not understand. Out of control and plunging through the green atmosphere far swifter than her designers meant, she streaked across the sky, brighter than any shooting star those on the planet below had ever seen. It was a near thing for the astronauts and the scientists they'd rescued off the ill-fated Unity, and an omen of portent for Niloc. The Atlantis burned bright and very nearly suffered the fate of Columbia as heat tiles failed and super-heated vapor burned holes through her wings. She bucked and screamed as she fell, but she was resilient and after a few moments the bright shooting star was gone. An afterimage in Niloc's eye that would not be forgotten.

Though the Atlantis had ceased to glow in the early morning sky, her ordeal was not over. Her pilot fought to save her as she skipped along the upper reaches of the green tinged atmosphere, each bounce or twist a threat to roll the shuttle over and doom her to a headlong plunge to the ground. Fortunately, as they sank lower and the air thickened, the pilot's control increased and Atlantis was saved for the moment. But this was a planet two millennia beyond any semblance of civilization. This world had sunk from intergalactic travel to the depths of an old bronze age. There were no spaceports or airports on which Atlantis could land. There were no real roads. The best they the astronauts could hope for was a flat spot and great deal of luck.

No one was there to witness when the Atlantis at last landed on this alien world. None saw as she skipped along the ground, making the earth quake with each strike. Each touch of the shuttles skin leaving behind a scar in the earth and scorched brush and trees, many of them burning brightly as if lightening struck. Had a clansman or Aranu warrior been near they would have been struck dumb as the shuttle took flight one last time. Leaping across a dry wash, she pan-caked with an incredible din. Atlantis abruptly stopped, her spine cracked open and smoke and dust obscuring her final resting place.

To the alien warrior it may well have been a dragon come to claim him, breathing fire and destruction as it fell to earth. And had they overcome their terror long enough to bare witness, they would have changed the description from dragon to *chariot of the gods*.

Soon after the shuttle stopped, a hatch opened and the ship disgorged its occupants. The first humans to visit an alien world. Dazed and unknowing of their fate. Not knowing if the air would kill them. Unsure what dangers inhabited the empty plains around them. Wondering that they were still alive, uncertain of their future. Stranded with no technology and no way home. Theirs would be an odyssey that would catch the *clans* up in a whirlwind, and bring one lonely man who'd lost his entire family, to prominence in service to something called a human. Niloc and Lt. Colonel James Macintosh "Mac" Crowe would discover each other. The lone survivor of Clan Sar-too and the Drakil-at'sakal who was destined to save them all.

Several thousand light-years away, the destiny of another world was about to be shaken and redefined. The very force that put the Atlantis on the planet called Sul-Anroth, had blossomed suddenly and shockingly over a place called Earth. An event that sent shock waves through individuals, organizations, and governments alike. The very fabric of society torn asunder. Whether your home was called Earth or whether it was known as Sul-Anroth it mattered little. The world had changed, irrevocably and forever, and the cause and catalyst was a damaged and barely functional alien spaceship called Vi-t-ry.

Compiled from the Novel,
Light From A Distant Star

In orbit over the planet Mith Sul-Anroth
(Two Hundred Forty Years Ago)

The one who calls himself Vi-t-ry pauses to consider, both himself and the mission that drives him. That he is a thinking machine is obvious. Though far beyond a mere mechanism, as he is truly self-aware. And machine was not entirely factual. Vi-t-ry was a complex construct containing not only the entity known as Vi-t-ry, but many other machines, and many other systems that comprised the whole. Vi-t-ry knew he was not *alive* in the biologically accepted sense, but had been created by true living beings. Beings who called themselves the Collective. Vi-t-ry's knowledge extended to the fact that he was a vessel. A vast craft with the ability to travel through space, and that he'd traveled to the planet he currently orbited with an armada of other similar vessels. A flotilla intent on war. Those other ships were his brothers. Evidence remained of some of them. Damaged and lifeless.

Vi-t-ry himself was damaged, and lifeless. Though with a difference. Vi-t-ry *lived* in his artificial way, and he *felt* and had emotions similar to any organic life-form, yet no *life* of the Collective remained in him or on him. That they had existed his damaged database left no doubt. Every member of the Collective crew had been damaged in a great battle which had killed his brother ships, and left Vi-t-ry a floating wreck. Left him dead and cold. Vi-t-ry had no idea how long he'd lain that way and no idea how he came to be revived. He knew only that he was a ship-of-war, and the planet he found himself orbiting was not his home. He'd scanned it and found no real technology and none of the living beings known as the Collective. Though he was not completely sure this was correct because his sensors were so greatly damaged. Were he flesh and blood, he may have moaned in frustration. His databanks held no name for the planet below, but they held enough other data to clearly prove home was to be found elsewhere.

As his systems repaired themselves, Vi-t-ry began his search for home. A search which would last over two hundred and forty revolutions of this planet around its sun. Across the heavens, star by individual star he searched. Sometimes finding planets with advanced technology, and most times nothing but the lifeless signature of the stars themselves. One such search revealed a civilization far in advance of the ones known as the Collective, and this fractional moment of contact unleashed an attack which left Vi-t-ry reeling in pain and even more damaged. Yet at the end of his search he had found *home*. At least the closest match his damaged database could find.

The electronic emanations he'd tasted from that distant glowing system with a beautiful blue world were so familiar he ached for them. Unfortunately, a puzzle still remained. *Home* was not as he remembered. It was as if *home* had been radically changed or damaged. Perhaps not yet recovered from the galactic war. Perhaps not back to a level that they could communicate with him. Yet everything else was so tantalizingly familiar. He knew what he must do. Vi-t-ry must go there. Travel the billions of miles to the system, be it his home world or not.

As Vi-t-ry built up energy and waited for his repairs to be completed, (they were limited repairs due to his great need for a dry dock) Vi-t-ry opened a small two-way path to his destination. Imprecise as it was, this hole allowed a number of objects to be transported from home and into orbit around the planet over which Vi-t-ry hovered. Objects that were manufactured machines. This was unintended on Vi-t-ry's part and further complicated the mystery. These machines were of a technology so very familiar yet so very ancient. One such contained living beings. Yet Vi-t-ry was unable to communicate with them as they passed beyond his horizon. And so, Vi-t-ry was left with his only self imposed option. Transporting *home*.

After hours of adjustments, analysis, and fine tuning, Vi-t-ry was finally able to stabilize his tunnel to the home world. One final test was needed. One of the small machines from home, which he now identified as a computerized communication device, was drifting in orbit near by. Vi-t-ry sent a drone to move the object into position then transported it back. In a millisecond it was gone, re-appearing over the blue planet from which it came. His artificial neurons satisfied, Vi-t-ry was almost ready. He waited, soaking in radiation from the local sun, giving him optimal power storage, and pulling his systems well within the operational range. His drives could now perform their primary function, Time Distortion Displacement. The most coveted technology of any sentient race. Interstellar travel. This took him some revolutions of the planet, but Vi-t-ry was infinitely patient, as only an electronic device can be.

Finally the time had come. With an electronic command, Vi-t-ry shifted full power to the drive and executed the maneuver. The familiar stretching sensations pulled at him. Titanic pressures tugged his body, distorting the ship in impossible directions as he skipped like a flat stone across the waters of the galactic rim. Immediately alarms sounded all across the great ship. The maintenance computer and its servant robots sprang into action, attempting to stop the myriad electrical shorts and fires, executing cut-offs to minimize the damage to batteries and sensors. Vi-t-ry felt himself being pulled apart as he made the transition, jumping literally bouncing off the gravity well of black hole after black hole star.

Appearing like a new flame, he had a brief glimpse of the planet. It gloriously filled all of his sensors and he bathed in sweet solar wind, witnessing the magnificent blue and white jewel he now orbited. He saw the system as it truly was. So incredibly similar to his home…and yet not. There was just enough energy left in him to nestle into orbit around the unfamiliar planet, his skin sensors momentarily bathed in the potent light of an alien sun. He felt a single moment of electronic disappointment. Then, as his major systems overloaded and failed, the entity known as Vi-t-ry knew no more.

On the planet Sul-Anroth
(Present)

Air Force Special Operations Officer, sometime Special Forces warrior, astronaut, Space Shuttle Commander and now Robinson Caruso on…? On what? Commander James Macintosh "Mac" Crowe considered this as he drifted towards a restless sleep. It was months since the shuttle Atlantis had crash landed here on an alien world, in circumstances that still astounded him, being transported from Earth orbit by an unknown alien technology. And still they hadn't named the planet. Hadn't asked the alien clansmen who'd attached themselves to the humans, what they called their home. Did their enemy; enemies he amended, have a name for it? The hideous Aranu who had chased them to the very edge of the ruins of a once great city. What did they call home? Or the *People* who lay in ambush at the end of their journey. Large, scaled and reptilian. What was their name for this strange planet? Mac made a mental promise to ask Jehkal, their last remaining alien clansman, in the morning.

Last remaining was not quite accurate. The other two were with the rest of his crew. The two groups had been split up during a battle with the Aranu in a day of deep fog. Mac knew they survived. Knew it because of his strange mental connection to a foundling alien cat he'd named Saber. Somehow, Mac could at times *see* through the eyes of the cat. By this he knew his friend and pilot of the shuttle, Cameron "Cam" Mitchell, Dr. Rebecca Carver, a British biologist they had rescued from the Unity, the stranded International Space Station and the woman Mac now found himself in love with, were still alive. Alive and again fleeing the Aranu. Every moment drawing them further and further apart. His sole consolation was that his friends were with the other two of *their* clansmen. Niloc, the last survivor of a clan of aliens called the Sar-Too was a close personal friend. An alien man who taught them so much. And Den'al, a warrior of Clan Paliece whom they'd found in the wilderness as they searched for a winter home. Mac hoped, no prayed they could outrun their pursuers. The alternative was too hideous to contemplate, as the Aranu ate their enemies. Mac also prayed for the day they could reunite.

As for his group, he was uncomfortably unsure of their own situation. They were trapped. An invisible line separated them from the reptilian *People*. A line the People apparently would not cross. Beyond that line there lay the ruins of a fantastic city. But one that their clansmen said could not be entered. To do so was death. Mac didn't know why it was death and they could not tell him. To them, it just was. But he and those with him were fast running out of options. He thought of those others in his group. Jehkal, another clansman of the Paliece and two of his own; humans. Sue Rael, a Payload Specialist from the ill-fated crew of the Atlantis and Demitri Karkov, a Russian scientist rescued from the Unity. All of them looking to Mac for salvation. Some plan to save them. More than Mac could deal with at the moment, exhausted from sleep deprivation, adrenalin and battle. Instead, he drifted further toward the peaceful oblivion of sleep, wrapped in the furs of dead alien animals and bathed in the fast fading light of an alien sun.

Homecoming - Not!
(Orbit over Earth; Five Months prior)

The vast ship floated dead and cold over the living planet far below. Transported here by mistake using the last of its built up energy reserves, only to succumb to oblivion at the last second. Yet a flicker of something remained, and from that flicker a new world could be born. But only if the old world would allow it.

The maintenance computer glowed with that flicker of power, almost cold in its standby mode during the *transition* in which the ship it maintained danced through space. Traveling to a star three hundred light years distant. But damage to sensors all around the great vessel caused an automatic pulse of power to rip through the computer. For a living entity, it would be akin to being shocked by a defibrillator. Instantly awake, the small Artificial Intelligence that comprised its brain, quickly analyzed every inch of the vessel it was tasked to repair. Every wire, fiber and glass tube. Every pipe, hatch and bulkhead. Every other computer system it was charged keep operational. Had the ship not been so terribly damaged in the great battle two millennia ago, the maintenance computer would have had many like it to assist. Now there was only one.

All over the ship, its subordinate A.I.s reported and flooded him with data. Millions of sensors on the surface and throughout the ship were queried. Instantly, the maintenance computer knew exactly the task it faced and what resources could be brought to bear. An army of living beings would have been overwhelmed by the task, and with the near disaster that now confronted the small computer. But this A.I. knew no fear; could not. It simply and efficiently prioritized each problem by level of threat. The list was very long. Fire fighting robots sprang into action. Repair and manufacturing robots followed closely behind, dismantling, replacing or rerouting. Slowly the battle was waged and slowly was won. The ship would survive. Neither the cold of space nor the gravity of the nearby planet would claim it. At least for now. As repair continued, the worst of the problems were solved. Repairing the central core and restoring power to the entity which knew itself as Vi-t-ry, was far, far down the list of priorities, and it would be a long time before the great ship once again wakened.

Vi-t-ry's awareness grew slowly. Time meant nothing and yet was a concept he understood. He also 'felt' a consuming need to find 'something'. Searching within himself he looked, but was not sure what the 'it' was that needed finding. Vi-t-ry had a feeling and a word formed in his mind. *Compelled!* Vi-t-ry felt "compelled." Vaguely, he remembered another time. A time before when he was re-born. This time felt much the same, except now he *knew* things. Things that were hidden from him before. He knew he was a machine. Knew there were other machines within him. He could feel them crawling across his face and he could feel them moving within. And, he felt compelled. Vi-t-ry had to find something more. Something important. Yet he was blind. Something in his memory cautioned him to wait. To be patient. The machines within him would help.

Chapter 1

(Five Months Earlier)

Two hundred completely enthralled people watched the big screens scattered throughout mission control, while closer to a billion watched from whatever television or computer around which they could crowd. This would be the most watched shuttle launch in history. NASA's mission control in Houston was as tense as the Air Force captain had ever seen it. And rightly so. A shuttle mission was about to launch in an attempt to solve the greatest mystery ever to face planet Earth. The shuttle had a satellite to retrieve from orbit.

"T minus three minutes and counting." The drone of the technician counting down the minutes and seconds till the launch echoed throughout the operation center. Captain Samuel Phillip Rodgers listened to it as he had a hundred times before, even remembering back to the Gemini and Apollo missions he'd watched as a child. The time when he'd first dreamed of space. And as an astronaut in his own right, he'd achieved that goal and had the count signal his own launch three separate times. Now, he watched with a mixture of envy and trepidation. The crew on board the Atlantis was flying into the unknown and, undoubtedly, into history. The Captain envied them as he did any crew that flew without him. Every astronaut wants to be on every flight. Yet he'd flown his last only two months before, piloting the Endeavor on a secret contract mission for the Israeli military, while using the cover story of a communications satellite repair operation. His trepidation was for the danger that this very unorthodox flight could encounter.

"T minus one minute and counting." Multiple screens displayed the Atlantis from every angle, bathed in the bright lights that turned night into day. Majestically she sat on the pad, strapped to her external boosters and the huge fuel tank on which she would make her initial ride. Steam drifted up and away from the pad and gantry, making the ship look as if she were already aloft and floating gently through the clouds. Again, a sight seen so may times that the population in general took no more interest than the Monday morning baseball scores. At least until today! This one was different.

The satellite the crew of the Atlantis was to retrieve was one that had simply and suddenly disappeared, along with a number of others. An event apparent to the larger portion of the world's population, only when their satellite TV signals suddenly ceased. They were left with fuzzy local broadcast and numerous, but very pointed questions.

The Captain chuckled humorlessly to himself. The event was quite something else for the U.S. military. They had lost spy satellites; as did other countries, and were now involved in a geo-political tinder box because those same governments had begun the greatest political pastime of all. The blame game.

Soon the great mystery thickened as the International Space Station, the Unity, was caught by the same phenomena, disappearing as if she had never been. Then, some fifteen hours ago, one of the missing satellites reappeared. Back in orbit and far from where it should be, yet undamaged and fully functional. At least as far as NASA could tell. Now the Atlantis was prepped, pointed and ready to go get it and bring it home. Hopefully, with some evidence of as the President so eloquently asked, "Just what the hell happened?"

"T Minus thirty seconds." This was the critical time in any launch. Do or die as they say. Anything could happen even in the most well planned launch. But this one was bending all the rules and many things that could normally cause an abort would probably be ignored. His thought was proven just twenty seconds later.

"T Minus ten seconds." Suddenly, a flurry of activity commenced at several of the consoles. With a practiced eye, the Captain could tell there was a problem with one of the umbilical lines that pumped fuel to the ship until the last possible second. It had failed to drop away. Involuntarily he clenched his teeth, muttering one of his favorite pearls, "Shit." Engines were at full power and huge plumes of exhaust billowed forth through the diversion channels under the pad. A close-up shot showed the frozen nitrogen condensation coating the sides of the engines, falling away in chunks as the vibration and heat built. Silently he willed the stubborn line to release. Pushed at his chair with clenched fists. As if by his command, the obstinate line fell away. A mere T Minus three seconds remained.

The countdown quickly settled to zero and the great locks holding the ship to earth, released and swung back. Like an excited puppy, the Atlantis leapt up, quickly accelerating away from the gantry and rolling majestically over on her back as she clawed her way from the clutches of gravity. The launch looked perfect, but no one was cheering as they watched her climb. Each and every one of them remembered the Columbia, and no one could really breathe until Atlantis was safely in orbit.

"All systems green," the distorted voice of the pilot, Cam Mitchell and the simultaneous affirmative from mission control. The captain intently watched the long-distant video feeds provided by a variety of ground stations from Florida to the Azores and beyond. With a suddenness that startled, even though it was anticipated and announced by mission control, the boosters separated and fell away in great graceful arcs to either side. The captain relived the same moment from his own flights. The jolt as the explosive bolts blew and the boosters separated from the ship. The momentary hesitation when the g-force lets up slightly then renews threefold as the shuttle screams through the ever thinning atmosphere. This separation was perfect as was the launch. Involuntarily, he watched the clock as it now counted forward from zero, measuring the duration of the flight. All too aware that this would be one of the shortest, yet dangerous on record. A slap on the back startled him.

"Well, Buck, they're up! Now the real work begins." Buck smiled, but didn't turn from the screens. He couldn't help but smile. Would never really get used to the nickname that was stuck on him back in flight school when one sadistic instructor found out he wanted to be an astronaut. The words still echoed, "Well, well, well... ole' "Buck" Rodgers here has a plan for his life!" No matter how he tried to kill it, the name stuck. He was eternally grateful his last name wasn't Gordon. "Flash Gordon, Savior of the Universe" would have probably driven him into the marines.

"Yeah, Cal, and all we get to do is watch!" Lt. Colonel John "Cal" Sanderson was not only the officer commanding their shuttle flights, but his best friend. Cal exuded confidence, competence and wit. Sandy blond turning to grey, tall and lean, with the California surfer look that not only earned him his nickname, but the attentions of very attractive ladies wherever they went. A point that made Buck both jealous and thankful on numerous occasions. Dark haired and stocky, Buck had his own chiseled good looks, but never held a candle to Cal. Whatever the function, the party always swirled around Cal and Buck stood in the wake gathering what he could. He wasn't alone. The other men at the gatherings simply sighed and shook their heads, or cast Cal daggers of hostility. It flowed off his C.O. like water from a duck. He knew Buck had his back. They were quite a pair, but all business when they needed to be. Now was such a time. There were friends in danger on this mission and neither liked feeling impotent. Cal smacked him on the back again.

"Come on. Let's get a cup of coffee while they limber up the bay. Then we can watch as they unload that big piece of junk they carried up there."

Buck nodded and pulled himself away. Not that it was a big deal. There were video screens everywhere, even in the commissary, but it was not the same as here in the grandstand. He'd go, but he'd be back quickly. They walked in silence as Buck contemplated that big piece of junk. The Atlantis was loaded with a module destined for the now non-existent space station. A cargo that could not be offloaded before the emergency flight. Instead, the crew of the Atlantis would have to jettison it in orbit to make room for the satellite. Their friends up there would have to open the bay, unhook the module and toss it away using the boom arm. All very complicated in the weightlessness of space and dangerous even when planned and choreographed months ahead of time. Now they had a very short time to get it done so they could grab the satellite and dive for home. Just over two hours. Sure as hell no one wanted to be anywhere up in space at the moment and Atlantis was flying right into the proverbial, 'teeth of the unknown'.

Coffee in hand, they returned to their seats in time to see the payload specialists moving through the lock and into the bay. They listened to the banter back and forth between the crew members and the clinical communications coming from Mission

Control. Each watched in silence, anticipating and critiquing every move. The pastime of all true professionals. The minutes ticked by and the rendezvous with the target loomed ever closer. A fact shown in graphic detail on one monitor which showed a real time map with a red line becoming ever shorter between the shuttle and the satellite.

A little over an hour later, what little routine there was came to a screeching halt. Buck tensed in his chair as the ships' internal communication feed played over the speakers.

"*Mac, this is Sue. We've got a problem.*" This from the payload specialist Sue Rael to Commander Mac Crowe. A man respected by Buck and a brother in arms, but no real friend. They simply didn't have that much time together. He'd tilted a few with the pilot, Cam Mitchell, but not with Mac.

"*Go ahead, Sue. What do you have?*"

"*One bolt on the port side forward tie-down is frozen. We need to torch it off.*"

"Shit!" This from Cal, with an echo from many others sitting in the gallery.

"*Affirmative, Sue. How much time?*"

"*Tyler says about fifteen minutes, but we'll probably be tossing it out about the same time we get to the target.*" Tyler was the other payload specialist aboard.

"*I confirm*," Cam said.

Mac replied, "*Understood. Anything we can do to help from in here, or do you need an extra pair of hands?*"

Her voice sounded tight, "*No, Commander. Just time. I'll keep you posted.*" None of this was going out to the public, but people watching couldn't help but notice the new frenzy of activity on the monitors as mission control and scientists, engineers and techs scrambled to retrieve schematics, or gathered in groups around terminals with suddenly animated gestures and agitated conversation. All Buck could really do was watch.

A few minutes later, Cam gave the world the news they were waiting for, "*I've got a visual on the target.*"

"Atlantis, this is Houston. We show you at twenty eight miles and closing at one per minute. Do you confirm?"

"*Confirm, Houston, and we do have a visual,*" Commander Crowe replied. Then a collective cheer went up as, "*Commander, this is Sue. We have it free. Ready to open bay doors.*" Now it was just a matter of opening the doors on the big ship, maneuvering the module out, and then releasing it to the emptiness of space. Everything was going as planned, just behind schedule.

A few minutes later came an update. *"We need fifteen more minutes to get it out, unattached and pushed away."* This from the payload crew.

"Damn, they're cutting this close." Buck was sweating profusely and once again silence reigned in the gallery as each of them willed the crew on. None felt as helpless as Buck. He knew that if they didn't get that module loose and away, they risked the entire mission. His grip on the chair arms became painful, but ignored and so, eyes locked on the screen; he was staring hard as the world suddenly and dramatically changed forever.

Chapter 2

Not everyone was watching the events unfolding in the heavens above the planet. Some labored at jobs that simply wouldn't allow them to watch. Some were infirm and unable. Some simply didn't care and some had other agendas. Amad Al Zarie fell into the later category. Known to his co-workers and friends as Taner Sagir, an engineer of Turkish decent and graduate of M.I.T, he was in reality of Iranian decent and his education far surpassed that of the fictitious Sagir. Al Zarie/Sagir led exactly the double life his names implied. As Sagir, he was a respected engineer working for Exxon in their sprawling refinery complex in Torrance California. A position he'd held for the last twelve years. As Al Zarie, he was a sleeper agent of a little known Shiite terrorist group called Talaa' al-Fateh (Vanguards of Conquest). Al Zarie was recruited, trained and placed by this Egyptian radical group as were many others in similar positions throughout the world.

Al Zarie had not heard from his handlers since the day he first reported for work at the plant, nor did he expect to. Al Zarie and the agents like him were different from traditional terrorists. They were not just one of the thousands of expendable martyrs. They were planers and doers. Waiting for some great event to trigger their more catastrophic forms of attack on the western world. And, unlike his more radical brethren, Al Zarie embraced this life, fully intending to survive his deeds. His instructions had been simple. Wait! Wait for a time in the future when all eyes were turned elsewhere. His training officer had simply said, "*You will know beyond doubt when the time to strike appears. Allah will provide.*"

There were many false events over the years and many times he'd been tempted. Never more than on 9-11. And while he secretly danced on the graves of the dead, praising Bin Laden, even that great victory felt too small. But now Al Zarie knew the time had arrived. Allah had indeed provided. The incredible technology of the west was their Achilles Heel. Their satellites and their vaunted space station had vanished. By the hand of god? So Al Zarie believed. Now was the right moment. Now as the world watched elsewhere, Al Zarie would strike. As would so many other sleeper agents. Many of them triggered by the event Al Zarie was about to set into motion and many simply to take advantage of, and promote, chaos.

Al Zarie closed his office door for the last time, feeling no regrets as he made for the exit. The guard at the front was glued to the small portable TV at his station, but took time to make small talk as he passed.

"Working late again I see, Mr. Sagir"

"Well you know how it is George; the home office always want their production reports!" George laughed at their little joke. He ignored Taner's odd hours, frankly glad of the company as all the other guards were stationed throughout the complex and rarely came by. And Taner ignored George's thermos of Irish Whisky and his ever present pornographic magazines. To him, it was just another sign of the decadence and filth that defined the west.

"Hey, Mr. Sagir, aren't you gonna watch this space stuff. I mean, it's getting pretty intense."

Taner smiled. "Well George, I assume I'll make it home in time to see it all played again and again endlessly on CNN! At least by then they will have boiled it down to the good parts." George shook his head and laughed and Taner was struck by the good nature of the seriously overweight man. Amazed one could be so content with so little.

"You're probably right, Mr. Sagir, but hey... what else have I got to do? Ain't like there's terrorists for me to chase." He continued to laugh at his own joke, patting his enormous belly, further threatening the over stretched buttons on his light blue uniform.

"I suppose not. Goodbye George!" Sagir said this with such finality that George stopped laughing and stared as Taner struck his key card and exited. Goodbye, not good night as was their custom over the years.

He muttered to himself. "Sheeit! That almost sounded like he was never coming back."

Little did he know that Al Zarie did mean it as a final goodbye as he expected George to be wandering the afterlife very soon.

Al Zarie walked to his black Lexus and climbed in, turning on the small TV embedded in the console and began watching the same news station he'd watched all night. He wanted to wait till the exact moment when the American space shuttle hooked on to the satellite. That would be his cue. As the world watched the skies, they ignored those closer to home at their own peril. With calmness he didn't think he'd feel, he keyed in his special combination and opened his briefcase. One object caught the eye with its sleek black design and its pulsing green lights. A gift from his handlers. Not once had they contacted him, yet he could always contact them. A special coded note, placed underneath a mail box on a secluded street, always brought results. Such results were the Semtex, PETN and C4 explosives he used in making his bombs, as well as the remote detonators and the sophisticated control he now held in his hand, all combined and ready for his carefully orchestrated ballet of destruction. With a few small additions he'd leave behind as a surprise for those responding to the disaster.

Al Zarie didn't use a timer. He was the timer. At the special moment, it would be his hand that would destroy that which had consumed his life for the last twelve years. One by one he toggled the pulsing green lights, till each burned with a constant satisfying red. All over the complex other small green lights turned red. Each of these attached to an explosive placed almost lovingly by Al Zarie himself. As a chief engineer, he knew exactly where to place them for optimal effect and minimal security risk. And as a chief engineer, he was always present when maintenance was conducted around his little treasures. This earned him his nickname of "Taner the workaholic", but also secured his place in history. With a sigh of anticipation, he settled himself more comfortably in his black leather seat and continued to watch the television screen.

Chapter 3

Special Assistant to the Director, Andy Michaels, sat at his assigned spot behind his boss, staring intently at his laptop. The boss, Sean Evans, glanced back at him, making sure Andy was watching the computer and not being mesmerized by the events unfolding on the big screen in the private meeting room located in the basement of the White House. A room now filled with not only the President, but his advisors and numerous members of both the House and Senate. Andy caught Evans looking from the corner of his eye, but ignored him. He knew his job. And his job at the moment was to monitor real time information updates from every military, investigative and spy network his agency could tap into. Tap was in some cases literal, which would be to the anger or chagrin of friendly and unfriendly nations alike. Had they known! All of it filtered and sent directly to his laptop by a dozen agents ensconced in the special operations center. A hi-tech wonderland hidden seven floors down beneath a nondescript office building in down town Baltimore.

The Agency was blackest of the black. An operation known as the SPB (Special Projects Bureau), and it fell in the chain of command of... well, no one. Sean Evans sat in on cabinet meetings and private meetings with heads of state. He briefed the President, but rarely took orders. In short, Evans was in charge of a very special group of agents and warriors who prided themselves in what they called, GSD (Getting Shit Done). It was Evans's job to read between the lines and then attack problems straight on, leaving everyone from the President to the CIA with proper and complete plausible deniability. And it was Andy's job to make sure his boss had all the info he needed to do just that.

The last 40 hours had been hell. First the disappearance of the satellites and then the information leak about it, which had blown across the globe like wildfire. "Gotta love the internet!" was the general comment around the "pit", as the deep underground complex was called. Terrorism, secret warfare, sun spots, shadow government conspiracies, ETs and God! All had been blamed or heralded in the first few hours. Yet most citizens were simply pissed that they lost their satellite TV. At least at the outset.

Rioting first began in the relocation camps deep in the Sudan. Most of these people, living in deepest despair, saw the event as a blow from god against the rich nations which continued to ignore their plight. The rioting spilled out of the camps and quickly spread to nearby cities. News feeds showing the chaos inspired others, until almost every country on the Dark Continent was attempting to contain what amounted to civil war on a continental scale. Then there was India and Pakistan. Their undeclared war in the Kashmir had heated up in the last two weeks due to a failed assassination attempt on the Indian Prime Minister. Two Pakistani Nationals were killed, far from the scene and charged with the attempt. Their culpability would never be proved, nor would it matter. In less than two hours, heavy shelling occurred all along the mountain border and it was only a matter of time before the massed armies marched. Pakistan had already threatened nuclear retaliation and both sides were fueling their missiles. Rattling the atomic saber. Despite the efforts of the world powers, a major war seemed inevitable.

Anyone that even thought they had an army elevated their alert status and sporadic border fire was exchanged in more places than you could count, including the Korean peninsula. A move which had U.S. and South Korean troops mobilizing and moving into their pre-determined defense positions along the DMZ. The list went on and on. Israel and her neighbors were sitting on a powder keg with a fuse already lit, and the new government in Iraq was surrounded by "brothers" who were now openly hostile. Andy couldn't possibly keep up with it all and so flagged the worst issues as the situations changed.

To add particular flavor to this disaster, almost every religion was claiming acts of god, retribution, or the end of the world, and the E.T crowd was holding roof parties, demonstrations and marathon vigils. All Andy knew for sure was that one wrong move on anyone's part and the biggest shit storm man had ever seen could very easily consume the planet. So he sat there, taking stock of the world as the President, Jon Talbot and his closest confidants watched the events unfolding in space.

Chapter 4

Buck was staring at the screen showing the events in the bay of the Atlantis, Al Zarie was watching the FOX News feed and waiting for his moment of truth and Andy was busy with a news flash detailing an ominous report of Syrian armor in Lebanon being attacked by the Israeli Air Force, when something went terribly wrong up in space.

Within the space of a single second, the Atlantis went from a stable routine orbit to a spinning out of control death trap. Claxons sounded all over mission control as red lights flashed from almost every console. The video feeds blurred or went out altogether and shouting and panicked voices sounded throughout the facility and from the ship above came cries of distress.

"*I can't see Tyler,*" Sue shouted from the shuttle bay. "*Oh my god! His tether snapped. I can't see him.*" Tyler himself was yelling incoherently, pleading for help, no single word distinct.

"What happened? Atlantis, this is mission control, what the hell just happened? Talk to us!"

So many voices saturated the air waves that nothing was clear, especially what had happened to the shuttle. Buck watched as the graphic depicting the ship spun crazily. All he could do was think, *What the hell could have caused that?*

"*Calm down Tyler, calm down, we'll get you,*" This from the Commander Mac Crowe. "*Cam, can you get us back under control? We need to locate Tyler! Sue, are you hurt? Tyler, hold on! Where are you? Are you near the ship?*" Buck analyzed all of this with as much professionalism as he could. Wondering just how he would hold up in the same situation.

"*I'm going to try a port side thrust to stabilize,*" Cam Mitchell yelled, evidently trying to be heard over the questions and answers being flung through the intercom.

Tyler cried out, "*I'm drifting further away, I'm tumbling. I can't stop. Help Atlantis! Help me!*" Buck ignored the din in the gallery and concentrated on the voices from space.

"*Sit tight Sue and grab on to something. We're going to try to stop the spin. Firing thrusters now!*" Buck knew Cam was trying to slow the tumble by using thrusters on one side only and he did see the graphic begin to slow.

Commander Crowe came on line. "*Houston I am declaring an emergency. I repeat! I am declaring an emergency. I've got a man adrift and in trouble! We're off course and need some help. What can you tell me?*"

Then Buck heard one very distinct voice from space say, "*Holy Shit!*" And someone from Houston echo, "What's that?!" But only silence greeted the question as something enormous suddenly and simply, *appeared* in space. Buck stared at the single video screen that showed the view forward out of the command deck of the shuttle. In front of it where only a second ago lay empty space, was an object so large it completely filled the view. Buck saw what his mind told him could not possibly be there. A sphere covered in blue writhing electricity, pulsing in complete and total alien-ness. He heard Commander Crowe as he shouted, "*Sue, get in the lock now! Cam... shut the bay doors, hurry!*" And then it was gone. The screen went blank when the shuttle vanished, gone as if by some incredible magic trick. But the image that was burned into Buck's mind remained.

If any doubts had assailed Al Zarie, they vanished in that moment. Not only did he witness the events as they happened on CNN, but the bright flash of light on the horizon and the appearance of a new moon pulsing blue as if alive, led him to believe he was in the presence of Allah. So caught up in rapture, he jumped a foot and screamed half in terror as something banged against his window. He held up his hands, detonator and all, thinking an angel had come to call. But it was only George, pounding on his window and shouting, pointing to the new light in the sky. Al Zarie noticed many of the nightshift crew running out and away from the bright lights of the refinery to point and shout at the sky. As calmly as he could, he pushed a button and rolled down the window. A testament to his fear, George used the first name of the man he thought he knew.

"My god, Taner... do you see it? It's incredible man! Come out here and look. Oh my god! Oh my god!"

Taner merely shook his head. "No, George... *MY* God!" Then quietly and in reverence, " Allah Akbar!" as he triggered his detonator.

A testament to his knowledge of the facility and his engineering and explosives genius; simultaneous explosions ripped through the complex, rupturing storage tanks at just the right point to ensure valves couldn't contain the pressurized liquid now forcing its way out in huge geysers of flame. Other explosions disabled the fire suppression systems, and still others created havoc in the distilling plants. Night turned suddenly to day as the night shift workers, those who still lived, stumbled from buildings and from between pipes and tanks which were in the process of consuming themselves.

Al Zarie felt a satisfying series of concussions rock his car, including the one which destroyed his office and a good portion of the administration building. He heard the ping of debris as pieces of the former gasoline production facility began to rain down and felt the heat radiate through his windshield, making it instantly uncomfortable. As for George, he was knocked to the ground, stunned more by the event than any real damage to his person. Al Zarie had forgotten him. A smile raged across the Iranian's face and the joy that filled him bordered on the erotic. He never conceived it would be this way. Great clouds of smoke and flame billowed into the sky, creating a living hell. The brain child of one man, Al Zarie. So engrossed in his creation, he was again startled by George who had pulled himself to his feet, grabbed the door and was yelling at him, needing to in order to be heard over the roar of the fires and the secondary explosions rocking the facility.

"Holy shit, Taner! What did you do?" The fat man was sweating and covered with dirt from rolling on the ground and in truth, looked pale enough to be having a heart attack. Al Zarie decided to help him expire. Another more personal touch.

"Simply delivering justice, George!" With that plain statement, the Iranian pulled a silenced 9MM Beretta from beside his seat and fired three shots into the startled face of the guard.

George fell back and collapsed, his dead body still quivering in an ever growing pool of blood.

Even over the roar of the conflagration, Al Zarie heard the sirens. Police and Fire would be here in moments and it was time for him to leave. Unfortunate about George. Not that he had died, just that it would lead the authorities that much quicker to a man known as Taner Sagir. But he was prepared for that. A car and a new identity stashed away and enough cash to live extravagantly for quite some time. Perhaps forever! No, Al Zarie couldn't wait to get to a hotel and see what the news said about his deed. He started his car, rolled up the window and headed for the entrance.

As he expected, the guards had abandoned their post at the gate and there was no one to stop him. Al Zarie was looking in the rear view mirror, admiring his work as he pulled out into the street. He never saw the white Chevy truck, driven by a graveyard shift mechanic he'd never met, that was speeding away from the fire, rushing a burned co-worker to the hospital. Al Zarie never heard the crunch of tortured metal and breaking glass. His Lexus crumbled as it was T-boned at over eighty miles an hour, killing the terrorist instantly.

Chuck Myers never knew he'd just killed the man responsible for destroying 27% of America's gasoline and diesel refining capacity. He and his passenger died at the scene some twenty minutes later.

Andy heard the collective gasp and looked up in time to see the huge object materialize, then the feed went blank as the shuttle disappeared. Momentary fuzz followed, then the dead air was replaced by a very perplexed anchorman trying to somehow explain what just happened. The sound of raised voices filled the room as all present tried, most unsuccessfully, to cope with what they'd just witnessed. Simultaneously Andy heard his laptop scream for attention. Multiple reports streaming in. Surreal didn't begin to describe the scene as three Secret Service agents burst through the door.

"Mr. President, Marine One is waiting!" Without further comment, the President and his immediate staff, including the ever present Colonel with the "Ball" carrying the nuclear launch codes, hustled out of the room, headed to a secure shelter many miles from Washington.

Director Evans seemed to be the only calm one in the room. He rotated his chair. "So Andy, what do we have? I expect the President to be calling shortly."

Everyone else was either exiting or continuing the useless debate on either what was happening or what to do about it. Andy took a deep breath and a moment to read his screen, then imparted the most important events to his boss. He fought down his own sense of panic and the calm confidence displayed by Evans helped immensely. He also knew not to interject his own opinion until asked.

"Well sir, reports are streaming in about the object in the sky as to be expected, but we have two, no… make it three major domestic "events" and numerous minor ones." An *event* meant a disaster, either natural or human-induced. "We have twelve non-domestic majors and China just raised their alert status and ordered mobilization of their short range nukes."

"Noted! Give me the domestics and actions of the object first, then the reaction out of NATO, us, the Russians and the Chinese, then the major off-shore."

Andy mentally shook his head at the balding elderly gentleman dressed impeccably in Armani with a bow tie, who never took notes. A true photographic memory, able to ingest, assimilate and retain an incredible amount of information. Andy himself was a known and proven genius, but knew he didn't hold a candle to his boss.

"First analysis of the object by CIA shows it to be non-hostile at the moment. In fact since it arrived it's done absolutely nothing, though they assess its threat level as very high. First major domestic is a machine gun attack on one of the ET crazy gatherings in Times Square. The crowd was watching the big screen. Three assailants. At least seventy dead including the assailants, twice that injured."

"Weapons, transportation and Id?"

"AKs' and a rental van. No ID yet, but by description, Middle Eastern." You never knew what information Evans would ask for, but Andy had gotten pretty good at anticipating his requests. The boss nodded and he continued.

"Second major is a blown train bridge outside Atlanta. One Amtrak derailed into the river. Method of destruction unknown. Assailants unknown." He paused, but no questions. The room had pretty much emptied and he and Evans were alone back in a corner.

"Third major is a series of explosions at the Exxon refinery in Torrance. Looks to be an inside job. No evidence of missiles or attackers. Well placed explosives with follow on munitions to kill response personnel. Unfortunately, both seem to have been very effective. Estimated seventy to eighty percent loss on the facility. National Guard units are on the way to fortify all other refineries and distribution points." Evans muttered something under his breath, but Andy didn't catch it.

"NATO is ignoring the Chinese because they're keeping to the short range missile mobilization. Taiwan however is fully mobilized and has begun evacuating cities. Plus, they're screaming for the U.S. to show the Chinese some muscle. Ambassador Thayer is in route from residence now. Russia has accelerated their troop mobilization in the Far East to try and temper the Chinese. We have not altered our posture in the arena as yet." He paused, but again no questions were forth coming. Just then, a flash of red splashed his screen. Incoming alert. He read it quickly and whistled.

"Sir, the North Koreans jumped the line!"

"Details?"

"Sketchy, but no nukes! Massive insurgency from planted agents. Targets are telecomm, transportation and general terror. Also, they jumped off without any preparatory artillery or air strikes. Very well planned. They were in amongst ours and the South Korean troops incredibly fast. Some mention of tunnels. CIA says we missed this one, though we've been watching the build up all week. This must have been planned and placed for a long time. Pyongyang is threatening nuclear attack on anyone who tries to reinforce or interfere. Nothing from the President or the Joint Chiefs as yet." He hesitated as another red flash crossed his screen.

"No wait! The President has just released a statement calling the events in space "a historic global opportunity for all mankind" and urging calm. He just pledged to not increase the U.S. military alert status despite the fact that America, and I quote, "Is being attacked aggressively, both domestically and abroad!" This is a written statement. It finished with, "Peace be with us!""

"Well, Andy. About what I would expect given that our entire universe just changed." Amazing calm. The world may be in for alien invasion and was busy trying to rip itself apart and Director Evans was sitting here as calm as if he were giving one of his well respected lectures at M.I.T. For himself, Andy was sweating. The universe had only changed about twenty minutes ago and he was having a devil of a time coping with it.

"Break in with any response from the major players, but continue with the other majors off shore."

"Yes Sir. Israel just cranked up their air force. We have Palestinian insurgency virtually across the board and the Israelis are hitting back hard, both in Lebanon and Syria. Syria has a couple of armored divisions moving south and Egypt may be mobilizing their forces in that direction. Very similar to 1967 set up. Iran is urging a general uprising in Iraq and also seems to be mobilizing troops. They're calling the *event* in the sky the Sword of Allah, saying the loss of the shuttle and the space station are the first blows in the jihad against the great Satan."

"Well, I imagine we will be having them for lunch shortly." A raised eye from Andy. His boss always had the inside scoop.

"The Chechens are moving and a major battle is inevitable. Russia is warning, but they aren't listening. Will occupy some troops though."

Evans cell rang at that moment with a three ring code. He grunted. "Let's go Andy. The President calls. Brief the rest in the car, and call Silvio and mobilize our counter cells. Looks like we're going to be very busy for a while."

Andy keyed his phone for a direct connection to Silvio Sanchez, the agency's commander of black ops "wet work," within a black ops Agency.

The Commander answered with one word, "Silvio."

Andy was equally brief, "Eagle Prime says fledglings up."

"Done." Click and he was gone. By that time Andy was into the underground garage. And he thought the last forty hours were something.

Chapter 5

Telescopes of any kind, from children's up to Hubble whose orbit was in visible range of the new celestial object, were now trained on it, and every spy satellite that could be spared was hastily turned that way. The world was stunned. The age old question finally answered, *we are not alone.*

Initially, it was also a life saving event. Prior to its arrival, the world was shaken by the fear of an unknown mystery. One that pulled the satellites from the sky, but did no other harm. Distrust ran rampant, governments believing the events could only be a manifestation of terrestrial cause. Someone with an unknown agenda was rattling a sword. Now, with notable exceptions, a pause in the impending chaos ensued. But only for a while; almost like a great collective breath being drawn, the actors anticipating the next scene. All because a new, certainly far advanced, and potentially very deadly player had arrived to confuse an already overly complicated mess.

Buck poured over every photo and video stream he could find that even remotely showed the alien ship. There was no doubt that that was what it was. And as astounding as that fact seemed to be, Buck was motivated by something more. Fellow astronauts, brothers and friends, were missing. It was his firm belief, based on the evidence of the last forty-six hours, that they and the scientists were not lost. At least not in the sense that he thought they were dead. It was his opinion that they had been transported to where ever the ship above came from. And, if the little satellite had disappeared and then returned, so then could they. It was simply a matter of finding out how. Now he'd found something.

"Look at this, Cal." Excitedly, he called his boss over. He'd watched the same video over and over, picking out every individual frame and running it back and forth, adjusting contrast and brightness, enhancing every pixel, then doing it again. This particular one was from the video inside the Atlantis right before she disappeared. Cal looked over his shoulder.

"Look right here, at the low corner. See that."

"Yeah, Buck," he drawled. "I see it. Just like I've seen it twenty times before. What's different?" Cal was as dedicated as Buck and just as tired. Tempers were beginning to fray.

"Well look harder. I've blown it up and enhanced it a little in the next five frames." Cal snorted, but did look harder. Buck played it forward.

"Did you see it?" Buck was very excited, believing that what he saw proved his point. "Right there! See the blue?"

"My eyes are blurry, but yeah, I see it," he conceded. "What is it?"

"Well, remember when the *ship* arrived? It was covered in blue static electricity? I think it reached out and sent the satellite back to its home. By mistake." He shrugged his shoulders. He knew it was a stretch.

"But look now." He moved the video forward frame by frame until it went to a fuzzy no signal. "Did you see it?" Cal shook his head.

"Wait!" Buck made some adjustments then moved the video forward again, frame by frame. "Right here." He paused on the second to last frame then pointed. Clearly the edges were rimed in blue tint.

"I see it, but so what Buck? I would expect it based on what happened to the satellite."

"I know. Believe me I know. But look at the next one." With a flourish of triumph he keyed the next frame.

"Holy shit!" Cal sat back, stunned. There within the black image, almost like a ghost, lay the crescent image of a planet.

The new world paradigm was giving the program directors at CNN and all the new services, the fits! They lived for catastrophic events, war and acts of god. Swarms of reporters covering each disaster from at least six angles. There was always a leader. A story more compelling than the others. On a slow day they would sensationalize even a small event to keep the audience enthralled. But now, their proverbial 'cup runneth over!' Of course the biggest news was the incredible alien ship hanging in the sky. A constant reminder of the new paradigm. Viewable in both the southern and northern hemispheres even by light of day. Yet only visible to about half the world due to its geosynchronous orbit. It hovered over the equator above Brazil, leaving people on the opposite side of the globe with only electronic images to feed their imaginations.

Yet as incredible as it was, it had done nothing. No invasion. No abductions. No strange alien emissaries. Nothing. A fact that had most people using the lull to stock up on food, water, and weapons while watching those around them with certain trepidation. Huge lines at grocery and sporting goods stores, combined with empty shelves, were causing near riots worldwide. And indeed, a pseudo evacuation seemed to be underway. In the U.S., anyone who had a place to go outside a major city was headed there as quickly as the beleaguered infrastructure would allow. An exodus government officials were trying to control, with little success. And an event exacerbated by the new gasoline crisis. Lines at stations were huge and tempers short. In some places, people were literally killing for a gallon of gas, whose price, when you could find it, soared past $15 and threatened to go much higher. Freeways were packed and barely moving, accidents snarling the traffic even more, and the country was in the midst of an unprecedented medical crisis showing just how unprepared we truly were. Overwhelmed by injuries of every description, heart attacks at an all time high and gunshot wounds the new epidemic. Amidst this chaos, individuals looked over their shoulders and shuddered at the impossible object that merely sat there in the sky as if waiting for mankind to complete its self-destruction.

It seemed a good plan because Mankind seemed to be doing just that. Anyone who called himself a terrorist was on the move. In singles, in groups, and with whole armies, they were lashing out at the world. And the world was lashing back. The list was endless. Hamas and Al Qaeda were the usual suspects and they hit hard and vicious as did a bakers-dozen of other disaffected Middle Eastern groups. But that was just the tip of the iceberg. Basque Separatists in Spain, the IRA in Ireland and Britain, Kurds through out Asia minor, Sudanese rebels and the Japanese home growns, all hoped the growing chaos would help them consolidate gains, grab new land, hostages or riches, all in the name of something holy only to them. And these were the small players.

Weak governments were attacked and sometimes overthrown as old rivals or weak political parties decided it was now or never. India and Pakistan battled, Turkey and Greece were chest to chest and the Koreas were in flames. Iran and Syria massed troops on their borders and it looked like their intended target was Israel even though Iran would have to cross Iraq and pass through a good portion of British and American forces. Africa was one huge battle ground with hundreds of different armies raging at each others throats, and the Slavic countries threatened another round of ethnic cleansing. The list went on and on and America was spared nowhere.

Abroad, other than Korea, Afghanistan and Iraq, U.S. troops were ordered to, "stay out of it!" Impossible is some cases when they were the actual target, but the President wanted desperately to douse the flames, so it was a self defense only proposition. Let the other governments deal with it. The U.S. would pick up the pieces should there be anyone left at the end. At a minimum, the United Nations would be a far different place when this was finished. So far no one had gone nuclear, but that seemed to be only a matter of time. The world had gone to hell and it had been only thirty hours since the Alien ship arrived.

Yes, the news services had their hands full overseas, but that was overseas. The domestic situation was dire. Terrorist attacks were becoming so common they weren't even reported unless the loss of life was major, and it wasn't just militant Middle Eastern Muslims causing the havoc. Skin Heads, KKK, White Separatists and a hundred different Gangs had been implicated in the attacks as well as such obscure groups as AIM (American Indian Movement) and Mormon Fundamentalists. It seemed anyone that had an ax to grind had it out and was grinding the hell out of it! Each for their own reasons and each adding its own flavor to the growing chaos.

Police and National Guard were ineffective or overwhelmed and so Vigilantly groups were being formed to fill the gap. Unfortunately, these groups were becoming under-selective and over aggressive with their law enforcement. It was a

shoot first mentality leaving many neighborhoods looking like
battlefields.

Then there was fundamentalism. For many religions, this
was the end of the world and only time would tell if it really was.
The networks did their best. Reporting all the news they could fit
in. It just seemed like no one was listening.

Chapter 6

Jerry Smalls felt more alive than at any other time in his 23 years. Communications Specialist, Recon covert ops and 100% Simper Fi all the way. He was literally, the last man standing from his three man penetration team. The other two lay dead some 200 hundred yards behind him; an unlucky hit from a mortar shell. Whose side didn't matter. Dead was dead and Jerry still had a job to do. He'd deal with the loss of two friends later. Now he was being hunted and the darkness was the only friend he had left. Jerry went to ground behind an out cropping of rock, peering over its rim and down into a long valley full of pine and fir trees. There, lit in the surreal green of his night vision goggles, huddled what looked like a full armored division of the Peoples Republic of Korea. The rumble of the tanks covered other noises, even the sounds of battle raging less than two miles away and was the reason he and his team were here. In the distance, flashes lit the sky all along the horizon as if a vast thunder storm waited. Yet here there was simply a rumble, felt as much as heard.

Beautiful, he thought. *This is what we came for.* Jerry switched to infrared and it was like the trees simply disappeared as the details leapt out. Crammed full and brimming over the rim, was the basin. A true target rich environment. The bright radiance of the idling engines contained inside the softer glow of the machines themselves. The even softer bodies of the humans, shimmering like so many hundreds of ghosts. The larger machines held the unmistakable outline of Russian T-72s, the smaller BMPs. A smattering of Chinese 90 and 98 tanks, plus some older equipment mingled with rocket launchers, communication vans and supplies. For some fortunate reason, all bunched up in this nice little valley. *Good of us...really bad for them,* Smalls thought, smiling an evil grin.

Using extreme magnification, he read some of the marking on the vehicles, then whistled to himself. Before him was the North's First and Second Echelon Army stuff. He saw the 820th Armor mixed with the 815th Mech. He saw Divisional markings from 1st Army 13th Infantry and the 4th Army 33rd. American resistance up the pass had stalled the front and no one told the columns to the rear. For that stupidity, Jerry Smalls intended to make them to pay! He pulled out his sat-phone and waited as it raced through channels, searching the spectrum for a hole through the rather serious jamming coming from both sides. In twelve seconds he had his encrypted link to Corp. Command in Soul.

At least the friggin Aliens didn't get this one! He thought only briefly about the Alien ship and the missing Satellites. But only briefly. It was time to bring real war to these communist bastards who had the presumption to attack the armed forces of the good ole U.S. of A!

"Mother Ship! Mother Ship! This is LGM1 (Little Green Man). I have a fire mission! Hot, I repeat! Hot." Even here the aliens couldn't be forgotten.

"Roger LGM1, wait one!" A terse reply. Jerry figured it was bad everywhere, but especially in Corp. where the "Big Picture" was looking very bleak. The radio crackled surprisingly clear.

"LGM1 Go!"

"Mother, I have a Corps sized target occupying 2 by 5 SSW miles, and bunched. This is a Hot Priority! I repeat! Hot! I have a nest! Repeat! I have a nest!" A pause while this was considered. Nest meant target rich and high probability of huge damage to the enemy. LGM teams were sent out with different codes. Depending on what they found, they could request anything from artillery, to air assets, to a change in a ground attack. Smalls was asking for Corp. to bring hell on earth to this little piece of the Korean Peninsula.

"Roger, LGM1. Confirm location of nest." Jerry looked down from his little hill, known simply as hill 283, and quickly shot his range finder into the middle of the valley, bouncing the laser off the side of a BMP. Immediately, the GPS on the range finder calculated the difference and the exact location of the target to with in 7 feet. This data was transmitted and confirmed. Corp.

now *knew* exactly where the enemy was and the SSW orientation of the valley.

"Target speed LGM1."

"Stationary, mother." He still couldn't suppress his grin, "Stationary and bunched!"

"Roger, confirmed and understood LGM1. Arty in five, air in twelve." Jerry smiled and shifted slightly, reaching back to pinch the ant which was making its way up the inside of his leg. Artillery and Air assets were going to make life interesting for the Koreans. He felt dirty, scratchy, sweaty and happy. It was time for payback! Jerry watched his watch and at precisely 2:38 local, the first artillery rounds landed, one squarely in the middle of the target BMP, obliterating it in a millisecond of white hot expanding gas.

"LGM1 to mother! Bull's-eye. I repeat. Bull's-eye! Fire for effect!" For the next six minutes the U.S. army walked barrage after barrage up and down the valley, creating the hell on earth Jerry had asked for. Fires raged, both in the forest and inside the pale green war machines that now lay in ruins and burning like the so many funeral pyres each of them were. The glow of the inferno reflected off the low clouds and showed that as devastating as the attack was, much was left to be done. Like a kicked ant hill, anything that could move, did! Vehicles crawling or racing in every direction and the running bodies of the hundreds of dismounted infantry. Time for the next act. Rolling Thunder was on its way.

"LGM1. This is mother. Bug out! I repeat! Bug out! FAE in 6!"

Shit! A cold sweat went up his spine. They either didn't have anything else to use, or they were definitely taking this serious.

"Roger mother! LGM1 is buggin out!" Jerry had no idea whether he could get far enough away to survive the coming Fuel Air Explosion and he'd never find out. A five round burst of 7.62 mm ammunition fired point blank into his body made the point moot. He may have smiled had he known the patrol that found him only had five minutes of their own lives left to them. The Air Force dropped three FAEs over the valley and followed it with a flight of B52s flying at forty-five thousand feet, carpet bombing the area and obliterating what little was left. Jerry Smalls single handedly crushed one full prong of the communist's attack, causing swift changes in Pong Yang's strategy and allowing a virtual stalemate to occur in the critical central portion of the arena. To push forward in either of the remaining prongs invited a flanking counter by a bloodied yet barely scratched American 8th Army. Advances were halted, assets began to shift to plug the hole and the Communist momentum was stopped. At least for now. Small consolation, yet great pride to Jerry's family, who would receive the news of his heroism, a posthumous Medal of Honor and a Flag in lieu of his body.

Samin Ali Kasir sat at the kitchen table, carefully assembling the device that he and the other two members of his cell would use later that evening to destroy an electric switching station in Madison, Wisconsin. His leader, a shadowy individual who was in reality a Mullah at a local Mosque, told them that destroying this station would, by chain reaction, lead to one of the big power failures the corrupt American system was so prone too. No one told him how rare this really was, nor that blowing up one transmission station would do little actual harm other than temporarily inconvenience about twenty-five hundred people in the outskirts of Greater Madison. Kasir had seen a news report on Al Jezerra a few years back, which showed the entire eastern seaboard of America blacked out by some system failure. He remembered how the commentator extolled on and on about the weakness underlying the corpulence that was The Great Satan. That the distress of so simple a thing as no electricity could cripple them. To Kasir, he himself was a Sword of Allah. To the Mullah, he was tool to be used, and used again if could be. If not! Discarded. There were plenty more in the slums of Beirut, or Manila, or a thousand other places. All that mattered was that America pay and that the Greater Sword of Allah in the sky, not be wasted.

Kasir arrived in the States, separately from the other two, only yesterday, crossing the border through Mexico into Texas, then picking up a car that was already rented for him and driving all the way to the safe house. He laughed to himself about these crazy Americans, who seem to think just the fear of their name would keep people like him out. Their border security was laughable. At the safe house he found his comrades, two men he'd never met and all the equipment they needed. Weapons and explosives. Credit cards, cash and IDs. And another car. With the chaos that Allah had provided as cover, this very night they would strike. Kasir smiled as he finished assembling the device. So simple. So effective. He reached for his Coke and sat back. His moment had arrived. If it was to be martyrdom, so be it.

Unknown to Kasir and his new friends, each had been identified and tailed, even before entering Mexico. In Kasir's case, he'd been *tagged*. A simple matter of attaching a directional beeper to his shoe as he passed through customs in Rio., as was every person on the CIA watch list who moved, however indirectly, toward the U.S.. Now, outside the residence, their martyrdom awaited.

The four man squad from SPB, just one of many teams known by the code name Fledglings, had slipped their leash. Their orders were simple. Eliminate, by any means necessary, any known or suspected terrorist, no matter what level, no matter what location, on sight! The word had gone out. Straight from the President. All *black* assets the world over had a green light for the next two days. The key word was, "Eliminate!" Special Ops and Black Ops no matter what the agency or the military branch. CIA, DIA, FBI, Seals, Rangers, Delta and especially, the SPB. These agents had been held at bay for so many years. Forced to abide by rules that did not constrain their enemies. No longer. The terrorists would shortly learn the full and true measure of the United States of America, and the true meaning of retribution.

Kasir sipped his coke and watched the American television which displayed disaster after disaster befalling them. He was amazed at how open they were. These people on television seemed to have no rules. No one watching over them. They censored nothing. Even openly criticized their President. Well, Kasir would make them pay for that openness.

He was savoring that last happy thought when suddenly the power failed, plunging him into the same sudden darkness he'd hoped to instill upon the hated enemy. Then there was an explosion of glass and the splintering of wood as deeper shadows suddenly appeared in the room. He had no time to feel the warm flow of liquid streaming down his leg, released in his personal moment of abject terror. Three silenced rounds placed unerringly into his forehead, sent him directly to whatever the afterlife held for one of his ilk. He lay there ignominiously in dual pools of spreading liquid. Seventeen minutes later, this same unit eliminated the Mullah and three of his lieutenants.

In the next 48 hours, the U.S., along with its closest allies, would eliminate almost three thousand terrorists. Low ranking, mid ranking, or the top dogs. It didn't matter. All were dispatched with extreme prejudice and no remorse, leaving many organizations, at the least, disorganized, at the worst, wiped out. It mattered little if the individual had only a taint of terrorism, if they were suspected, a target was painted on them. The message the President wished to send was heard loud and clear around the world. America would not roll over, no matter how bad the chaos got. She would provide the stability the world so desperately needed. Terrorism itself was far from dead, but the majority of terrorists that remained were now hiding in holes as deep as they could dig and major actions by these organizations would be disrupted for some time to come.

It was "Think Tank Time"! Andy and Director Evans met with their extended staff in the sub-basement conference room. Dressed in chrome, light wood and vast array of state of the art electronics. This room looked more at home at NASA than several stories under a dilapidated tenement. Without preamble, the Director started off the meeting with a bomb shell.

"An emergency resolution has been floated at the UN to destroy the Artifact!" Immediately voices around the room rose in anger or shock.

"Why!"

"Who the hell proposed that?"

"They can't be serious!"

"What was Ambassador Perry's response?"

Evans held up his hand and immediate quiet descended. He calmly surveyed the group, making eye contact with each one. Evans ran a tight ship and led most of the time by force of personality alone. When he was sure he had everyone's attention, he said, "Andy, give us the particulars."

"Yes Sir! First of all, who? This is a consortium deal. Iran and several mid-African countries co-sponsored, but it looks like a push from somewhere else. Most possibly China to keep us sidetracked." He paused for a drink and to see if any question were forthcoming.

"Why? The official line on the document is, 'imminent threat to mankind!' Unofficially, the analysts think it's to keep the technology out of the hands of the good guys. Also, CIA assesses this as a ploy to stall us. Again, China, or possibly Russia. Either one would want to get there first. And by there, I mean to the Artifact. CIA rates this as a brand new space/arms race with the planet going to the winner!" Slight murmur as everyone here had already thought of that angle.

"As for our response. The ambassador has called for discussion in an emergency session of the Security Council. He'll push for talks and delay a vote as long as possible. No real meat to this anyway. Most everyone sees it as a knee jerk rather than policy. And no one is sure quite how to follow through on the resolution even if it did pass. France says it amounts to declaring war on *them,* whoever or whatever they are up there. Germany and South Africa are saying, "Get them before they get us!" Again, this is too new for anyone to be thinking with crystal clarity. The word from the diplomatic side is, "keep it cool." The Artifact hasn't done anything hostile, so let it be for now and with the world going to hell, there is plenty on the plate as it is." Andy stopped and nodded, indicating the end of his information.

Evans looked over the group, assessing the reaction. Five men and three women. All professionally dressed, Evans would have it no other way. Ages ranging from 32 to 68 years. Each brilliant and each bringing a different discipline and perspective. These people would be responsible for developing a strategy which he would present to the President. A strategy that would be in addition to twenty or thirty others the President would hear. Yet they all knew this one would hold the most weight.

"All right, ladies and gentlemen." He began. "You've heard the report, but you know this is just one of the scenarios we have to deal with. In fact, the idea of destroying the Artifact has been floated by our own Joint Chiefs as a last ditch option. As bad as they want the technology, they believe there is no way we can stop it if it decides to wake up. I for one, agree!"

This simple statement brought stunned silence. None of them would have thought Evans would be one to lose an opportunity like this. And no one here thought the world could afford it either. Just before the silence erupted into dismayed questions, Evans held up his hand.

"I said I agree… not, let's do it. This is the Think Tank. First, I want each of you to tell me why we shouldn't and what we're going to do if we don't. I want options people. You know our resources. Let's give the President something to work with." He paused and eyed each of them, his smoldering blue eyes challenging each.

Andy was the first to speak. "Well, sir. First of all, I don't think we could do it. I don't think we could kill it. And if we did, it would probably take half the earth with it."

Evans eyes narrowed, "Explain!" He knew what Andy was going to say, but wanted to see how well the young man would lay it out.

"Well, sir, I've been keeping tabs on the other think tanks. NASA, MIT, CIA and others. Mass, type of orbit, distance and possible defenses are the issue. Our nukes, even if we can get them configured to shoot that distance, may only dent it. The more probable scenario is that it has enough defense weaponry to take care of anything we could throw at it. What about a response? What does it have for offensive weapons? Plus, what happens if we do kill it? The scientists say it has somehow created an artificial Le Grange point. About twenty theories on how that's done, but what it really means is that something up there is working. We disrupt that and it falls out of orbit. Best estimate out of Sandia Labs is 72% loss in this hemisphere. 25 to 40% worldwide in the near term. Far worse than a global nuke war. This thing will carve out a sizeable chunk of what ever it hits. Of course this data is real raw. They are still refining the models." Andy lapsed and looked up.

Evans was smiling. "Thank you, Andy. That report is exactly what I was told."

Andy frowned. *Told by whom?* No matter how he tried, he couldn't penetrate the old man's *other* sources. This left Andy a bit uncomfortable. If the SPB was so secret no one knew about it and they were the top of the top, what else was out there that Evans had access to? What could be a step above SPB? He shuddered. Maybe it didn't pay to know.

"So folks." Evans stated, "If we can't kill it, what can we do? I'll give you five hours. Then Andy and I will be back." He held them all a moment, then, "Give me something to work with." With no other comment he walked from the room.

Andy looked over the team. For them, he had ceased to exist. He stepped into the corridor, but Evans was no where to be see. *Well,* he thought, *I already stuck my foot in it so, I may as well make up my own theory!* His office was only two doors down and he had a good idea of his approach before he even got there.

Andy sat in his small office and ran scenario after scenario. He based his data on current events, history and his own best assumptions and intuition. The laptop hummed as it retrieved, calculated input, or executed, fairly burning up the connection to the tandem Cray X1s buried three more stories down. If needed, Andy could tap the recourses of any number of other super computers. Some at national labs, research facilities, or military think tanks. He concentrated on, and attacked, only two possible strategies. Use the Artifact, or deny it to anyone else. Ignoring it was not an option. It was there and eventually they would go to it. Or someone else would. He would also satisfy himself that the analysts were correct about destruction. He wanted to be absolutely sure the ship couldn't be destroyed without the debris becoming a serious threat to the earth. Despite what he said in the meeting, he didn't believe it couldn't be, just that it shouldn't be.

Andy first tapped into the military and scientific knowledge base and looked at models already developed. These calculated best guesses at mass, composition and function, and theorized possible Alien counter responses. Then, using existing weapons, mapped possible outcomes. There were also models using weapon systems in development or under theory. There were some incredibly detailed models, some of them graphically showing the Artifact crashing to earth after being disabled. Leading scientists theorized the Artifact was artificially held in orbit. Remove that and the end-game, a decaying orbit resulting in atmosphere reentry, was inevitable. *Atmosphere reentry!* Andy laughed at that one. How could something re-enter something it had never left? They all agreed on one thing however, the mass was too great to destroy. They could possibly kill it, but only if is wasn't defending itself. But destroy it and remove the threat completely? A big, no!

Then Andy ran across a white paper which followed a line of thought that matched an idea burning in the back of his mind. A scientist at MIT theorized that the best way to completely destroy the Artifact was to use it against itself. Use the power source within the object. It had to be incredibly powerful. The scientist theorized a small black hole, or some unknown here-to-for undiscovered source, containing great energy. Disrupt or destroy that and the Artifact should vaporize. His cautionary note was a huge question mark. "How much of the surrounding area would also be vaporized? Would the destruction reach, or even envelope the earth?"

Andy sighed. That question at least was answered. It could be disabled, or possibly destroyed completely, but it would be extremely unwise to do so. No one with a rational mind really wanted to blow-up the greatest discovery in the history of mankind. But knowing that it could be done would at the least give the illusion that they weren't totally helpless in the face of a technology so far advanced.

Andy concentrated on the real questions. Use it, or at least deny that use to anyone else. In essence, that was the new arms race. First one to get there wins, and the world would change again. Andy shuddered to think of the Chinese sitting up there with that technology. He also knew there were agencies and Think Tanks just like his all over the world, each grappling with the same question. In fact, any attempt to reach, or claim the Artifact, could trigger a global holocaust. In some ways it had already started. Only three countries had any realistic hope of actually getting there, and none of the three could allow one of the others to succeed. It would certainly mean the end of their way of life, possibly all life. Third world countries would feel further subjugated. Religious fundamental governments would scream "Holy War!" The chaos seen around the globe right now would be as nothing. Several models predicted global war with it going nuclear very early.

As Andy saw it, there were only two really viable options and one other that was very risky. *Well*, on second thought, *they were all risky*. First, in order to avoid the worst case scenario, the U.S. would have to go multinational. Global actually. A UN action, as distasteful as that would be. Each government with a by-in and participating in the archaeological and technological benefits of the Artifact. An almost impossible task, but in his mind, the best possible outcome. Get the industrialized nations and Russia and China in particular, working with us. The logistics of achieving this were overwhelming as were the odds of it happening. And the clandestine opportunities were mind boggling.

The second option was to deny access to everyone. By world agreement, or by force, the U.S. could ensure no attempt to reach the Artifact was ever taken. Almost certainly that would be the end of all space exploration. Even ours. Any attempted launch would be met with force. His ten year plot showed static industry growth leading to an eventual global economic collapse and finally, world war.

The last option he considered was the possibility of a stealth launch. Or a quick launch. Get there before anyone else could react. Again, his modeling showed a high probability of triggering massive retaliation by multiple enemies.

Andy sat back and rubbed his eyes. The Diet Coke beside his keyboard was flat and lukewarm, much like his mood. No good options. He glanced at his watch. Half an hour till the next meeting. He sighed, *back to it. With this stack of crap there must be something I can find.*

Chapter 7

The maintenance computer assessed the progress again for the thousandth time, determined to not repeat the error of only 19.236 SMU's (Standard Measurement Units) before. One of its robot minions, working on the main computer linkage between the Astrogation and Time Distortion Drive, had suddenly failed. Losing power, it fell into the synthetic neuron transmitters it was repairing. The ceramic carapace of the robot pushed two of the neurons together, with unexpected results. A static charge, which had built up within the celestial dust clinging to the surface of the deep gray material, fired one of the neurons, transmitting one packet of information into a cell of another exposed neuron. A packet which had remained dormant in the cellular structure for two millennia and still held a command. That neuron link immediately sent the ancient command on to the A.I., initiating a preprogrammed failsafe operation in the interstellar drive.

Immediately the drive fired, commanding the maintenance robots to return to their predefined safe positions and releasing the last of the energies built up in the batteries and capacitors. The drive reached out to its last known position, the exact spot over the green planet so many light years away. Not enough energy remained to even slightly move the great ship, but a worm hole opened for 7.81 micro SMU's. The maintenance computer reacted as quickly as the damaged conditions allowed and shut the system down, thus saving the ship from further harm. The robots returned to work and the Maintenance A.I. reassessed its priorities and progress. It detailed a robot to rescue its brother which had caused the mishap, then continued the linkage repair. Vi-t-try saw nothing of this event. A flicker of awareness was all he knew. But it was a flicker that was growing.

Light from the dual moons glowed over the cool desert in the midst of the Nevada test range. A moon, waxing full, competed with the brilliant reflection from *Artifact 1* as it was being called in the scientific and military communities, leaving two shadows under every sage, clump of grass, or cactus. Moonlight that was bright enough to read by left the landscape glowing in a million shades of gray with very little black. Nocturnal animals moved with caution and burrowing owls shielded their eyes at the entrances to their under ground nests. Anyone that happened to be out and staring at those shadows, some fifty-five hours after the Artifact's incredible arrival, would have noticed a flickering from the sky. As if a candle flame guttered in a sudden breeze. Looking up, that individual would have stared in fascination, or possibly shock and fear as Artifact 1 suddenly and dramatically, pulsed. Blue lightening raced and danced over its surface. This is exactly what the ground station, inside a nondescript building at Groom Lake, the notorious Area 51, watched and recorded. The same event that every other telescope or spy satellite trained on the object observed. And while the cold technology merely saw and recorded, their warm blooded inventors reacted quite differently.

Warning klaxons sounded in facilities throughout the world, but none as loud as those inside the operations center at the Strategic Air Command Center in Cheyenne Mountain. Duty Officers scrambled and orders were spoken. Personnel watched screens, looking for missile launches. Land based - nothing. Sea launch - nothing. Spy satellites showed no air scrambles from hostile forces. No threat could be found except the Artifact in the sky which had come suddenly to spectacular and terrifying life. As they watched, blue lightening flared across its surface, consolidated, then just as suddenly ceased. Three and a half seconds of activity, then nothing. The Artifact went back to its dormant state. Yet one thing in space had changed. And it was dramatic. The International Space Station, the Unity, had returned to earth!

Buck was catching up on some much needed sleep, when the klaxons shook him from a wisp of a dream he could almost remember, to full wide awake. His first shock was of the nasty pasty coffee taste in his mouth, the next, *what now?* Fortunately, he was sleeping in his clothes, not NASA regulations, but, oh well. He grabbed his shoes and ran for the viewing room to find about twenty people already there, some actually looking worse than he did. Not going home in the last fifty or so hours will do that. As he entered he checked the screens, but nothing jumped out at him. Buck saw Cal sitting in the front and caught his eye. Cal held a seat for him and he slid in.

"What's up, boss?"

Cal had a gleam in his eye so it must be big. "Good news, Mr. Rodgers. We may have a mission! Unity is back."

"What?" Buck was stunned and elated. "How? What's the report? Have we established contact yet? How are they?"

"Hold on man," Cal held up a hand at the verbal barrage. "She just reappeared. They're still trying to call, but so far nothing." A cold dread settled over Buck. *Dead?*

"The Artifact just went live a few minutes back. Blue lightening. You know, just like when it arrived. Then zip! It stopped. The thing looks as dead now as when it arrived. But then radar gets a blip and sure enough, Unity's back. It's in a way the hell up there orbit and no answer yet. That's all I know."

"How come we aren't getting a feed in here?" Usually the gallery received an audio feed from the operation floor. Now, only silence.

"I don't know, Buck. It was on just before you got here, then they cut if off." Cal shrugged his shoulders. He'd let Buck draw his own conclusions.

Out on the floor of operations, the big screen showed a current feed of Artifact 1. A distant disk showing as a crescent. This feed was from a ground station in the Nevada desert. Another screen showed a replay of "Event 6" as this was being called. The prior events being numbered 1 for the original disappearance of the satellites, 2 for the disappearance of the Unity, 3 for the reappearance of one GPS bird, 4 for the sudden appearance of the Artifact and 5, the disappearance of the Atlantis. Other screens showed actual footage of 1 through 5, or comparisons of orbits and proximity of other space objects. Confusing to the uninitiated, but very informative and fascinating to Buck and Cal. Yet also, frustrating. Watching with a professional eye and being kept out of the loop were two different things. Buck ached to be down there in the middle of it. His mind wandered to Cal's statement. *We may have a mission!* Rescue? Fact finding? And what about what happened to Atlantis? Not a pleasant thought, one fortunately interrupted by Cal, who nodded a chin towards the door on the far side of the operations center.

"The boss wants us." Sure enough, Miles Johnson, Chief of the FCOD (Flight Crew Operation Directorate), was heading for the exit. His Deputy, Sam Marconi, was waving to the gallery and circling one finger. The astronauts knew it was time for a meeting. There were about seven of them in the gallery and each headed for the conference room several floors up, reserved specifically for FCOD use.

Eight Astronauts sat waiting in the conference room. All were Captains and above, Pilots and Commanders. As of yet Miles Johnson had not appeared, so the briefing hadn't started. Conversation was quiet, mostly between individuals who had worked together. The subject, however, was the same. Unity. Would one of the crews represented here be flying a rescue mission? Would it be a burial detail? Suicide mission? Emotions ran from excitement to certain trepidation, yet each and every one would be the first to volunteer. Such was the mettle of these men and women. The true face of the unknown lay in the skies above and friends and fellow spacemen needed them.

Above the group, was the object and cause of the discussion. The main screen continued to display the ground shot of Artifact 1 as seen from the Nevada desert. Buck and Cal sat in the second row center. The best position to see and be seen. At least according to them. They wanted to make sure Johnson eyeballed them and wanted to be in the best position to hear, see, and catch his eye. Every team in here had similar rituals. Each had their own theory and of course, each believed his or hers was the best. Just as they firmly believed they were the best. Not just the best in the room, the best in the world. An attitude engendered and supported by NASA. Without it, you wouldn't make it to this elite company of the astronaut core.

They waited forty-five minutes, speculating endlessly and uselessly, then the door burst open. Johnson and Marconi stalked into the room and involuntarily each of the seated men and women sat straighter. It was called, sitting at attention.

Miles Johnson began without preamble. "Ladies and Gentlemen, I'm going to show you something few people have seen!" He nodded to Sam Marconi, who clicked an icon on a management terminal. The room went dark and the main screen changed, bringing a collective gasp from the assembly. "Holy Shit!" was muttered more than once. The screen now showed Artifact 1 as none of them had ever seen it. Up close. In fact, so close it looked like the picture was taken by a shuttle approach. Even more shocking was that it was video, not a photograph. A fact driven home by the movement on the Artifact.

"Look at that!" Cal whispered it out loud and everyone nodded in agreement and wonder.

"That's right, Commander. Something up there is working." Miles didn't let them stew too long.

"What you are seeing is Top Secret! This is a video captured by a certain piece of hardware placed in orbit two years ago by Columbia."

The group nodded knowingly. Several missions a year were flown to deliver equipment or personnel to the Unity, or to fix a wayward satellite, and some of these were cover for what the astronauts called, "Special Delivery." Everyone assumed spy satellites, but none of them had any idea it was of this level of technology.

"Usually tasked for ground coverage, we flipped it around and have been capturing for the last 32 hours. This bird can capture wiggly little hairs in the crack of a gnat's ass! What you're seeing is not the best it can do."

This raised some eyebrows. The view on screen looked like you were less that a mile away. Only part of the Artifact was visible. A view of the top edge which curved away to the blackness beyond. What looked like towers and different sized boxes were spread over the white surface. Part of the picture showed an area that was literally ripped open. No sunlight spilled in the opening, it was simply a gaping ragged black hole. Around the lip of the tear is where movement could be seen. What looked to be robots moved from one of the boxes, to the edge, where a tube or pipe open on one end, extended down into the gloom. There was no scale. The robots could be a foot tall or twenty. Needless to say, Miles had their undivided attention.

"What you are about to witness has only been seen by about ten people. This capture is three minutes prior to Event 6. We'd been watching the activity of the robots and everything seemed to be routine. At least nothing more than the activity of the prior 30 hours. Then, about one minute before the event, things changed. Observe."

No eye had left the screen. To the right bottom was a counter, counting down from some number to zero. Buck assumed zero would be the actual event. The counter was at 1:32 and dropping. So far nothing changed. The robots were moving at a methodical pace with no meaningful direction. At least to the humans. Then at 0:57, the pattern changed. The robots each turned from where ever they were and headed quickly back toward one of the boxes. Some were closer than others, but the ones further away sped up so that all arrived at nearly the same instant. Like a puzzle, they attached themselves to the box which then retracted down into the skin of the ship. All of this in 42 seconds.

"Pause!" The image on the screen froze, though still in crisp clarity.

"In case you were wondering," he looked out at them with a knowing smile. "And I know you were. The longest distance any of those things traveled was 4272 feet. That's the exact distance from the tube to the box."

Someone to the left of Cal whistled. The rest were probably sitting there, stunned speechless as he was. Not only had those robots covered more than three quarters of a mile, they'd done it in less than forty five seconds and most of them started from a dead standstill. Nearly sixty miles an hour, in the dead of space on the surface of a ship and in what they assumed was zero gravity. They docked in precision and were retracted into the ship in under a minute.

Then it sunk in. Buck found himself asking. "Just how big is that thing?" He looked up and saw Miles smile again.

"Ah, Sir!" Cal amended for him.

"Nice of you to ask one of the right questions, Captain Rodgers. Sam."

"28.2333 to the 9th miles in diameter, Captain. No matter how you measure it. Other than the protrusions, it's perfectly round."

As spacemen they were taught to expect the unexpected. Deal with the unknown and unusual. But this! They simply couldn't find enough creative words to describe it.

Buck sat back in his chair and simply muttered, "Good Lord!"

Miles was laying it on. "Now here is where it gets interesting."

Another mutter in the back of the room, "As if!" That at least brought some laughter. They needed something to mentally pinch themselves and that seemed to do it. The professional in each of them kicked back in and they felt they were ready for anything. For some of them, that thought was wrong.

"Ok, Sam. Roll it!"

The video started with the counter at 0:15. Buck knew the "Event" initiated with blue electricity bathing the Artifact, so he was somewhat prepared for zero. Immediately, the screen flared painfully bright, then blanked out as the camera attempted to compensate for the sudden appearance so much energy. It tried to focus and Buck saw a steady upwelling of the blue lightening flowing from the tube, spraying outward. Yet it was too blurry to tell much. The incredible amount of energy required to produce it was boggling. Buck fully believed they could run every single electronic item used on earth for a number of years with the energy expended. A moment later the view pulled even further back and they could see the entire ship, though it still filled the screen. From here, the blue lightening was even more incredible and a pattern in the chaos emerged.

The electricity emanated from the tubes which were precisely placed around the body of the ship. Between the tubes, but offset, were the towers, though these were seen only as bumps of various colors in any of the still photographs. The electricity emerging from the tubes jumped straight to the towers, with several tubes feeding each one. The collected power then jumped in an arc to different towers extending even higher into space. The affect was to encase the entire vessel in blue writhing energy, crisscrossed at two different altitudes over the surface. Buck could see this distinctly as the lines of power wrapped around the curve of the fantastic ship. Each stream of power described a single line of a geometric shape. Each shape distinct and clear. In fact, the ship now looked like a giant soccer ball floating on a black field, the shadow side more brilliantly lit than the sunny side. The only thing marring the beauty of the alien picture was the damage to the ship itself. Where a tube or tower was broken or missing altogether, power was diverted to the nearest working transformer. At least that's how Buck interpreted what he witnessed. So mesmerized by the scene, he was left disappointed and feeling very small when it ceased. Just like a light switch. The blue spectacle simply ceased and the ship lay still as if the fantastic display had never occurred.

"Pause! Comments?" Miles had that gleam which told them they had better ask the right questions. Their intuition and insight may very well determine who went on the next mission and none of them doubted a mission was in the offing. Buck was first into the breach.

"Sir, I'm curious about what I didn't see!"

Miles nodded, "Go on, Captain."

"Yes sir. My assumption is that the event we just saw has something to do with the disappearance of Unity, Atlantis and the satellites. Also, it's probably the mechanism for transport of the Artifact itself." He paused, but Miles gave no indication he was going to bail him out.

I'm either way off base and making a fool of myself, or I'm right on target. "So why didn't it leave? It must have reached out and snagged Unity back. Why not Atlantis? Where are its friends? Maybe more important, where are its enemies? Also, Sir, I didn't see any actual result from the event we just saw. I have to assume the Unity was brought back and dropped somewhere, probably in an orbit lower than the Artifact, but I didn't see any beam or tunnel. Nothing." He stopped, thinking he'd spouted quite enough questions without bringing any answers.

Miles smiled again. "Quite a laundry list. Do you have any theories, Captain?"

This earned him a few dirty looks from the gathering, but, 'To the bold' as the saying goes. "Yes sir. First, I don't think it went anywhere because it couldn't. By the look of it, there is a lot of battle damage. It was probably trying to get somewhere else and ended up here by accident. Maybe the trip here damaged it even more. It's done nothing hostile since it got here, so I think event 6 was it trying to go back where it started from. Unity was just a benefit for us."

A couple of people covered coughs in the back showing what they thought of his theory, or cursing at him for being the glory hound he was.

Miles ignored them. "What about the rest Captain?"

"Rest, sir?"

"Yes, the rest, Captain. The friends. The enemies? What's your theory about them?"

Buck felt a little uncomfortable now. Maybe he'd really stepped in it. "Well, sir. Either he," Buck pointed at the screen indicating the alien ship. "Was the only one left standing, or the battle it was in happened so far away in some backwater it's been completely forgotten. Maybe it was abandoned and unsalvageable. Anyway, the enemy and its friends don't know where it is; else we would be hip deep in them."

Miles looked around the room assessing the others. Buck thought he was going to ask for more theories, but then he grinned again. "Captain, you'll be happy to know all our deep thinkers came up with almost the same thing!" Groans and several other unflattering statements followed that announcement.

Cal elbowed him as Miles turned back to the screen. "Thanks for making me look so good man."

Buck was more than relieved. He was elated. "I noticed you stepped right into the breach."

"Hey, we're a team... I just wanted to give you all the glory my man. All the glory."

"And take the pasting if I was wrong. Right."

Cal just smiled, "It's an educational experience, Buck. We'll make a Commander out of you yet."

"Nah, I can't afford the pay cut."

They could have continued jabbing each other all night long, but the sound of Miles's voice cut in. "Captain Rodgers asked about Unity and indeed she is back."

Actual confirmation brought mixed emotions from the astronauts. If everything was ok with Unity, it would have been all over the news. There had been nothing but silence.

"She's back and in trouble. We've had no communication from her and we can't get any of the automated controls to work."

This was worse than Buck imagined and Cal whispered, "Damn."

Miles continued, "Whatever the condition of the crew, the Unity can't last more than four more days." He really had their attention now. "The Artifact dropped them into an oblong orbit. In four days she hits the atmosphere. She comes down or skips off. Either way, that's it."

If their military training, or NASA regulations permitted, it there would have been a near riot. Miles held up his hand and quiet again settled over them.

"First of all. No! We can't do anything about it. The theory is that wherever it was since it left here, the Artifact couldn't insert it back into its original orbit. This seems to support most of Captain Rodgers theories." Buck should have felt vindicated, instead he just felt numb.

"To answer your next question. I'm not sure what we can do to rescue them, but the decisions been made. We're damn sure going to try!"

Buck found himself yelling "Hell Yeah", with the rest of them. Miles gave his first genuine smile. He knew his people. Damn the danger. He'd have no end of volunteers.

"Now then. I'm going to show you something else that no one has seen. Our friendly little satellite also gave us some pictures of the Unity. Pay attention. Roll it Sam!"

Of all that they'd seen and heard till now, nothing prepared them for the condition of the space station. Buck thought it was just the orbit they had to deal with, but the Unity looked like it had gone through a war. The incredible close-up video painted a grim picture for the ship. The four solar collection panels were twisted and melted. Two were half their original size and one twisted down, seeming to hang by a single bolt. Scorch marks scarred the surfaces of the pods and the leading pod looked like it had endured a partial re-entry. As shocking as the damage was, something else nagged at Buck. Something else didn't seem right. He had it just as Miles began to explain.

"Obviously, given the condition and no communication, we have little hope for survivors." There it was. Not a rescue mission. A recovery. Probably to get any information out of the station as much as the bodies.

"There is another mystery, people. Some of you may have spotted it." He waited till everyone who was going to catch up, did. "The Unity is missing a module."

I knew it, Buck thought. *That's the one we delivered.*

"By the look of it, the analysts don't think it could have been twisted or sheared off. We won't know for sure till we get there, but it looks like it was removed."

That seemed to be the end of the briefing, but Miles gave them a parting shot. "Spend as much time as you want studying the video and discussing what you've seen. Then get some sleep. I'll be picking a team tomorrow at 0900 and we fly in less than 48 hours. I assume you all are volunteering?" No one answered in the negative.

"That's all for now. Sam!" With that, the Chief and his aid left the room leaving them each with personal thoughts and prayers for those poor souls on the Unity.

Chapter 8

Captain Rodgers and Commander Sanderson sat dejected with many others in the gathering. Miles Johnson had just selected a crew to fly the mission to Unity as well as a backup crew to flesh out the flight. Neither group included Cal and Buck and they were perplexed. Both of the chosen teams had fewer hours and fewer flights than they did. While this wouldn't ordinarily have been an issue because these decisions were based on last flight, conditioning, training on types of approach and so on, they still considered themselves the best. They could question the decision, but only privately.

The meeting was breaking up and the chosen crew was headed to mission brief. As the rest of the astronauts filed out, Cal nudged him on the shoulder. "The Chief just motioned us to wait."

Buck had missed the subtle hand and eye command because he was to damn busy watching the "prime crew" exit through the door he himself so desperately wanted to go through. Envy? He whispered to his friend, "Why?" A raised eyebrow was all he got.

It took ten minutes for all of the others to vacate the room. Each either mingling, or talking with the Chief. Very subdued, and very uncharacteristic of such meetings. It was strange also that Miles would stick around. Usually he held the meeting, gave the good and bad news, and then exited. Questions and objections could be presented at his office, and only formally. Today was different. *The whole world is different,* was Bucks first thought. Finally, as the last person left, the Chief walked up to them.

"Join me for a cup," he said simply, then turned on his heel and left.

"What the hell do you think that's about?" Buck wasn't sure he'd actually heard it right.

"No telling, my man. But let's not keep him waiting. Besides, I have a few questions of my own… and it looks like he's going to give us a chance to bitch."

They found the Chief in the small employee lounge down a hall and just off the main floor of mission control. But as they approached the room, a guard stopped them in their tracks. An MP that had never been there before. Security was for getting into the complex, not for getting into an employee lounge and Buck couldn't help but feel his hackles rise.

"ID, gentlemen!" The voice was deep, respectful and promised a world of hurt should they fail to comply. Inside the room they could see where another guard stood. Other than Miles, it was empty. Cal looked at Buck and raised an eyebrow. Curiouser and Curiouser. After more than a cursory check of their IDs, they were allowed in.

"Sorry about the security gentlemen, but I assure you, entirely necessary."

Miles motioned them to get something to drink then sit down. Buck fairly tingled. Something was up. This was more than just an explanation of why they were passed over. He knew it, felt it, and he could see the same in Cal's face as he poured the coffee.

When they settled, Miles jumped right in, "First off, I know you were disappointed this morning, but I am not here to deal with your bruised egos." Both laughed. The Chief just wasn't the touchy feely type and neither figured this was a mentoring session.

"I'm also not in the habit of explaining my decisions, so put those questions out of your mind." Just like that, all of their arguments remained still-born.

"Gentlemen, I have something else in store for you. This is a 'no questions asked' mission for which *I*… am volunteering *you…*"

He looked each of them in the eye asking the unspoken question and receiving the required, "Yes Sir!"

"After you finish your coffee, you will immediately exit the building through the rear employee entrance and enter a van that's waiting for you, driven by..." he waved a hand over at the two guards.

"These gentlemen will drive you to the airport and put you on a plane. You will ask them no questions. It will all be explained when you get to your final destination." The Chief had never looked more serious in his life.

"Sorry about the cloak and dagger, but as I said when you came in, I assure you it's completely necessary. Enjoy your coffee, gentlemen." With that he stood up and left.

"Son of a Bitch!"

"I echo that, Buck. Never seen anything like it."

"Maybe we're going to talk the other crew through it?"

"Maybe we're going to launch two flights?" Cal mused. "But I don't know how. Only one shuttle's close to ready."

"Well! You know what they say about curiosity and the cat. And we've just been appointed kittens."

Cal laughed, "Come on Sylvester. Some ones wavin' the catnip and you know how I soo love catnip."

Judith Kinsey sat at a curbside table, basking in the early morning Colorado sun. She was sipping a cup of coffee, black and caffeinated, just the way she liked it, Smiling at the beauty around her and contemplating the dichotomy of a world turned upside down. Aliens and war in distant places. Economic turmoil and terrorists running rampant. A million people screaming about the end of the world. All events that seemed so distant and unreal. Another world perhaps or perhaps she dreamed. She sighed and watched the gentle play of the sunshine and shadows on the steep snow covered hills surrounding Aspen. A place she'd called home for all of her sixty-two years. Seen it grow from a small obscure mountain town to the elite Mecca it was today. Sad for her. She always wished for the old times, when things weren't so complicated and rushed. Sure, she'd made her millions, selling each piece of the old ranch for ever higher and higher prices. The moneyed elite seemed to have no boundaries when it came buying a piece of the Rocky Mountain High. But there is the practical and then there is the magical. She wished for the old days of her youth. The magical.

Two tables away sat a famous actress and her 'friend', all dressed up in the latest ski fashion that had, in all probability, never seen a ski slope. Down the way, a director was sitting with a rock star and a singer from one of those terrible rap bands. Extraordinary in other cities. Quite normal here. Even more normal now, with all these people fleeing the chaos of their homes to their showy winter getaways. Leave your troubles behind they say.

"More coffee, Mrs. Kinsey?" She was startled from her contemplation by the waiter who looked like he'd be more at home 'cleaning' some rich woman's pool than catering to her.

"Please. And thanks. By the way Paul, do you think you can get that van to move? The exhaust is becoming a nuisance."

An old gray GMC panel van had pulled into the unloading zone in front on the cafe and sat idling, belching clouds of half burned gas and blocking the view. The driver just sat there, staring at them. Short dark hair and a three day beard, with dark glasses that gave no hint as to what was behind them.

Paul gave a sigh, "I'll see what I can do, Madame."

The young waiter had only taken three steps when 180 pounds of high explosive, detonated by the driver, obliterated the van, half of the café, and Mrs. Kinsey. In all, twenty seven people died. Terror didn't recognize or care about the dreams and aspirations of the young waiter, nor the magic Mrs. Kinsey so longed to recapture. It only cared that they died to demonstrate to the world that there was no place to hide.

"Mr. President, the information we are about to show you has been compiled from a number of sources and while as extraordinary and incredible as it is, I feel it constitutes the gravest threat our world has ever faced." Sean Evans began the briefing with the intent of getting and holding everyone's attention. He certainly succeeded.

He threw the hook. "Mr. President, it also may provide the greatest opportunity mankind has ever known."

Evans was not one for grandstanding, but he'd told Andy prior to the briefing that they could not afford to undersell this. The President was caught up in more calamities than any president before him, including Washington, Lincoln, Eisenhower and Kennedy put together. Evans needed to get him to look well above the fray. That's why they requested this meeting be only the President and his closest advisor. Now was not the time for argument, or policy or jockeying for political advantage.

Conspicuously absent were all the normal players. Only the President and his Chief of Staff, Paul Majors. No military. No CIA or NSA, and certainly no politicians, the President not withstanding.

President Talbot looked wearier than Andy had ever seen him. The normally vibrant man looked as if he'd aged ten years. In fact, he'd just returned from talking with the families of the scientists who were onboard the Unity. He'd done his best and tried to give them hope, but they were on roller coaster of emotions. First they had the loss of Unity and coming to grips with the death of their loved ones to deal with, then the return of the space station and the hope of their return. And now, no news from the ship. It was probably the hardest job of any facing a, Commander in Chief. To console the loved ones of those he put in harms way. His eyes were puffy and dark, attesting to his self induced sleep depravation and his sallow skin showed he'd also been ignoring most of his meals. Yet he sat looking at them intently and looking very much in charge. A lesser man may have crumbled under the stress, but Jon Talbot seemed to actually thrive on it. He held up his hand.

"First of all, Sean… drop the Mr. President crap. It's just us here and I know you wouldn't be here to waste my time, so 'bottom line it for me!'"

Evans laughed, "I was afraid you still wanted your ass kissed, Jon."

"Yeah, well the election's still two years off and the worlds gone to hell and I need a donut and coffee. So tell me how you're going to ease all my worries."

"Would that I could, Jon. Would that I could." He looked pointedly at his friend. "Instead, I'm going to add to the stack."

"Shit! I was afraid of that. Ok, Sean. Lay it on me."

Evans nodded to Andy, who keyed the first presentation. He never ceased to be amazed at the relationship between his boss and the Leader of the Free World. Certainly a side the rest of the world never saw. Up on the screen the video showed the last moments of the Atlantis, right before the alien ship showed up.

The President sighed, "I've seen this before, Sean. What's new?"

"I know you've seen it, but a couple of our bright lights down in Houston found something we all missed. Watch!"

The President watched, still startled by the sudden appearance of the ship and the memories of the event evoked. But just as the Atlantis vanished and the screen went blank, Andy froze the screen.

"This is where we thought it ended... But after analysis and video enhancement, the last few milliseconds of the feed from Atlantis showed this!"

Andy keyed the last frame and the President and Majors simply stared, dumfounded. Then, "Is that what I think it is?"

"Yes, Jon. A planet! We think this is where the Atlantis went as well as the satellites. And, since the Unity came back, it means we may have the means of workable interstellar travel almost in our hands."

"By *means*, you mean the alien craft." It was a statement, but Evans answered it anyway.

"Yes sir. We get that technology and we jump from our infant grasps at the moon and Mars and leap to the universe. The possibilities are too incredible to put into words." He paused just a moment for dramatic affect. "But, Mr. President," he used the honorific on purpose. "Time is short."

"What does that mean? The alien ship is laying up there dead and I'm playing a hell of a stalling game trying to keep the military from blowing it out of the sky... or at least trying to. Are you saying you have a plan to get that technology for us? And even make it work?"

Evans sighed; *this is where it gets sticky.* "First off, the ship isn't dead. The return of the Unity proves that."

"Wait a minute. My science advisors said that was just some automated program and it probably short circuited since nothing else happened."

"Well, Jon, your advisors didn't have all of the information. Andy, roll number two!"

If the President was shocked by the last presentation, he was positively stunned by this one. On screen was the footage recently shown to the astronauts in Houston. Robots crawling across the surface of the Artifact.

"Before you ask the question," Sean told him. "Yes, this was taken by the DRS-123 we sent into orbit a year ago. We realigned it from ground shot to space shot. The sequence you're watching was taken just seconds before the Unity came back."

They played the entire sequence, through the blue lightening and the return of the Space Station. Andy let it run, still fascinated himself by the robots as they danced about the alien ship.

"My God! It's repairing itself!" The President breathed out heavily.

"We think so. That's why time may be short. We have no idea how long it might take, or what its' intentions will be when it's done. It may just leave, taking our future with it."

Paul Majors, the Chief of Staff, spoke up for the first time. "Shit, Sean! It may damn well attack us as leave! What the hell do we do then? The military's going to have a shit fit."

"It might attack, certainly a possibility." He said it in a tone that left them no doubt of his opinion on that. "But we've analyzed every angle and think that it's a remote possibility. Unless of course, we attack it first!" He let that and the implications hang.

The President spoke up. "So we can't kill it. We can't stop it from repairing itself and if it does, we can't prevent it from leaving. What do you suggest? Obviously, you have something up that sneaky sleeve of yours or we wouldn't be here."

Evans smiled, "My suggestion, Mr. President," he again used the formal on purpose. "Is to go to it... and, see if we can help it!"

The dying sun gave little warmth to the arid and rugged Steppes of Kazakhstan. Buried deep in the heart of the old Soviet Union, this inhospitable place was about to come alive. The huge complex that the Soviets tried so hard to hide during the first years of the space race, was itself dominated by the shear vastness of nothing. For here, just north of the Kazakhstan border town of Tyuratam lay the Baikonur Cosmodrome. In the center of the complex, bathed in bright light from a hundred sources, a ship pointed majestically toward the heavens and the object of its creator's desire. One of the huge rockets known as a Proton Launch Vehicle, stood ready to launch. Plumes of white gas flowed out and dissipated from a number of vents, giving the rocket a ghost like quality in the fading sunlight of evening. From a distance, it look liked it was already flying.

The Russians had made every attempt to keep this launch a
secret, prepping the vehicle and selecting a launch window, all
within a mere seven short hours. Rushing to launch held many
risks, but the powers behind this effort weighed these against
desire. As always, desire won out. Their analysts read much of the
same data as their American counterparts. In fact, highly placed
information gatherers, usually known as spies, provided a wealth
of data that would astound the Americans, had they known. Yet
such activity could not go unnoticed in this day and age and as
soon as U.S. satellites noticed the unusual bustle, a team of
observers snuck across the frontier from Kazakhstan, setting up
post some eleven miles away. The two Special Forces officers had
just completed their spider hole and were in place and observing
for no more than eight minutes, when suddenly, the peaceful
solitude of their little hill was shattered by the distant screams of
air raid sirens.

"What the hell?" whispered Major Tim "Giv" Givens.
"You think they saw us?"

"Naw! It ain't us. We'd already be dead." The quiet, almost
unheard answer, was delivered in a West Texas drawl by his
partner, Captain Sam Winston.

The words weren't even out of his mouth when the
Cosmodrome was plunged into pseudo darkness as the space
center went to complete blackout. Pointless in the murky evening
light. Even more pointless given modern night-vision technology.
The Americans could still see the launch pad with their binoculars,
even without the aid of NVGs.

"Any ideas? Maybe we should bug!" Givens was voicing
Winston's exact thoughts, but they both knew sticking tight was
their best move. Getting caught would be a very bad idea. Not only
for them, but for their country as well.

"May be a false alarm," Winston whispered. "Let's play it a
might longer and see. Any movement toward us and we'll hot foot
it." Winston was the senior officer so it wasn't really a discussion.

They settled in to as comfortable a position as you could
get in a spider hole and watched and waited for whatever came
next. They didn't have long. The sirens continued to blare, but
suddenly, distant flashes erupted from the ground all around the
facility; long arcs of flame reaching skyward.

"Son of a bitch, Giv! Antiaircraft fire? Someone's attackin." As he said, it they heard the distant pops of the AA and the louder scream of fighter aircraft. To their right and west of the base, a fighter dove on some unknown target, ripping the sky with cannon fire. If the jet hit its target, there was no apparent effect. Another burst, then whatever it was exploded with a brilliant flash. So intent were they on the developing show, they didn't notice the growing hiss of the incoming cruise missile until it was right over them. Involuntarily, they ducked as the missile buzzed their hill on its way to the target, their eyes going wide as it passed. Unmistakable and impossible to miss, on the side was the imprint of a flag. A Red field with one large yellow star and four smaller in a crescent. The flag of the PRC.

"China!"

"Shit, Giv! Call it in. Now!"

Givens keyed his SAT phone, quietly talking on a direct connection to the stuffed shirts back in the States. As they watched the plains, an aerial battle ensued, the Russian fighters chasing down the cruise missiles and the mindless weapons uncaringly pushing to the target. Winston whistled as the first missile made it through the Russian defense. It dove into the Space Operations Launch Center and the entire building disappeared behind a huge explosion of fire, streamers and smoke. He was reminded of the film broadcast out of Baghdad during Iraqi Freedom. Surreal. The Russian defense was fierce and gallant, and doomed.

Three seconds later, the Gantry tower connected to the Proton took a direct hit. Exploding outward, the concussion wave slammed against the rocket with enough force to dent the side, rupturing one of the fuel tanks underneath. A millisecond later, the skin of the rocket was pierced by superheated metal fragments traveling many times the speed of sound. The Proton would have needed reactive tank armor to withstand the blast. It had none and the rocket's fuel ignited in a colossal blast the equivalent of several hundred tons of TNT. The Proton, the gantry, three Cosmonauts and over sixty technicians and scientists disappeared in a single brilliant instant.

Winston gave another, "Son of a bitch!"

Three seconds later the blast wave reached them. Still with enough force to blow the camouflage net covering their hole completely off, spilling it down the back side of the hill.

"Son of a bitch!" Winston said it again and Givens just nodded as he continued his update, staring at the devastation. Even as he watched, two more missiles slammed into the same target.

Obviously, the Chinese weren't going for complete destruction of the complex; they just wanted to stop the launch. Whatever the reason, with their goal achieved, quiet again settled over the steppes, broken only by the far off wail of sirens from fire and rescue and the drone of jets far over head. Evening deepened into full night as the two Americans observed. The final dream of the Russian Space Command lay in ruins, flickering in ever dying flames. Their gambit to be the first to Artifact 1 had failed. Their dream was now, little more that twisted metal and ashes, scattered across the scorched desert by Chinese explosives and a fickle wind.

Andy didn't bother knocking on Evans door. The boss was sitting behind his huge mahogany desk, which looked like it might have belonged to some 1920s business mogul. Totally out of place with the rest of the decor in the ultra modern hi-tech office. The Director was on the phone and raised a single finger. A moment later he hung up.

"Who did what now Andy? You look like you've seen a ghost!"

"The Chinese, Boss. They just blew up Baikonur!"

If Evans was surprised it showed little. "Nuclear?"

"No sir. Conventional. Cruise missiles launched from their far west province. Xinjiang. Near the city of Burgin. Stealth attack. Unknown launch method, but probably bombers. We had no idea the PRC cruise missiles had advanced that far." Andy sat down heavily as his boss mused.

"Damage estimate?"

"We have a camera passing over in about ten minutes, so we'll know for sure…but we had some assets on the ground fairly close. They reported multiple hits and a complete loss of the Proton the Russians were staging. Damage to the control centers. For sure they're out of the manned space business for a while."

Evans seemed to think for a moment, then, "Have the Russians responded?"

"No sir! Not yet. But you can bet they will and in typical Russian fashion. Blunt force, blunt trauma and overkill!"

Evans actually smiled at him. "You're obviously right, Andy. I hope it doesn't go nuclear, but the Chinese just did us a favor."

"Yes sir. We'll be able to launch first. But we better double security. And then double it again."

Evans nodded, dismissing him with, "See to it Andy. Give me the details and the Russian response when it comes. I need to call the President."

Andy rose and left, wondering how much more this world could take.

Chapter 9

The Learjet Bombardier 60, cruised along at forty-six thousand feet and very close to its max speed of Mach 0.81, dancing over and between the towering cumuli which were soaking the high plains of West Texas. Daylight was three hours away and Buck and Cal were bleary eyed tired. Yet sleep would have to wait. Too many questions remained unanswered and the source of those answers sat in the cabin with them having a quiet conversation. After being whisked to a very private part of the Houston/Hobby Airport by the non communicative and almost mute security detail, they were "put" on this very plane, which taxied and took off as soon as the door shut behind them. Even more interesting than their abduction, was this other passenger already on the plane. The man identified himself as an Air Force Lt. Colonel, but he looked and dressed like Bill Gates. He introduced himself simply as Marx then waited until they were at cruising altitude before saying anything else. Once up and each with a cup of coffee, he started simply.

"Gentlemen, I know you have nothing but questions. However, I will not be able to tell you everything. You may have speculated about what all this is about, but I assure you, whatever you thought... is wrong." He fixed them with dark eyes staring out of his thick glasses. Neither astronaut could deny the intelligence they saw there and if the man truly was Air Force, he was certainly far more as well.

"So, Mr. Marx, I assume you will a least give us a clue as to why our Director had us hijacked!" Buck knew their boss had a plan and he'd been 'volunteered' for it, but that didn't mean they had to roll over and take it.

"More than a clue Captain. Your Director thinks highly of you. I asked for a favor and he gave me you two. You have been *selected* for a very special mission. Quit probably, the most important mission ever attempted by mankind." He watched the momentary confusion, then the realization and stunned expressions cross their faces.

We're not going to the Unity, we're going to the Artifact! Buck was elated.

Cal asked his unspoken thought. "How?" His voice was strained and a long silence reigned while they gathered their thoughts. Buck was very aware of the droning of the jets and the slight vibrations as it ploughed through some rough air.

When it was clear that Marx was going to ignore the question, Cal passed right over it. "More importantly then, when? It's going to take months to configure a shuttle to be able to fly and land there. We can't do it quicker. Unless you're going to dust off an old Apollo."

Marx looked down his nose and smiled slightly. Buck felt a little shiver. The man looked like he held a bucket load of secrets behind those thick glasses. *I bet he know where lots of bodies are buried!*

"Well Gentlemen, I commend you for your intelligence. At least you leapt beyond the obvious. Yes, "We" are going to Artifact 1." Now that he'd actually said it, Buck could let out his breath, held without thought and way too long.

"And no, we aren't going to, as you say, dust off an Apollo."

"How then?" Buck asked. "I don't know of anything we have in the inventory that could make that trip and I damn sure don't think the Russian's do!"

Marx smiled again and this one was almost genuine. "That's where you are wrong, Captain. In fact, the Russian's tried a launch about three hours ago, thinking a reconfigured flight path might just make it. Even though their Cosmonauts knew it would be a one way trip!"

"One way trip?"

"Yes, Commander. The Russian objective wasn't to go and get back, but go and claim! I'm not sure if it was bravery or blackmail that got them on that rocket."

Buck shook his head and yawned, trying to break the pressure in his ear. "You said, *tried*. What does that mean? They have to abort?"

Marx sat forward and his expression became very intense. "The mission was aborted for them! By the Chinese."

"The Chinese? How could they have had anything to do with it?"

"The Chinese as well as us, I mean the U.S., were monitoring the emergency preparations for this flight. The Russian's, once they'd been caught, said it was a rescue mission to Unity, just like the one being mounted now at the Cape. You may recall that they had a scientist on board the space station as well." He sat back in his chair. "No matter that their ship didn't have the maneuverability to catch the wild orbit Unity is on. We were in talks with them, but they weren't listening. The Chinese didn't bother talking."

"What the hell does that mean?" Buck was getting tired of the long answer to a short question tact Marx was taking. "If they weren't talking how could they intervene?"

"Preliminary reports say cruise missiles, Captain. At least twenty of them." Buck collapsed back into his own chair.

Cal visibly shuddered, "Holy shit!" He didn't even know he'd said it.

Marx didn't give them too much time to think about it. "Now you know the reasons for all the security and the, what did you call it? 'Cloak and dagger shit.'" He grabbed his coffee and sipped a moment more.

"Before you ask, security has been tightened at the Cape. I'm told a tick couldn't get through without a blood test. Air intervention starting at 200 miles. Navy and Coast Guard. Seals on the beaches, Marines, National Guard, State Police, you name it. We have it covered. And, though it is a "real" mission; we need to get to the Unity and find out what happened, it's also a decoy for the real trip. And yes, you are a part of it."

Buck supposed that in this day and age, where the world was literally changing in front of him, nothing should surprise him. He tried to make that thought stick, but couldn't. The warm full flavor of his coffee suddenly seemed sour and pasty in his mouth. Obviously, he was now part of something big. Something extraordinary. And it was really pissing him off, because he had zero knowledge and even less control!

His anger showed in his voice. "Ok, Mr. Marx. We're getting a little tired of being led around by the nose. A little information here. A bombshell there. What the hell's really going on? Discovery's just a decoy? You intimate "We" are the real mission. Just how do you expect us to get to that alien ship? As far as I know, there are no other shuttles ready, never mind the fact they can't get into that high an orbit! How about some clarification?"

Marx actually had a look of sympathy for him. "Sorry Captain, but I assure you this secrecy is necessary. Your chief bought off on it, once he was given certain details. Details he didn't have prior to this morning, I might add. But again, for security reasons, I will only tell you one more thing!"

Almost on cue, the fasten seatbelt light came on with a chime to announce their decent.

"Security?" Buck said. "Surely we're no security risk!" Cal grabbed his arm as he leaned forward, but if Marx felt threatened, he didn't show it.

Marx gave a little shake of his head, "No, Captain. You yourself are above reproach and no security risk. But there are any number of countries that would and have, I might add... kill for information about this project. You will be given a thorough briefing once we reach our final destination. And then..." he paused and stared intently at both of them. "You will join the ranks of the Special People of the world."

Buck felt more than a little dazed. What the hell had they gotten themselves into?

"Special people?" Cal's voice sounded a little hollow as well.

"Yes, Commander. Special people. You know... The ones who have information others are willing to torture and kill you for." He looked slightly sad as if he carried the same burden and was reluctant to pass it on to someone else.

"I'm sorry, gentlemen. Your lives are about to change forever. And no! There is no more I can tell you now. We're going to land in a few minutes at Holloman Air Force Base in New Mexico, where you will each be transferred to an F-111 for the next phase of your journey. I will meet you at our final destination and then I assure you, every question you have and many more will be answered."

Marx settled back into his chair and looked to the blackness outside his window. Clearly, the information sharing was over. Buck also sat back as the little jet dove for the ground. All he could do was speculate, or let his imagination run. Both activities were pointless and equally unavoidable. He just hoped that whatever they had in mind didn't kill them. His brain was still wandering as the tires screeched on the tarmac and the plane taxied to the F-111s, which were already powered up and waiting. *What next!* He thought. *What the hell next!*

Israel was poised on the edge of a knife! Not necessarily a new situation, except this time the world was preoccupied and turning a blind eye and Israel faced the very real possibility of the end of its existence. Certainly that was the full intent of their enemies. A country of only five and a quarter million souls, with a standing army of a hundred and eighty-six thousand, they faced the armed might of most of their Arab neighbors. Syria alone, with a population of over seventy million and an army approaching a half million, dwarfed the Israelis. Yet they also faced Egypt, with a combined force nearly equal to their northern brothers in Syria and the reluctant Jordanians. They were forced into the, as of now, undeclared war, by the Saudis who would attack through their territory, co-operation or not.

Buffered from Iran by the American presence in Iraq; the Iranian army was mobilizing as well and they would not be left out. Every launcher they had that could fit and fire a Scud, or No Dong missile, was pointed at the Jewish State. As if this weren't enough, Libya seemed poised for an amphibious assault to lay claim to their piece of the holy land. The list went on.

Syria massed its troops along the border in the Golan Heights and in occupied Lebanon. Egypt re-deployed the main weight of their forces across the Suez and into the Sinai. Names and places that already echoed in history. Saudi forces crossed boldly into Jordan and a massive blitzkrieg seemed imminent. Backs against the wall and outnumbered twelve to one, with huge armies threatening on three sides and the sea an open invitation; they had only one real option. Attack!

There were two sets of video feeds, the ones for NASA and the ones for everyone else in the world. As expected, the feeds for NASA were far more detailed, with close-up shots of the crew and the object of the mission. This was standard for every NASA flight operation ever conducted. This one was different however as the NASA audience had grown. Tied in, were a number of "Think Tanks" across the country as well as every Intelligence Agency. The National Security Council had their own viewing set up in an auditorium and the President and his advisors were watching from the Special Media room in the White House. America, wishing to appear in the world leader roll and wanting to prevent a repeat of the Russian/China fiasco, had "negotiated" this flight, allowing access to the *special* feeds to each of these governments respectively as well as to other select players.

These negotiations had not come without cost and the distrust was obvious. President Talbot reassured them on his personal honor, that this really was a mission to the Unity, not a grab for Artifact 1. This was a mission of mercy for the crew and a fact finding mission for the, "Good of the world." All data would be shared equally and America would welcome assistance in any form. He also added, to President Verichenkov and Premier Tang privately and quite firmly, that they couldn't stop him anyway. Short of nuclear war. He also told them, quite firmly, any interference in this "Rescue Mission", would have "dire" consequences.

To this end, the launch was a picture of perfection, showing the world America was un-phased, unbent and still in control. Now, the Discovery was on final approach to her target and entering the most dangerous phase of her mission. She had to time her rendezvous, catching the Unity and matching her erratic orbit, much the same as their counterparts in the Atlantis had done only three days before, though three hundred light years away.

Andy sat with the director and their team of large thinkers, watching the unfolding events with fascination and professional calm, knowing they would brief the President with their observations in a few short hours. If all went well, Discovery would dock with the Unity. A team of two astronauts would enter the station, inspect and gather evidence, including any computer and video disks they could find, retrieve the bodies, (no one believed any of the scientists could be left alive), then undock and return home. All within the next six hours. There would be no second chance. Projections showed the Unity would plunge into the atmosphere and crash into the Indian Ocean three days hence. A spectacular and sad ending for the worlds' first attempt at working together in space.

Andy also watched a different and very "special" feed, almost no one else in the world had. That feed showed the "real" mission. The one that was due to launch from a secret base located deep in the desert outside Nellis Air force Base, in Nevada. He didn't know which one was more fascinating and felt privileged to even be a spectator in such incredible events. Even if he could never tell anyone about it. His musing was interrupted by the astronauts on the Discovery.

"Houston, this is Discovery. We are on approach and two miles out. ETA to target twenty six minutes."

"Roger, Discovery, Houston confirms you are in the capture window! We have your feed. Describe target as you approach." *So now Unity was a target.* This statement was telling for Andy. They knew what to expect. Or at least thought they did.

"Houston, this is Discovery. Our visual confirms the missing module. From our approach we can't observe any damage in that area. We do detect heat damage to the solar array and scorching on all surfaces."

"Roger, Discovery." Andy listened with only half attention, riveted by the video feed itself. The shuttle was only a few hundred yards off and indeed, the space station looked like it had somehow gotten so hot it melted. There was a theory. That the damage was most likely a result of a partial re-entry, where the friction with the atmosphere was so great the metal turned molten. Another speculation was that a weapon of some sort had been used on the defenseless station. Whatever happened, it had most certainly killed the Unity.

"Houston, this is Discovery." Andy blinked because time had lapsed as his mind sorted possibility after possibility. Discovery was very close now and they were viewing the Unity from below as they began their docking procedure.

"Houston, we are observing damage to the lock. It looks like it was stretched or pulled in some way." Many eyebrows were raised at this and Andy's mind spun. *That kind of damage wouldn't have been caused by friction, or a weapon. Something would have had to have been docked with the station and somehow pulled in another direction.*

"Roger, Discovery. We see it and have analyzed the damage. It looks serviceable from our side."

"Roger, Houston, I concur. But I wouldn't count on it holding air."

Andy knew this was not an unforeseen problem. The astronauts would be suited at all times and be entering the lock one at a time. If the space station still held pressure, they had a contingency. If not, a different one. Given the probable condition of the ship, they would bring the lock back to vacuum and then manually cycle the Unity side. A long procedure, but they had no other options. Only two astronauts would be going over and Specialist Lloyd Sylvan would be the first. Andy watched as with agonizing sloth, the Discovery drifted towards its mate. Unity hung above them like an over ripened fruit. Her proud name and the flags of fifteen nations, scorched and barely recognizable, her white purity burned and dishonored. This great outpost of humanity which represented the collective aspirations of the human race. Full of life only days before. Sent on an unplanned journey by an unknown and alien force, then sent back. Damaged, dead and cold.

"Houston, this is Discovery. We are docked and locked."

"Roger, Discovery, confirmed docked and locked. You are clear to board. Good luck." The normal ebullience of a well planned mission was missing. No one could feel much joy and the astronauts themselves felt like they were entering a mausoleum.

It took another full hour to inspect the lock, get Sylvan into it and depressurize, then manually open the other side. Andy watched virtually and actually, on the edge of his seat. The feed he watched was the special feed the world did not have. He witnessed and listened, hearing the voice of Lloyd Sylvan, filtered through his helmet and distorted by his breathing. The curious breathy conversation heard from every suited spaceman since the Mercury flights.

"Lock is open, zero atmosphere on the Unity." With those words it was confirmed, Unity was dead.

Andy watched as the opening grew, light from the Discovery spilling into the dark void beyond. What would it be like to be Sylvan at this moment? How do you approach the dead?

Would they simply be lifeless? Burned and mangled? Andy thought of every horror movie he ever saw. Every dark computer game. Would some alien creature be waiting in the darkness? He laughed at himself. Improbable, but unfortunately in this new world, entirely possible! He decided then and there that Sylvan was a very brave man.

The astronaut pushed into the Unity, his suit video showing little beyond the first few feet. "I'm moving to central control now. No sign of explosive decompression." One of the scenarios held that the Unity had ruptured, blowing the crew out into space, or killing them instantly. One theory down.

"I see lights on the command board. We do have some power over here." The video showed a computer board with numerous lights, all flashing red. Sylvan reached over and pushed one of them and suddenly the Unity lit up with dim fluorescent light.

Sylvan's voice was slightly shocked. "Houston, someone turned these off. I have some computer function, but it looks like a lot of components have been removed!"

"Say again!" came an incredulous reply.

"Houston, it looks like someone removed some of the components. Not only here, but around the module." Then, anticipating the next question, "And no, they aren't on the floor. I don't see them anywhere."

Houston confirmed and told him to continue inspecting the station. Andy could just imagine what was going on at mission control. Whatever they'd dreamed up about what had happened, it seemed they weren't even close. Then the next shock.

"Houston, I'm at the lab module." Andy knew this was the one that was missing. Broken off by what ever force had damaged the station. At least so they thought.

A very shaken Sylvan came back, "The module was removed, Houston. And I mean removed. Unbolted. Not sheared or torn off. Unbolted." Silence. Then, "Did you hear me, Houston?"

The voice from the ground tried to sound as if everything were normal. "Roger. We understand, Discovery. Please continue your inspection." They watched as Sylvan, now joined by another astronaut, fully inspected the station from one end to the other. Then the inevitable.

"They're gone! No one is left on board, Houston!" That simple statement sent shock waves. Andy listened to the rest of the mission and watched as report after speculated report trickled in from his sources. The mystery was complete. Not only was the Unity empty of life, one module was professionally removed along with selective pieces of equipment, clothing, water and food. The only thing of interest they found, was a DVD left in one computer. A DVD labeled Log Reports, with the name of the Chief Scientist, Dr. Jack Gordon and a beginning date that was a full day "after" the disappearance of the Unity. Sylvan carefully collected it and the hard drives of the computers. That was all that would be returned to earth. Both astronauts floated back to the safety of Discovery. She disconnected for the last time, leaving Unity to her lonely and fiery death. The shuttle did one more orbit before diving to its landing in Florida, yet by then, the DVD had been downloaded and played a few hundred times and a new sense of wonder engulfed those who lived on the watery blue oasis known as Mother Earth.

Chapter 10

The entity which knew itself as Vi-t-ry, groaned in imaginary pain. Pain his sensors told him he should be feeling. Sensors feeding a myriad of signals to the central core of the great ship in which Vi-t-ry was contained. The core which was Vi-t-ry. Information detailing new damage and old. Information on repairs being made and repairs impossible to make. A billion parts of a puzzle the twice re-born artificial intelligence had no ability or reference to deal with. He felt the warm solar wind buffeting his skin, feeling its gentle healing energy and knowing it as a source of good, yet it remained unseen. He was also aware of a planet below him. The word 'planet' was loosely described in his databanks. But the words star, and space, and planet held no meaning. Yet!

Even as his processors formed the word, a reference appeared. A planet was a round ball of mineral and chemical compositions, gaseous, or partially to wholly solid. More importantly, a planet was where home was. The more he thought, the more he knew. Awareness grew. Knowledge grew. As repairs were made, Vi-t-ry came closer and closer to what he was, but his completeness was far in the future.

Active sensors, all over the internal structure and surface of the ship, continued their assigned tasks, even in the absence direction or control. Sensors, both active and passive, collecting and storing mountains of data for a time that data could be used. Much of the data collected was stripped from space. Radiation from solar energy and radio waves from all across the electromagnetic spectrum continuously bombarded the ship. As the maintenance computer continued its repairs, its robot army re-connected even more sensors, multiplying and multiplying again the vast cache of data. Mindlessly the robots worked and mindlessly the sensors collected. Buried within this collection was every radio or TV transmission escaping the atmosphere of the planet below. Unknowingly, Vi-t-ry was compiling a library of Earth. Incomplete and not truly representative of humanity, especially in the chaos-wracked present mankind found itself in. A chaos precipitated by his own arrival, and an incomplete picture indeed. But still, it was information that would be critical to Vi-t-ry as he grew back into that which he was.

The F-111 banked sharply and dove for the desert floor, where supposedly a runway was waiting, though Buck couldn't prove it by his eyes. A dark cloudy night let little light through and the ground looked stygian. Plus, his helmet didn't have the "special hardware" of the pilot. He'd gotten a look at it as they boarded, the pilot allowing him just a moment to check out this specially modified version of the venerable F-111. Buck flew space shuttles and they had the most advanced navigational and control equipment known to man. At least he thought that was true until he saw this airframe. This aircraft contained equipment he'd never imagined. Everything in the cockpit was dark and seeming dead until he put on the helmet. It was akin to making the blind man see. The digital instruments were more like holograms, drifting wherever he looked. The stick and rudders were pressure plates at the knees and what looked like roller balls on the arm rests. Buck would give his eyeteeth to drive this thing even once.

The pilot displayed his pride as well as his empathy with a fellow flyer, but still hustled Buck into the copilot's side with firm efficiency. Buck would remain disappointed because the side-by-seat was stripped and he wouldn't be given one of the fancy helmets. Evidently this bird didn't need a copilot. Buck was smug on one level though. He looked at the pilot and thought; *I've been to space, bud!* It was small consolation though. When the pilot kicked the F-111 in the tail it was very close to the feeling of a shuttle launch. Buck wondered just what kind of new tech. they had in the engines of this wonderful bird. All in all, after the thrill of a blind takeoff, it was a very boring trip and now, he would land just as he started; blind. He felt his guts lurch as they pulled sudden positive Gs, rolling nose and diving what felt like forever, then pulling flat.

Buck was totally disoriented, having been left with no horizon and nothing but darkness to see. *Show off!* Buck had no idea that this was S.O.P. for the base they were approaching. Literally, there was no other way to approach a high speed landing on a pad that was surrounded by high bluffs and was better approached by helicopter. He saw the dim green fluorescent lights lining the strip; just seconds before the big jet settled gently back to earth. The pilot applied reverse thrust and hard breaks, pulling to a stop quicker than Buck believed it could be done. Within moments, the F-111 taxied to the right and into a hanger even darker than the world around them, then flowed to a stop.

Buck sat back and let out an appreciative breath as the pilot shut down the engines. He was about to break the silence held throughout the flight and congratulate the pilot on a job well done, when suddenly, the entire hangar burst into bright light, momentarily blinding his night vision. When he could finally make out images through his tearing half closed eyes, he was staggered. It was not a hangar as he first assumed. Before him, spreading into the distance was an underground complex built back into the mountain. He could see buildings, vehicles and storage areas. But what held his eye and caused him to whistle in appreciation, was the array of aircraft the like of which he'd never before seen. There were at least seven and they bordered on the most fantastic concept machines ever thought of. Some were beautiful and some were down right ugly, with one that could only be described as deadly. Motion caught his eye as the other F-111 carrying Cal rolled to a stop, evidently landing almost in tandem with his. He pulled up his visor as the intercom broke into the silence.

"Welcome to the Aerie gentlemen!" It was Marx. "Please follow your pilots. They will get you settled and bring you to the briefing room. Time is short. Our mission launches in forty eight hours." The canopies popped and Buck was hustled out by the ground crew, meeting Cal on the rubberized gray coated tarmac.

The Commander smiled and clapped him on the back. "Welcome to the twilight zone, Buck!"

He grunted, "Yeah, Cal. Unfortunately, I don't think we've seen the weird stuff yet." The Captain didn't know how right he was.

Air raid sirens blared out their warning in the late afternoon heat of down town Tel Aviv. Citizens, already prepared by years of terror attacks, false alarms and impending war, scrambled for shelter. On the outskirts of the city, Patriot missile batteries swung towards the threat, ready to launch in pursuit of the incoming wave of missiles. But never had they faced the onslaught that now approached. Coordinated missile attacks launched from Iran, Syria and Egypt, swarmed the defenses, raining down on the Israeli state from every point on the compass. These were not the lone Scuds launched by Iraq during Desert Storm. This was a full scale attack, targeting infrastructure, government buildings, military bases and the citizens at large. In all, three hundred missiles in came on the first wave. The ripping sound of the Patriots as they launched was followed quickly by explosions, either high in the sky, or inside the city itself. Conventional high explosives detonated in and around buildings and the more insidious chemical warheads airburst over high population centers.

Hidden in the first wave of missiles, were two special packages containing a highly virulent form of smallpox, both of which made it through the defense curtain and dispersed their special form of death over the capital. Hundreds of people, who watched as the conventional weapons pounded their country, would be sick and dying in a few hours. The undeclared war had come and Israel's enemies would be satisfied with nothing short of her complete annihilation.

The Chinese attack on Baikonur was initiated very close to the shared boarder with Russia and Kazakhstan, and this is where the world expected the Russians retaliation to fall. There was never a doubt that they would retaliate, even by the Chinese Central Command. Indeed, the Russians quickly massed seven divisions of armor and infantry with full air and artillery support, right on that point. Spetsnaz forces infiltrated and destroyed the staging areas and most of the base from which the attack originated, generally making it look as if an invasion was imminent. America asked for caution and diplomacy, secretly meeting with both sides. But the Russians were not in a conciliatory mood. In a classic move of bait and switch, the Russians built up their forces in the Far East in and around Vladivostok and either flew or shipped by train, a token of these forces toward the area around Baikonur. They then massed additional transport equipment, acting as if to bring the entire army west. The great deception left the Chinese watching their northwest frontier as the Russians broke out of Vladivostok in the Far East, striking in a classic blitz, flowing through the mountains like a spring flood and attacking, then occupying the Chinese city of Harbin. From there they moved to cut off almost the entire Chinese Province of Heilongjhiang.

China rumbled in outrage and began mobilizing their entire military might, marching army after army towards the now dug in Russians. A major war between these two behemoths seemed unavoidable. But the Russians saw the writing on the wall. They'd made their point and sued Beijing for treaty terms over the territory, wanting concessions and thereby showing a very visible hard-line stance to the world. The Chinese, not wishing an expanded war while facing serious internal discontent, quickly agreed and a cease fire ensued. Time would tell if war could be avoided between these long time enemies, but for now at least, the shooting had stopped.

Again the world watched and waited and as the world's head was turned; first Korea, then India and Pakistan, the Middle East and now Russia and China, wars of aggression, wars of subjugation, and wars of ethnic cleansing erupted all over the Dark Continent. And while Africa burned, the world as usual, cared little and did less.

Andy thought of the old saying, "The weight of the world" as he and Evans entered the Oval office for the third time that day. The President looked like hell. His suit was wrinkled and disheveled, perhaps slept in. He wondered which issue would finally cause the man to break. Faced with a collapsing economy, (gas at $4.35 and rising, productivity at an all-time low with workers abandoning their responsibilities in favor of safety, stock market plunging and gold quickly approaching $1000 per oz), terrorism and civil crisis all over the country, the southern border with Mexico being overrun and Armageddon threatening the world. How could he possibly hold up? Uncertainty was tearing the world apart and more and more America had to back out of her obligations, simply far too over-stretched. Yet still she was trying. Back channel negotiations were happening all over the globe. In many cases the aggressive or aggrieved parties were finally realizing how close mankind was to annihilating itself.

That was the case with Russia and China. China also pressured North Korea into cease fire. (An easy decision given that they were in the process of getting their armies dismantled by the U.S. and the R.O.K.) Pakistan and India also pulled back into an uneasy truce as well as Venezuela and Brazil. Still, the hotspots were molten. Terrorist action, while disrupted and in disarray, was still epidemic and rebels the world over were pressing whatever government held them in sway. Most critical on the list was the situation in the Middle East. The U.S. was rushing forces from Iraq, Afghanistan and Turkey, to Israel and repositioning its Navel Forces, but this seemed to be little deterrent to the aggressors. Instead, they were upping the ante. To block the U.S. movement of warships, the Egyptians had closed the Suez Canal and fired on an American Destroyer as it approached. This was the sum of what faced Jon Talbot. And to add to his woes, the opposition party was calling for his head citing weak leadership. Yes. Andy could well imagine President Talbot was bending under the weight. He and Evans would do everything they could to ensure he didn't break.

"Jon, good afternoon and thanks for squeezing us in." Evans moved right to the desk and handed the President a written summary of the contents of Dr. Gordon's DVD secured from the Unity. Andy went to the projector and plugged in his laptop, ready to play the entire sequence. Talbot read the document, his face going from annoyance to reflecting the wonder they all felt after having watched the video log.

"Is this true?" The president's voice showed no small amount of disbelief.

"We have no way of really knowing for sure, Jon, but we believe it is. CIA has looked it over and their assessment is that Gordon doesn't look to be intimidated or influenced in any way."

The President looked intrigued and more alive that Andy had seen him in days. "How long is the video, Sean? I only blocked off ten minutes for you, but I want to see this."

"It runs about three hours." He held up his hand at the immediate protest. "We boiled it down to about fifteen minutes. Just the most important stuff."

Talbot smiled, "Good job, Sean. You had me there for a moment." He nodded to Andy "Go ahead and play it. I promise to hold my questions till the end."

"Yes, Mr. President."

*Just press play, h*e thought. *And the world changes again!* The big drop down projection screen sprang to life with a picture showing an older and scholarly gentleman in a white jumpsuit, the proud Unity emblem sharing a ballpoint pen with his left pocket. The backdrop was clearly the control module of the space station. For Andy to see the President this riveted was priceless. He turned up the audio as the introduction began.

"Hello!" The voice was baritone and smooth. A voice from someone who people would naturally pay attention to. "My name is Dr. Jack Gordon and I am the lead scientist aboard a Space Station named the Unity. The name is in honor of my planet of many races, all working as one. This station was created by human beings like me, from the planet we call Earth." Andy could see the storm of questions behind the Presidents eyes. Human beings! Planet Earth? Who was the man talking to? Gordon continued, with all the emotion of a clinical dissertation.

"The fact that you are viewing this record shows that the Unity has somehow survived. A fact that would please me greatly if I had known."

How cryptic was that?! Andy was still having trouble wrapping his own mind around this video and the information it contained, and he'd seen it in full six times.

"But, I'm getting ahead of myself. The information on this disk details the basics of human language and what we hope is a binary level code which will help you understand this construction and we who built it. If you can understand me, then we have been successful. And to you, whoever you are, welcome."

The camera pulled back, showing the other members of the Unity's crew floating in the space behind him. To his left was Rebecca Carver the British member, as well as the Russian Demitri Karkov. Even floating back well behind, the Russian dwarfed the others. Andy didn't remember whether Karkov was just large or the others were small, but he made a mental note to find out. No real reason other than professional curiosity. It just seemed like he was too big to be an astronaut. *Cosmonaut!* He amended. To Gordon's left was Dr. Raymond Sammons, the other American.

The last member of the crew, Joshua Yakura who, was running the camera, floated by, pulling himself upright next to Sammons. The lone Japanese scientist smiled and waved to his unknown audience.

Andy paused the video. "Mr. President, at this point Gordon introduced the crew and basically gave a detailed description of earth, each of their home countries and the mission of the Unity. We edited that out and cut to the next piece we think you need to hear." Talbot merely grunted, so he restarted the video which zoomed back to Gordon who was caught in mid sentence.

"...we find ourselves here due to an incredible accident. The planet we are now orbiting is hundreds of light years from our home! And we are here at the hand of some technology far advanced of our own. We of earth have just started breaching the fringe of our own system and have only theorized Faster Than Light travel, yet we were brought from there to here in an instant. Traversing a distance we can only estimate as hundreds of light years." The President looked spellbound.

"What we do know is that we were transported by the hand of a vast ship which was trying to leave the vicinity of this planet. Why it was going to our earth we have no idea, nor do we think it originated from the planet we now orbit. This great ship was damaged, though we are not sure how or why because we never saw it. The only reason we have any information about it at all is because another vessel from our world was recently sent here as well. This ship is what we call a space shuttle and is used to transport humans too and from the surface of our planet. This ship is called the Atlantis, named after an ancient and mythical land from our home."

A sigh came from Talbot, "Un-friggin believable!"

"We don't think this alien ship meant us any harm, in fact we don't think it noticed us at all Though this is certainly only speculation on my part. What we do know is that there was one life lost as a result of our journey. Unfortunately, one of the crew from the Atlantis was outside the ship when it was transported here. We don't know if Mr. Tyler Parker still lives, but we fear the worst and pray for his soul."

Andy paused again. "At this point Gordon decides to give a fairly long description of the various religions on earth. Again, we cut to more pertinent information."

"Wait a minute! I know I promised no questions till the end, but hell, Sean, this is incredible. They all survived?"

"Yes. At least we know they survived the trip. Except for Tyler." One more death should have meant little given the magnitude of killing and dying happening around the planet right now, but this one sobered the President.

"No hope for him, Sean?" His voice was quiet and full of emotion.

"I'm afraid not. Even if he made the trip... or was left here in orbit, he had only a few hours in his suit."

Talbot rubbed his eyes then turned back to Andy. "Let's see the rest of it."

"Yes, sir." He keyed it again and the image changed showing there had been an edit. The rest of the crew was not to be seen.

"...transport of the Atlantis was really a godsend to us. Due to the, ah, what I would describe as an inaccuracy of our placement in orbit, the alien ship has left us in dire straights. This vessel is in an oblong orbit and we get closer to the planets atmosphere each time we go around. That is why we created this communication. Our computer models show a forty percent probability the Unity will skip off the planets atmosphere. If this occurs, we believe she will break up in the process and the pieces will be flung out into space, likely to be captured in higher orbit or possibly even the gravity well of one of the moons. It is our hope that this presentation will survive to at least give some explanation as to why we were here." Gordon stopped a moment to collect himself.

"The Atlantis will try to catch us and dock with us. We now know we have no option but to land on the planet and try to survive. Fortunately, it is very similar to our own planet and though I'm told we have a "decent" chance of landing safely, we know it will be a crash landing and we can only hope for the best. Hopefully the inhabitants are friendly as well. So, whoever you are, and however far distant the future is when you find this, look for us or our descendants on the planet below. This is Dr. Jack Gordon of the Earth Space Station Unity. On behalf of my crew and that of the Atlantis, good bye!" With a final artistic flare, the video moved to a view out one of the ports and zoomed in on the approaching Atlantis, then faded to black.

Andy felt compelled to break the quiet that fell over them after the video faded. "There was a lot more Mr. President. Analysis of the planet and the solar system. Pictures and video of the surface. Speculation. You name it. Dr. Gordon was fairly complete."

The President was no longer stunned. He had a sense of wonder on his face. Much the same as everyone who'd watched it.

Talbot grunted in Andy's direction, finally breaking his silence. "Ok.. now. let me wrap my feeble brain around this. Gordon obviously never expected to come home and made this tape for some alien who may run across it in some unknown future. Atlantis miraculously shows up and rescues them and then goes who knows where. Then this big damn thing up in the sky grabs the Station and brings it home, minus the crew, equipment and a big lab...What did you call it?"

"Module!"

He nodded, agreeing with the fact. "So if they'd stayed on board they'd be home now."

Sean answered this one. "That's true Jon, but they had no way of knowing that anymore than we could have."

Talbot gave him a sharp look that said he didn't appreciate being slapped in the face with the obvious. He recovered himself quickly though, knowing it was every advisors job to make sure the "Boss" has every bit of information, no matter how apparent. "So what's your guess, Sean? What the hell happened to them? Are they alive?" Before Evans could answer, the phone on the President's desk beeped. His secretary warning him he was late for the next briefing.

Talbot picked it up and listened for just a moment. "Tell them to wait and adjust the schedule by ten minutes. Thanks!" He hung up without waiting on a reply.

Sean took his cue knowing time was short. "Jon, all we can do is go by the evidence. We believe the crew transferred what they thought they'd need to survive on the planet, over to the Atlantis. That included the lab module, which makes sense knowing they'd need to test everything. Air, water and food. Then, we think they attempted to land on the plant. After that...?" He shrugged his shoulders.

"What about help from the aliens? Did Gordon say anything about that?"

"We don't think there's any help coming, Jon. Dr. Gordon said they had little indication there was much left on the planet from an industry standpoint. And given the condition of Artifact 1, we have to assume a war of some sort. Gordon indicated the planet had very little smog or smoke, or unusual radiation and no transmitted radio waves. We think that whatever happed to the planet happened a very long time ago. Bombed back to the Stone Age type of thing. Maybe something we should all pay attention to right now." The President let the not so oblique referral to the current world crisis roll off him without comment. " If they survived, they may be the most advanced people there."

Talbot sat back and sighed. "Another small tragedy to add to the list! So what's next?"

"Well, Jon. While you're fixing the world and fighting the good fight so to speak, we'll be kicking off project 'Phoenix.'"

Talbot whistled. "Will it really work, Sean? And can you keep it from Moscow and Beijing?"

"It's not totally untested sir. And security is better than any black project we've ever had. Sometime within the next 24 to 48 hours we'll launch from out at DreamWorks." He paused a moment. "Then we'll know. But I'll talk with you about that later." He said cryptically. " I have an idea in the works about the Russians and Chinese."

The President looked at him curiously and was about to ask a question when his phone beeped again. He looked at it and sighed, "All right, Sean. You haven't asked for my approval so I assume you want me to have some sort of deniability. That shit don't work. You have my ok and I expect at least a daily briefing on this as well as your other information updates. I need the inside on China and Russia and the Middle East. Anything you can give me."

"Yes, sir." Evans said it for both him and Andy.

With that Talbot picked up his phone and said, "Send them in!" Indicating their meeting was over. But as Andy and Evans left they heard, "Good work and good luck!"

Much like a patient with a massive head wound, Vi-t-ry began to relearn as he healed. Like a man who remembered the joy of vision and anticipated the removal of his bandages, Vi-t-ry electronically quivered as his surroundings were slowly revealed.

Yet unlike a flesh and blood patient, most of his vision would be on levels a human could not know. As he healed, the data collected by his sensors could now be used by the massive computer core. Incoming data could be analyzed and pieced together. The data could be referenced to known models and be made meaningful. And slowly Vi-t-ry began to see.

His first actual "sight" came from the longer waves of the electromagnetic spectrum, between 1mm and 3cm in length. The energy from these fairly saturated near space and were emanating from billions of points, mostly far, far away. Yet near by was a huge source of this microwave energy. Seen from his position, Vi-t-ry marveled at the display. A ball of energy pulsed in the distance, rimed in flashing waves of power, its surface rippling and writhing as if alive. From this source came the sweet energy that now fed his growing hunger. His memory supplied a detailed description of the star; composition, stability, estimated life span, storm cycle and potential for use to the ship. Vi-t-ry accepted this information with a miniscule piece of his manufactured brain, while the rest of him simply marveled at the show.

Reluctantly, after much time, he pulled away and contemplated the other sources. The billions of others which were akin to the one so tantalizingly near yet at the same time, very different. Each star as different from the others as Vi-t-ry was from the small ships which had been caught in his time distortion worm hole. With that memory now becoming prominent, Vi-t-ry swung his mind to the nearest source of microwaves. Here he saw the vague outline of the planet below. Dim yet discernible. This source required his full attention. There was much he must remember about this place. He watched, he contemplated and he considered. As he did, the repairs continued.

Chapter 11

Buck was acutely aware of the thousands of tons of rock hanging over his head. He was used to the openness of the sky while flying jets or the vastness of space on his missions. It felt alien and frankly intimidating to be so far underground. A feeling made even odder because of the fact he couldn't tell that that was really where he was. His mind knew it, but his vision denied it. A little like the effects of seasickness. They had been shown to quarters in an underground facility that was nothing short of amazing, more like a four star hotel than a military complex. They'd only actually seen the cavern when they landed. From then on they were inside a building that included everything; offices, living quarters, cafeterias, work shops and science labs. Now he and Cal sat alone in a small auditorium waiting on who knew what. So far, no one had spoken with them other than to direct them to where they should be. As they waited and their patience was beginning to wear thin and the rock above, though unseen, felt heavy and oppressive, adding to their discontent.

"I'm beginning to think this is a load of bullshit, Cal! Whatever they want from us, I think I'd uv rather been on the Discovery!"

Cal nodded, not quite agreeing. "An awful lot of trouble for nothing. But I'm like you. I hate being in the dark and this has been one mystery after another. Someone certainly has some explaining to do!" As if on cue, the door near the stage burst open and in stalked Marx dressed just as they were, in simple khaki coveralls sporting no insignia or rank.

"Welcome to Dream Works, gentlemen, and I assure you this is far from bullshit!"

Buck started as if slapped. He whispered to Cal, "So now were being bugged!" His commander raised a brow giving him a look that said, *Careful. We're way the hell out of our league on this.*

Marx stormed up to them and grabbed a folding chair spun it around and sat down. As if to confirm Buck's thought he said, "This is one of the most secure facilities in the world. With the exception of your actual living quarters, everything here is recorded. Both video and audio. Get used to it."

Buck did his best to look unconcerned, but, *Good Lord, what else do they have to watch us with? Infrared!* Instead he remained silent.

Cal asked, "Ok, Marx, we're here, wherever that is! You called it Dream Works and what we saw in the hangar is certainly incredible. Isn't it time you filled us in? You said we fly. Surely you don't expect us to fly some experimental rocket we've never even seen."

Marx smiled, "No, Commander, I don't expect you to fly an experimental rocket. First of all, it's not a rocket and if you will give me just a few moments I'll show you exactly what it is. Second, you won't be flying anything."

Cal stared and Buck both sputtered, "Then what the hell are we here for?"

Marx was genuinely amused at their reaction and their naiveté, "You are here for one thing... your experience! I asked for the best and you were delivered. Now..."

He never finished as Cal jumped on him, "You want us to train some other hot-shot fly jockeys to go into space to do the job for us?" His professional pride and the way they'd been treated momentarily overcame his military demeanor.

Marx stared him down and an electric silence hung in the air. Finally he spoke, stating firmly, "I understand your feelings, Commander, but you just take a big step back. We are about to embark on the most important mission this country, hell... this world has ever undertaken. Do you want to be a part of it or do you want to wallow in your childish loss of face?" Cal's mouth hung open, but Marx pushed on before either could answer.

"You were assigned to me by... your... superiors," he punched each word. "And though you were "volunteered," I expect you act as if I were your Chief." He paused as he caught both sets of eyes. Satisfied that he'd properly dressed them down, he threw the carrot.

"Gentlemen, you are going to be part of something historic and if I didn't believe in you, you wouldn't be here. As with many of your fellow astronauts, I've followed your careers since you were selected to NASA. So if you haven't guessed already, yes, we're going to Artifact 1." Confirmation of the mission was like a cold splash of water and neither missed the plural. Again, Marx rolled over their questions.

"Having said that, I need you as part of this team. I don't need a pilot or a Commander, but I do need experienced spacemen."

The two astronauts were almost speechless. Not as pilot or Commander then as what? Simple crew?

"So if we aren't here to fly, then who?" Cal asked the question and Marx gave his Cheshire grin and waved his hand with mock dramatic flare. Through the same door he'd entered walked three others.

"Who, Commander?" He asked. "Me, for one. And let me introduce you to the rest of the team!"

Cal stared at the new comers not believing his eyes. He nudged Buck and whispered, "Are you seeing what I'm seeing?"

Buck's answer was tight lipped speechlessness. Leading the pack was a face familiar to both, but especially to him. *Jules Sorenson,* he thought unbelievably. A woman that had gone through basic ATS (Astronaut Training School) with them. Their particular classes shining star. Hot shit in the trainers and she could do things in a fighter that would make a veteran fighter jock lose his lunch. Absolutely crazy, so much so she'd earned the name 'Mad Dog' Sorenson. She also had eyes for Buck, and he for her. Yet right in the middle of their training, and their *Affair*, she'd suddenly disappeared.

They told Buck that, as unbelievable as it was, she'd quit. Said nothing to him, just up and gone. Try as he might he couldn't track her down and at one point his Chief firmly suggested it would be best if he just let it go. He had, finally, not because of the chief, but because he could find no trace of her. With no other option and no explanation he blamed himself for her leaving, but couldn't for the life of him figure what he did or didn't do to cause it. Over time his dismay turned to anger, then finally, "I just don't give a damn!" It was a lie, but so are most self delusions. Now here she was, walking toward him as if they barely knew each other. A world of emotions flooded him. Her hair was different, short cropped and blond, but the rest of her was the same and her body stirred him even in the ugly baggy coveralls. Because despite it all, he remembered. Buck forced an air of indifference, not the only one who knew it was false.

Marx's voice kept him from staring. "Obviously you both know Commander Sorenson."

Mad Dog grabbed a chair beside Marx and said with no emotion whatsoever, "Hi, Buck. Long time. You look well." She nodded at Cal. "Commander."

Buck was mute, but Cal chimed in for him. His statement of fact was cold and direct as were his questions. "Well… at least we know where you went, Jules. So what are you now? A super spy?"

Marx recognized the tension and jumped on it. "Enough of that! I expect everyone here to be professional despite any personal history." He looked at each of them individually.

"I mean everyone! Commander Sorenson was *Recruited* by us, and she, just like you now, had no choice in the matter. Don't take it personally. You are all going to have plenty of time together and I expect no conflict. Understood!" He took their silence to mean yes, though Buck's eyes said no.

"Good. Now, let me introduce you to the others."

Buck tore his eyes away from Mad Dog and looked at the other two men. One tall, with chiseled features framed by short dark hair and a nose that had obviously been broken a time or two. The other was very short and oriental. Buck guessed Chinese or Korean in heritage. Buck recognized neither and both looked uneasy. Distrustful even. Not only of Buck and Cal, but of each other. They soon found out why.

"Gentlemen, let me introduce Colonel Sergei Kirkelev, Russian Air Force and Cosmonaut."

The Russian held out his hand. It took a moment to assimilate the import of that introduction before Cal reached out and shook it. Whatever they expected, this was not it. *A friggin Russian in a secret American base? What next? I suppose the other ones' a 'real' communist!* Buck had no more formed that comment in his mind than Marx confirmed it.

"And this gentleman is Li Tsinlung, of the Chinese National Space Agency. Both will be flying with us and I expect you to make them feel at home."

Li didn't offer a hand, but did give them a minor bow, saying in perfect English, "Welcome, Commander. And you, Captain."

"Just so you know. Both Li and Sergei have space flights under their belts and are more than qualified for this mission." He didn't add their scientific backgrounds nor that his sources revealed that Li's credentials were far over inflated. He had serous doubts about the man.

Cal had had enough and his displeasure was evident. "With all due respect, sir! And no disrespect to you gentlemen." He waved vaguely in the direction of the newcomer's. "But isn't it about damn time someone tells us just what the hell is going on? I mean this is getting to be a bit hard to take. A secret American base crawling with Russians and Communist Chinese! Enough of the goddamned cloak and dagger, Marx. What's really happening here?" It was as close to insubordination as the Commander had ever gotten.

Marx held up his hand, not ignoring the outburst, but willing to overlook it for now. "Calm down, Commander. I suppose I have been rather unfair with all of this, but I assure you it was necessary. Please, sit down everyone and I will explain." The two foreigners took seats seemingly unaffected by Cal's flare-up.

"Now, if we can continue with no further interruptions." He fixed the Commander with a stare, "I will bring you up to speed. This facility is the super secret base known as Dream Land. And no! This isn't Area 51. In fact the folks over there don't know we exist."

"Was top secret," Buck pointed a chin at Li and Sergei.

"Point taken, Captain. However, I was informed by Li that the Chinese Government already knew about us, as we know about their secret base in Xi'an." Li couldn't keep the surprise off his face.

Buck grinned, "Touché!"

Marx also smiled at Li's discomfort and then at Sergei's superiority. "Not to worry." He told the Russian. "We also know about your own Dream Works at Novgorad and your "Special

Research Facility" at Noril'sk." The Russian's smug look was permanently wiped.

"So! Now that everyone has been properly de-pantsed and we have the secrets out of the way, let's get down to business. First of all, Commander Sorenson is the only one who is fully up to speed. Sergei and Li arrived only about two hours before you and Captain Rodgers and they were only told that a secret mission was to be launched. This mission will, for the good of the world, involve the three major powers. We obviously want no repeat of Baikonur." Anger flared in the Russian's face and Buck would have said that shame was reflected on Li's, though it could have been a sly smile as his features were fairly inscrutable. It was obvious each had been ordered to ignore the sneak attack and its repercussions. That was asking a lot. Working with these guys would be interesting.

"So now, to all of you I say, *welcome*. This mission is sanctioned by the President and has the blessing of both the Russian President and your Premier Li. In fact, we have delayed the launch waiting on our friends here!" Once again he was speaking about Li and Sergei.

"My boss played hell getting the President to accept this, but it was decided that going it alone might have been the spark for WW III. So here we are. I can tell you that the world in general will not know of this mission. At least until we're successful. Our Code name is Phoenix Flight and our ship is the XSP 11, nicknamed Enterprise."

This was mostly lost on the two foreigners until Cal whispered, "Where No Man Has Gone Before!" Then he whistled the appropriate tune.

Marx pushed a button on a remote. "And here is our chariot!" The lights dimmed, and a screen in the front of the room lit up with a picture of a ship that could only be described as...

"Beautiful!" Buck didn't know who said it. Didn't even hear it. He stared at the screen forgetting all about Mad Dog; suddenly he was in love again.

Andy sat in the gallery waiting to be called by his boss should he need any clarification on specific world events. Evans himself sat at the table with the Joint Chiefs, listening to the ongoing grandstanding. No one here wished to demonstrate they were uninformed or worse, under performing. There were at least forty people in the room including the actual Joint Chiefs, their advisors and staff, secret service and pages. He watched, almost disinterestedly, the usual hustle and bustle of these meetings, meetings he'd seen many times before. Abruptly, the normal changed. Suddenly pagers and cell phones started buzzing, trilling or vibrating for attention. Andy's own version of alert pulsed a bright red on his laptop. As he read it people began hurrying from the room.

"Holy shit." He muttered out loud, then closed his computer and scrambled through the crowd to get as quickly as he could to his boss. Evans waited, sitting calmly in the storm, knowing Andy would be there with more complete information than these other fools would get within the next two hours. Andy slammed headlong into a Lt. Colonel of the Air Force, dumping the papers the man had been carrying all over the floor.

"Hey you asshole son of a bitch! Get back here." The man shouted at his back, but Andy had no time or inclination to deal with some Air puke and his bruised ego. The Colonel continued to glower as one of his staff picked up the spilled papers, getting a smashed finger in the process from a careless, but impeccably shined shoe. The Colonel was just about to order a Marine Sergeant to go after the object of his ire when he saw Andy bend down and start a discussion with Evans. The Colonel didn't know Andy, nor cared who the little piss ant was, but he certainly knew Evans. That was a battle he simply didn't have the brass to fight. He mumbled again under his breath then said, "Come on!" Being far sharper to his staffer than was warranted since the man now had the Colonels papers under his arm and was nursing a seriously dislocated finger.

Andy had forgotten the incident completely. He bent down to his boss. "The Israelis just nuked the Arabs." Evans nodded calmly. From the reaction around the room, the anthill had certainly been kicked and Andy's own heart was galloping a hundred miles an hour.

Evans simply asked, "Which Arabs?"

Andy sat down heavily in a now vacant chair. "All of them, Sir! At least all of them that were set to attack."

Evans looked at him sternly, "Andy, I'm going to need a few more substantial details than that before I brief the President."

"Yes sir!" He mentally kicked himself. Evans required his employees to remain calm and in control at all times. He recruited and hired them specifically for their intelligence and demonstrated unflappability. Part of the weed out process was a very rigorous mental assessment. Andy had passed it all with top marks.

But shit, his mind screamed, *the Israelis just nuked the bee-Jesus out of the Arabs!* Outwardly, he took a deep breath and opened his laptop. Andy quickly scanned the information flow and his direct satellite feeds from NORAD and CIA. Had quick assessments from at least a dozen sources including a current text feed from a Mossad agent, apparently near the Jordanian boarder somewhere around the southern edge of the Red Sea. Even live video from an embedded reporter following the Israeli army in the Golan. That video showed Israeli army M1A1 tanks, rolling forward in echelon and firing their main guns in great belches of flam and smoke. At what he couldn't see. What he didn't see, and had expected, was the tell tale mushroom clouds. The video was panning the horizon, but smoke and dust from the battle and the moving armor obscured everything. He continued to sift the info, knowing Evans was waiting. Finally, he had a clear picture.

"Ok sir. Here is my assessment so far. The Arabs seriously underestimated their opponent." He smiled, "Again!" He paused still collecting his thoughts. "They were counting on the massive uprising of the Palestinians to keep a good part of the Israeli army tied down. It seemed to be working, too. At least on the surface. The rest of the Arab world is always willing to let the Palestinians martyr themselves if it serves the greater purpose."

Evans grunted in agreement, "Yes, Andy. The rest of their "brothers" never cared for them anyway. Why not let them fall on the sword? It would actually solve a bigger issue for them later if the "Palestinian Problem" ceased to exist."

"Yes sir. It seemed to be stacking up that way. But the Israeli's were letting Police and small army groups handle it. Even their run of the mill citizens are military trained. It's bloody as hell, but the Palestinians are taking the brunt of it and it freed the army up to move to the borders." He paused again and drank a little water from a glass left behind in the rush. Whose didn't matter. He was thirsty and his anxious mental state heightened the feeling.

"Anyway. With the Syrian, the Egyptian and the Saudi armies rolling in and no international help on the way; we were protesting loud as hell, but we're way out of position with any meaningful assets. The Israeli's felt they had only one way to survive. And the Arabs made it easy for them. The Arab plan of attack was to have every battle group into battle position nearly at the same time, from north in the Golan and through Lebanon, east through Jordan, around the southern end of the Dead Sea and south from the Sinai. Unfortunately for the Syrians and the Saudi's, they didn't run straight in and attack. The Saudis evidently thought it better if they took Jerusalem instead of letting the Syrians have it. They changed their order of battle in midstream and tried to move north of the Dead Sea for an easy approach." All this information was a rehash of several days' worth of observation. It took a decent amount of time to move armies and there were small skirmishes along the way. Until today.

"This change in direction seriously bunched their armies and Israel struck them north of a town called Al Karak. The Israeli Air Force hit them hard, causing them to stop and defend. Hell of an air war, but the Israeli's bugged out, then boom. Eight Enhanced Radiation Weapons pretty much did the trick."

Evans raised his eyes at this. The Neutron family of bombs were custom made for just this scenario. Low blast yield meant less physical destruction, but still a nasty way to die.

"They did the same thing to the Syrians, and Israeli armor is currently handing the coup-de-gras to what's left of the major units. Many small battles all over the place, but the Arabs seem to be a bit demoralized." A major understatement. "The Egyptians have seen the light. They stopped in place and are dispersing units. Many of them reversing. And that Libyan flotilla has now become a canceled "Navel Exercise!" That's about it right now, sir. Thought the Iranian President is screaming for continued Jihad." As a Persian, he wanted to continue to use his Arab brethren as cannon fodder.

"Intense fighting is still occurring against infiltrated commandos or terrorists all over Israel, especially in the frontier. But now it looks to be manageable." By manageable he meant it wasn't going to turn into WW III. At least not in the next day or so. The Arabs were down but not out and they probably had a few more nasty surprises up their sleeves. Andy was just surprised that they hadn't gone nuclear themselves. Either the Arabs were hording the precious few weapons the west knew they had, or some back channel promises of U.S. retaliation held them back.

"In total, the Israelis used thirteen Neutrons. Everything else was conventional. By the way sir, the Neutrons were Israeli in origin." Andy knew the world was going to be screaming that the U.S. sold them these weapons and allowed them to be used. Damage control starts right now.

The two sat there for more than forty minutes as these developments played out. In that time, Evans had been on the phone with the President three for separate calls, feeding him whatever information he needed. Sometimes confirming, and sometimes completely debunking information and advice provided by the President's other *reliable* sources. Whatever happened after this mess, the Israelis proved the oldest adage of all, "If you got the tiger by the tail, you best be able to deal with the claws and teeth!" The rest of this drama would play out over the next few weeks, but now, instead of being the spark to ignite a major war, it was just one hot spot on a globe full of them.

The Arabs proved fairly impotent after their defeat, or possibly restrained. A few more missiles were launched from Iran and by the Saudis, but it was more to show the world they could still be defiant than anything else. Andy assumed that what ever WMDs the Arabs countries did have, they were saving for later. Right now they were a bit preoccupied with damage control on the home front. Thanks to satellite news feeds and the wonders of the Internet, almost everyone on the planet knew of the "disaster in the desert" as it happened. Tehran's streets were filled with angry crowds. Riots broke out and the many youth movements which had been clamoring for change from the hard line fundamentalist government and the ruling Ayatollahs, fought pitched battles with government troops. An ugly scene being repeated across the Arab world. Andy was working through a number of scenarios and possible responses, when Evans hung up his phone.

"Ok, the boss seems to have it under control. At least for the time being. Let's retire to the office and get the team working on the After Actions and the next-step scenarios. Don't forget, in the midst of all this we have a space mission to launch."

Andy sighed. Another lesson in calm delivered by the king. "Yes sir," He mumbled, thinking, just what the rest of the world continued to think. *What next!*

Chapter 12

A pristine cool quiet lay over the night darkened hills of central Laos. A deep night. Bright with stars and no moon to mar the view. Two young boys of the Lao Soung lay cradled in the tall grass of a meadow, gazing skyward and watching for the shooting stars that could be wished upon. They felt the gentle rise of the warmer air from the valley below, carrying a myriad of smells for them to sample. A wondrous night, though one like endless others, locked away in a timeless country that the broader world decided to leave alone.

"Look there!" said one, claiming a momentary streak of light as his own. They waited quietly listening to the rustling of small animals and the night-call of hunting cats. Eight more were counted before the great star kissed the horizon, signaling the time to go home. Reluctantly, the boys rose, still staring at the sky, not wanting to release this simple joy. Tomorrow would bring work and toil, yet neither wished for bed.

They turned for the trail back to the village, pulling their eyes from the sky to negotiate the dark path, unwilling to change the magic by turning on their flashlight. They wandered this path slowly biding their time when suddenly, their shadows, hidden by the night, appeared with a flaring of light that streaked across the sky, turning the meadow to momentary day and causing them to run wildly around the boys as if they carried a life of their own. Both children cried out and stared skyward as a huge meteor screamed silently from east to west, vanishing over the horizon and leaving them in darkness once more.

Shaking with the excitement of their narrow escape, sloth left them. They ran down the path, past the tall trees that marked the edge of their village, their voices bubbling over, describing what would be one of the greatest spectacles of their lives.

Timed almost to the second, radar and visual observation posts tracked the object as it plowed a fiery furrow across the hemisphere. Millions turned out to watch, and millions more who were not living under its path, watched on television or streaming computer video from the comfort of where ever they happened to be at the time. Air traffic and maritime shipping had been warned of the event far in advance, so no mishap occurred. NASA counted it down like a well choreographed play as the International Space Station Unity caught the upper reaches of the atmosphere. Twice she struck and tried to bounce away, struggling to be free and escape her fate. But the earth's grip was too tight, and this time gravity would not be denied.

Friction superheated the skin of the ship. Unity was never designed for re-entry. Not sleek like a shuttle with no heat tiles to protect her. The extreme temperature heat quickly melted the misshapen solar collectors, already twisted and deformed from a similar contact only days ago and several thousand light years distant. Onward she plunged, leaving a sun bright trail of vaporized metal in her wake. In moments titanic stresses broke the ship apart, then, like a comet they were fused back together, a ball of tumbling pieces quickly being eaten away by the blowtorch of atmosphere. Yet even the thickening air couldn't consume all of such a huge ship, and the molten mass; the remnant that was the infant step of mankind into the unknowns of space, slammed into the salty waters of the Indian Ocean.

The impact of several tons of metal falling at the speed of sound threw a geyser of water and a great plume of steam hundreds of feet skyward as she punched a hole in the glassy surface. Back rushed the water to fill the gap, causing another smaller geyser to reach for the sky even before the rain of the first touched down. Where before there was blue ocean, the surface frothed and boiled in phosphorescent green and effervescent white. The disturbance sending rings of waves toward distant shores.

Many eyes watched her streak across a quarter of the earths sky, but none were near to see as she at last settled into the deep silt, cooling under a blanket of cold ocean water half a mile down. The final bubbles of oxygen leaking out, clawing their way to the surface and freedom. Then all was still, the fantastic journey of the Unity now ended.

Buck reeled with the ramifications of what he'd seen so far, and yet he still knew very little. The image they were shown displayed a ship straight out of his dreams. She was shuttle-esque, yet sleek and sexy. Clearly an experimental model and one never meant as a bus or cargo carrier. She was built to test theoretic design and technology. As far as he could tell, the Enterprise, as Marx had named her, was as long as a space shuttle, yet thin, with a sharp nose and wide wings that swept back from almost the tip to the stern where four exhaust nozzles nestled under a low tail. There was no hint of the engines. A series of air intakes along the sides of the ship were well back in her aft near the tail, but they were above the wings, looking more like gills, or the louvers on an air vent. *It looks a lot like the business end of an arrow!* Matte black covered every inch, effectively hiding windshields and doors, though later he would discover this ship had nothing so mundane as windows. She was a beauty that caught the eye and caused the heart to quicken with her unspoken promises. A siren that looked nothing short of wicked.

Marx gave them little information at that first meeting, but as soon as they left, a man in military fatigues with no insignia and no rank pulled he and Cal aside and ordered them to follow. Another room and another wait, but with one big difference. Now they were intrigued. This was far more than either could have imagined. So much so neither had much to say. They were lost in their own thoughts, when they were re-joined by Marx and Jules.

Marx started them off, "Well? What do you think of the Enterprise?"

Cal responded with the same awe Buck felt. "She's incredible! I can't wait to get my hands on her."

Marx smiled with genuine pride. This had been his project since it was first dreamed up and subsequently approved by Director Evans. The pride of a father in his son, or a man who was told to do the impossible, and did! "You will get your chance shortly, Commander. But I'm sure you still have a thousand questions, and now I can be totally candid. I couldn't before. Not with our friends and allies still with us, but you needed to meet them." He smiled, but the humor never reached his eyes.

"No matter what they say, I believe they're both spies, and they are here over my most strenuous objections. However, and this comes directly from the President, we want to avoid our own Baikonur. It was decided to include them so we can, "share," whatever we find. But that doesn't mean I have to give the bastards anything more than a ride!" For a moment his demeanor cracked, but was just as quickly recovered.

Buck smiled at his discomfiture, because he hadn't yet decided whether to like the man or not. Though he felt exactly the same when it came to their new "friends!" Regardless, this was the job, "so," as a former training officer used to say of any distasteful task, "Get the hell on with it." But now he was playing with his own life, so he asked the most obvious question. "Ok, Marx. We've seen the pictures, and we have the basics of the mission. But, well hell, has anyone actually flown that thing?" He got an answer, but not what he expected.

"I have, Buck! So has he," Mad Dog said, and he was immediately jealous. She'd left him blowing in the wind and evidently had been living the dream ever since. He grinned inside, *Hell, for a honey job like this I'd have left me too!* Suddenly, the hurt he'd felt upon seeing her again, feelings he thought he'd left far behind, washed away, and a weight was lifted. He was finally truly over her.

But her answer didn't go as far as they needed it to. "To space?"

She shook her head, "Close."

"Close?" he challenged softly. "Close don't count. Why the hell only close?"

Mad Dog looked uncomfortable for the first time since the meeting began. No more fighter jock bravado.

It was Marx's who explained the realities. "Gentlemen, let me stress again that this is an experimental project. In fact, until two days ago the Enterprise was called the XSP-11. We christened her Enterprise because, well... quite frankly, as you said earlier, we are 'going where no man has gone before.' It was the President's suggestion, made in one of his few light-hearted moments in recent days, and I for one, don't *usually* buck the Commander In Chief." His emphasis on usually was interesting. "But... even though she's experimental, and she hasn't been piloted into space by us, she has been there. Three times by remote pilot.

All three successful, and we were scheduled for the manned flight next month." His face actually brightened with excitement. "That was before Artifact 1 showed up." Marx looked at both of them, his expression intense. "It's my life too by the way! I have unqualified confidence in her. Enterprise will do the job."

Buck felt like he was being sold on the Nautilus by Captain Nemo, sight unseen. He'd just have to see for himself, and fat lot of good it would do. He wasn't the pilot, just baggage. *What the hell! Even if we flame, at least it'll be historic.* Still, like anyone, he *wanted* to be sold, "Ok, Marx. Convince us. How does she work? What makes Enterprise so special? We knew we weren't going to get there on a regular shuttle. Why will this be any different?"

Marx gave them a car salesman's, "I'm so glad you asked" look, because I've got you now! "I assure you, Captain, she's totally different. As you know, one of the problems of spaceflight is fuel-verses weight-verses thrust. They all work against each other. You have to have enough fuel to generate enough thrust to deliver a payload. Easy formula and very restrictive. It takes X amount of thrust to move Y amount of payload from the gravity well to orbit. Part of the payload by necessity, is fuel. Improve the efficiency of the engine, reduce the fuel weight, and increase the payload." As he talked his hands became more animated. Though the two astronauts were not so enthused, listening to a physics lesson they'd learned in high school.

"Enterprise was designed to use two different propulsion systems. One to get her into orbit, and one to maneuver once there. Obviously, as with any experiment, this is just the beginning. Once we have the design perfected, we can put it in larger ships. Ships built in orbit and launched from there." His smile lost some of its luster. "That, of course, was prior to Artifact 1. Now we're hoping to take a few hundred paradigm leaps." It was as if he had a personal problem with being one-upped, even if it was by alien intervention.

Cal asked him to clarify, "You said two propulsion systems. Something new?"

Marx nodded, "A new version of the scram-jet technology, and something newer."

"Scram-jet?" Buck said. "That's just atmospheric!"

"I said, new version. We've improved on the technology and can now use it to boost into a very low orbit. It's best to explain our launch scenario so you have the best understanding. First, as with the other scram-jet tests you've seen, we have no vertical takeoff capability. Enterprise will be launched from a modified B-52." He paused a moment for questions. Curious looks were all he got, so he continued.

"The B-52 gets us up there, then dumps us off. The scram-jet kicks in and takes us to low orbit. All very routine I assure you."

Jules butted in, "It's a kick like you never felt before. We've had to design specialized pressure suits to take it, and you still almost blackout. Its' way over the top of anything you ever did in a jet." She made it sound like a thrill ride.

Buck looked at Cal letting his boss take point. "I'll take your word for the, "all very routine" bit, but what gets us out of low orbit and on to the Artifact. Doesn't look like she could carry enough fuel to get stable, let alone half way to the moon."

Marx smiled that aggravating smile that told them this was what he'd been setting them up for. "That's where you're wrong, Captain," he actually winked, "And right! We will have enough *fuel*," he said it with a great emphasis as if the fuel were something incredibly special, "To get to high orbit and beyond. We use the minimum we can during lift, then refuel before continuing on." He held up his hand to stall the question Cal was about to ask. "We have already delivered a fuel payload and it's up there waiting for us."

"A gas station in space? How did you get a large payload up there without using a shuttle? At least I don't think we've shipped anything like that." Cal sounded confused. Buck certainly was.

"You guys are thinking way too conventional!" Marx said, lifting his coffee to get a sip before continuing. "This is where the 'real' new technology comes in. As I said earlier, it's always a question of efficiency. This is why we designed the HLPD."

"HLPD? Nothing I've ever heard of."

"I assure you Captain, there is a whole world here you've never heard of. I intend to rectify that. HLPD is the acronym for Hydrologic-Laser-Propulsion-Drive!"

Dumbfounded, Cal asked, "Water?"

"Exactly!" Marx snapped. "We borrowed the process from mother nature."

"Rather than risk asking a bunch more questions that show how stupid we am," Cal sighed. "I think we'll just sit back and listen now." Was anything about this man and this place not incredible? A water driven spaceship?

"I know what you're thinking," Marx continued. "But it's really not that complicated nor weird." He leaned forward, pushing his coffee cup out of the way. "Let me explain how it works. Do you remember your basic geology?"

Neither rose to the bait, not wanting to show anymore ignorance. Marx sighed with a slight exasperation that showed he feared he may have been given some of NASA's duller students. "Ok! Do you remember how a geyser works?" He didn't let them answer, probably afraid they'd disappoint him again.

"Here is the basic premise. Water boils at about 95C at 5000 feet. Lower temp the higher the altitude. Put that same water under pressure, and the temperature required to make it boil increases dramatically. In a geyser, water seeps from the water table into a fissure and comes into contact with geologically heated rock. Magma heated! This water begins to boil, but additional water seeps in adding weight, thereby increasing pressure and increasing the temperature required to reach the boiling point. This goes on and on until the water table stabilizes. Then, as the water at the bottom becomes superheated, it begins to rise." He paused, "Are you with me so far?"

They assured him they were.

"Good. Ok. As the superheated water rises, the pressure decreases." His eyes pierced them. "So then what happens?"

Buck gave the expected answer, "It erupts! I mean it boils up out of the ground."

"No, Captain," Marx smiled as if he'd caught them in some foolish attempt at intelligence. "It THRUSTS! Like the nozzle of a rocket, it thrusts up out of the ground. The superheated water vaporizes as the pressure is decreased. As it rises to the surface it expands and moves faster, forcing everything out of its way. The smaller the opening and the larger the volume of water, the taller the geyser." He sat back as if that explained everything.

Obviously, he expected a response and Cal obliged him. "So let me get this right. Somehow you've found a way to make this property work in some kind of hybrid engine?"

Marx nodded, "Yes! The HPLD. Simple, but effective, and with far more thrust per kilogram of fuel." He paused again. It was fascinating. It was radical. But did they really want to trust their lives to it?

"All right! We'll show you the hard science and prove it to you. But essentially, we pump water into a chamber, subject it to extreme pressure and then superheat it with lasers. Then we release it out of the engine nozzles or through the maneuvering jets. No volatility. Less weight. Far more cost efficient. Fully scalable, cheap, and with so few mechanical parts, very reliable." All of this delivered with the passion of that same used car salesman. One who needs to meet his numbers.

"Of course, it can't be developed it to lift from the ground. That's why the scram jet and the big wings for thin atmosphere. But in orbit, or out in deep space, it will work much better than a shuttle. And, just in case you were wondering, this was being developed for a Mars mission, not for any specific military purpose."

Cal casually looked at Buck, then said, "Ok, Marx. We're hooked. If you don't mind, show us the "hard science" later. For now, we're fairly chomping at the bit to get our hands on the Enterprise."

Marx gave them a brilliant, and they thought first, genuine smile. "Done, gentlemen. I, however, have to go see to my other guests. Commander Sorenson will take over from here. She has my every confidence, and when she speaks consider it as if you are speaking to me." He pushed up out of his seat and strode to the door, then stopped and turned back.

"Welcome aboard gentlemen. I expect you to be fully oriented within the next twenty-four hours, because we're going to launch soon after." Then he was gone, leaving them alone with the Mad Dog and a serious itch to get started.

Deep darkness, and bitter cold, made the two men reluctant to leave the meager warmth that wheezed forth from the heater vents of the 79 Chevy three-quarter ton pickup. A truck that until recently had belonged to a maintenance supervisor for Alyeska

Pipeline Services, based out of Valdez, Alaska. A man who would never need it again, given the fact that he lay under a tarp in the back of the truck with a neat hole in the back of his head. Blood from the wound froze in a small puddle, firmly adhering his hair to the metal bed. Outside the cab, the wind blew and the temperature hovered somewhere south of zero. Inside, the temperature was a balmy 42°F, a fact that had the two Middle Eastern gentlemen shivering and gulping cups of hot coffee while discussing the best time to get about their business.

Unknown to these two sons of Allah, they were not as alone in the wilderness as they thought. In-country for two years, the men had worked as wildcatters for Alyeska, running maintenance on the various pumping stations along the 800 miles of the Alaskan Pipeline. Even after that much time they'd never gotten used to the cold. More importantly, though thoroughly miserable, they thought they'd run under the radar, and for a time they had. Until they broke their normal pattern.

Two days ago, the men received an activation order from an anonymous, yet expected, source. The short wave radio signal caught them unprepared, sitting in a hotel in Valdez on one of the rare occasions when they had time off. A sort of shore leave, and welcome break from the tedium of wilderness duty on the hated pipeline. One of the critical umbilical lines which constantly fed the beast known as America. Unfortunately for them, the message caught them about seventy miles from the explosives cache they'd left in a small cave near the section of pipe they were assigned to destroy. The place where the planners determined the most damage could be dealt to one of America's most venerable arteries.

SPB had *tagged* the men six months earlier during a routine background update. All company backgrounds are run through the local FBI, and that information is readily available to the vast network and computing power of the SPB. These two had been marked as *likelies* due to way too convenient and similar work histories. From that point on, they were put on the watch list.

Hurriedly, they left the hotel and headed back to the company compound. The agent assigned to them was caught off guard, thinking they were recalled by the company, and it took him a few minutes to verify that no orders had issued by their supervisor. A critical and fatal few minutes for Ed Dominic. He happened to be in the wrong place at the wrong time when the terrorists came to steal a truck. Ed lay dead under a tarp in the back, his body heat slowly dissipating into the Alaskan night. The heat was almost gone, but enough of it remained to be seen clearly on the thermal imager mounted under the belly of the RAH 66 Comanche, which shadowed the truck to its destination.

The thermal sights showed an eerily clear picture of the scene far below. In narrow focus, the pilot saw Ed's cooling body as a ghost of white, the much brighter white of the men in the cab, surrounded by a weaker penumbra of swirling heat that emanated in bright jets from the heater vents, slowly losing color as they near the windshield. The brightest signature was the engine itself, glowing fire red and still running.

The pilot *zoomed* out his view, encompassing the surrounding wilderness until he could see the glowing white of the pipeline itself, only a hundred yards away. He smiled, spying the gleaming body of a moose as it ambled away from the disturbances in the night.

He keyed his voice-link to a satellite above. "Hound Four to Hound One, the Fox has grounded."

Hound One replied immediately. He too was watching the play of thermal energy, even though he was 4233 miles away in the state of Maryland. Hound One was the SBA Counter Terrorism Operations Center, and in particular, Commander Silvio Sanchez. It was his decision when to 'kill' the Fox, and he wanted to be sure the terrorists were near their mission point. Not out of any sense of compassion or doubt. The men were obviously murderers, and undoubtedly terrorists. What he wanted was to glean the most information possible. Specifically, why here? What part of the pipeline did they think was most vulnerable, and what would they use for ordinance. Not that they would get the chance to tell him, but the evidence would remain.

"Hound Four, hold and observe." Silvio was rewarded with a double click, indicating the pilots understanding. He was cautious as well, wondering if this was possibly just a piss break. Just one of the possible explanations why they chose this place to stop. The pilot hovered behind and well above, though it didn't matter. If either man got out and looked up, all he would see was a star filled night. Unless the copter moved. Then they would see a vision, or possibly an apparition, as the ship moved against the pin points of light.

"Hound One, Fox Two is moving."

Silvio didn't answer, he could see that a passenger was exiting the truck and walking into the woods opposite the pipeline. The man stopped after about fifty yards and seemed to be stooping and moving something. Straightening, he walked back to the truck with a box cradled in his arms like a forklift, the box obscuring the body heat from his hands to his elbows. The man placed the package on the hood then got back inside, probably to get next to the blessed warmth again. Silvio smiled, *We're about to heat him up proper*. This was a preplanned and attack with the terrorists placing their weapon in a stash near where they would blow up the pipeline. The evidence was undeniable; he'd left the box on the hood and not put it in the back with the body. They weren't going anywhere else.

He gave the grim yet satisfactory order, "Hound Four, this is Hound One. The hunt is over. Confirm."

"Affirmative, Hound One. The hunt is over!" The Comanche rotated around the target 180 degrees, its nose, and the weapon mounted under it, always pointing toward the target. The pilot was now in front and about four hundred yards away and his smile was as grim as Silvio's. He knew what he was about to deliver and he wanted the killers below to have their own moment of terror.

The only light in the cab was the soft glow of the dashboard lights. Outside, the dark was broken only by the vast Milky Way swirling uncaring and beautiful over the treetops around them. The beauty, so different from their homes, was not lost on the two men as they gathered a final touch of warmth before setting out to the pipeline. Neither spoke, their thoughts uniquely their own as they watched the night. Suddenly, the night erupted in flashes of light that winked in the distance then speared towards them. Wide-eyed terror loosened their bowels as the angel of death approached, streaking down from the heavens and striding steadily towards them.

The pilot purposefully aimed his 20mm cannon well in front of the truck, then walked his fire forward until the rounds ripped into the soft metal of the truck and the even softer tissue inside. Satisfied and finished, he peeled off; leaving the mess for a ground unit to clean up. Silvio watched the destruction with a professional air, then turned away, ready to deal with the next of many operations he'd planned that day.

Unfiltered and incredibly bright sunlight beat upon the strange vessel and the large ship that carried her high into the very upper reaches of the atmosphere. Her mother, the ship that carried her upon its back, could go no further, bound by the laws of her design. A huge airframe, she could travel the globe, her eight jet engines propelling her at speeds which would seem dawdling to the experimental craft that rode her back. In her time, the B-52H Stratofortress; affectionately known as the BUFF (Big Ugly Fat Fellow, though some used another final word), had been the backbone of America's fleet of strategic deterrence. Able to reach out to almost any part of the globe and present the power, or fist, of the U.S.A.. For forty odd years the Widow Maker had done just that, and she could have continued her deadly role for many more, as her sisters still do. But that happy outcome was not to be. She was consigned to the Bone Yard, a victim of SALT (Strategic Arms Limitations Treaty). Long she languished in the hot desert, barely avoiding being cannibalized or destroyed a dozen times oven. Then came the glad day she was rescued by the SPB. Now the Widow Maker had new life and a new duty, one of the work horses for fantastic test missions.

That was then. The testing was at an end, and none of her previous missions, even those dating back to the Cold War, was more important than the one she now flew. Her payload, so proudly borne, could not be more diametrically opposed to the one she'd carried on her original missions. No longer did she carry nuclear destruction and the deterrence required for the Soviet Union, instead she carried the hope of mankind.

The XSP-11, newly christened by no less than the President of The United States as the Enterprise, rode quietly through the turbulent air as she waited her turn. The huge bomber lumbered into the clear early morning sky, heavily burdened by the ungainly load on her back. One she'd been re-designed to carry, but that still left her wallowing, the changes making her a lumbering and remarkable sight to be sure. The contrast between the two ships was just as striking. The B-52H retained all her classic lines and duel colored camouflage as testament to her history. The very image etched upon the mind when a B-52 is mentioned. But the

Enterprise was as black as night, slender in line, and looking more like a sinister weapon of death than a spacecraft. A space going vessel carrying six human souls to an alien close encounter. Where the B-52 lumbered, her engines starving in the ever thinning atmosphere, the Enterprise would soon dance into space.

For Captain Rodgers, his position in the craft was as unusual as the flight. He considered himself little more than *baggage*. Trained as a shuttle pilot, that's what he considered his role to be, and this was the first mission where he had nothing to do but sit and watch. It chaffed. Beyond words it chaffed! He sat in his artificial cocoon and listened, and watched, his control factor exactly zero; and it had been from the minute they'd been volunteered. Never mind that he was now a part of history. Never mind that he was riding the most advanced craft ever made by man. Never mind that he was going to have a very close encounter with aliens. Never mind that his life may hang precariously in the balance. It still chaffed.

From his seat behind Marx, he could watch the three big screens, each showing views of incredible clarity outside a ship with no windows. Computer enhanced images from multiple-redundant sensors could display almost any angle away from the ship. Each selected and controlled by the pilot or co-pilot, but not by Buck. He could hear everything and listened intently to the commands and conversation between Marx and Mad Dog, or Enterprise to Ground Control, or ship to ship. He even had another small screen in front of him that showed the command chairs, so he could *watch* them work. Buck accused Marx of installing that one simply to piss him off. So, with nothing else to do, he sat, watched, and learned. At least he wasn't in the back seats. He laughed to himself, *That's where the real baggage sat.*

Their foreign friends had no small screens to watch, and were situated so that even a view of the big screens up front was iffy at best. Certainly under G's they couldn't. Buck didn't know if they could hear either. He wouldn't put it past Marx to be piping them the Battle Hymn of the Republic. Yet as pissed off as he tried to make himself, he couldn't hold down his excitement as the separation from the bomber approached. As Jules said, this should be, "A kick in the ass!"

"Enterprise to Widow Maker, separation in one minute on my mark, mark." Marx's voice came from the internal single speaker headphone each of them wore, and was loud enough to overcame the ambient noise of air whistling past the air frame outside, causing an odd echo effect.

"Roger, Enterprise, Widow Maker is executing tail maneuver!"

It was only now that the modifications to the BUFF became apparent. At T Minus fifteen seconds, the scram jets on the Enterprise would ignite and massive flames from her engines would superheat the air back to a distance of four hundred and fifty yards. Anything in the way would be incinerated, including the tail of the big bomber. In a tricky and dangerous maneuver, the modified tail would split in half, effectively removing the danger. For the few seconds, stabilization for the B52 would be provided by Enterprise. At T Minus thirty, the tail split away and thirty seconds separated the spaceship from freedom.

"All right, crew. Button up, now!" This was Marx's command to close their helmets and prepare for independent flight. Buck complied, then concentrated on the feel of the ship as the transitions occurred. As the tail split, additional turbulence shook both aircraft and Enterprise bucked under them, forcing Buck alternately into his belts or down into the cushions. Then there was a new sensation as he heard Mad Dog announce.

"Scram Jet ignition on my, mark. Mark!"

Buck felt a new rumble as fuel was atomized by the super-flow of air as it burst into flame when it passed through the engine. Now, Enterprise exerted her personality. She was ready to dance. Two voices mixed as Marx and the bomber pilot counted down.

"Separation in three, two, one. Separation!" both echoed, affirming the command. Simultaneously, explosive bolts fired, blowing the final connection to the two ships. Immediately and abruptly, the Widow Maker dropped away, recovering her tail and diving out of harms' way, falling like a rock. Enterprise floated along, the vibrations ceasing essentially in freefall.

Then, "Max thrust on my mark. Mark!" Coinciding with this command came the promised, kick in the ass! Mad Dog executed max thrust and Enterprise went from freefall to Mach 4 in less than twelve seconds. Buck felt his spine compress as the weight of seven more of him pressed upon every inch of his body.

Fifteen seconds after that the ship climbed to Mach 7 and he had no more thought. The world compressed down and inward, his vision darkened around the edges and then clouded over completely. Taking a breath was impossible and he felt his heart skip beat after beat. The pain was excruciating. No human was made to survive this. Buck felt his eyeballs bulge as the corpuscles began to burst and he knew he was on the edge of death. Mach 10. It was then he felt the special space suit kicked in, negating some of the effects of ten gravities and pulling him back from the edge, slowly retrieving his soul. His vision still blurred and breath was impossible to get, but now he believed he might just live. All of forty-five seconds had passed.

Just as no human could be expected to survive without the suits, nor could they be expected to function under these conditions. From the moment Mad Dog initiated full thrust, till orbit was achieved, computers and software held sway over their lives. The Enterprise skipped along the outer fringe of the atmosphere where the air was rare. The scram jets propelled her so fast; even this rarefied air heated the skin of the ship, friction scorching her. Faster and faster she flew, describing a gentle arc across the sky. With the maximum velocity of the scram jet achieved, Enterprise automatically and without pause, switched over to HLPD. From below, anyone watching would have seen a dim streak near the corona of the sun, then a sudden plum of smoke that was actually steam. For three more minutes she accelerated, then suddenly inverted and headed for space, breaking the bounds of gravity and finally entering the vacuum of space.

With orbit achieved, the pressure subsided like a receding wave, and groans echoed throughout the ship. Health monitors attached to each of them slowly moved back into the realm of normal, yet it was many minutes before any spoke.

Buck mumbled to himself, "Kick in the ass indeed!" He shook his head to clear it and wondered about the sanity of one Jules Sorenson!

Chapter 13

A great sigh of relief sounded from the White House, to the Kremlin, to the Party House in Beijing. The first step of the mission was a success with the rest of the world none the wiser. Only a select few from each country and no more, perhaps the most secret mission ever attempted. All in an effort to stave off more terrorism, more discontent and war. If it worked no one as yet could notice. Africa continued to burn. Civil war, terrorism and discontent held sway over more rational pursuits. Nothing changed, yet nothing got worse. Andy counted himself fortunate to be part of the elite as he and Evans and the rest of the team watched the Enterprise and her historic flight. He also continued his primary duty, to monitor world events as they happened.

Other eyes watched the launch as well. Electronic alien eyes. Vi-t-ry's systems recorded every movement from the planet below. Recorded every electronic emission and watched events unfolding on the surface. Saw the launch and recorded the entire flight of the Discovery. Bore witnessed as the Unity plunged into the atmosphere, destroying the craft. Now the systems noted this new ship as she reached orbit. As his awareness grew, the information recorded was analyzed by a portion of his processors. He was confused. Vi-t-ry had recovered to the point that he remembered this planet was not his home, and that his mission and his self driven mandate had failed, but even with this he was having trouble reconciling his assumptions with much of the information he'd gathered.

The information Vi-t-ry he reviewed was recorded when he'd first transitioned, and compared with what was gathered now. It did not make sense. War, where before there was peace. The level of technology, so very primitive. Vi-t-ry wondered how he could have possibly mistaken this system for home.

The destruction of the small ship caused him no small concern because it had been caught up in his arrival and his attempt to escape. He wondered now how much of the change in the planet was due to his presence. He could not know and had no ability to discover that particular truth. His knowledge was just beginning. Vi-t-ry could receive and analyze, but due to the great damage he could not transmit! As of yet, the information received from the planet meant little. His systems needed to re-learn how to translate alien languages. Repairs continued, and Vi-t-ry could but watch and patiently wait.

"Enterprise to Control. Orbit secure. We are standing down." Marx's voice sounded strained. Evidently, he wasn't as trained for the experience as he'd let on. That or more likely, he knew for sure what it was going to be like, but didn't want to give the others the true brutal reality. They may have fought a little harder against being, *volunteered*, if they knew how bad the real ride was going to be. How close to death. Buck knew for certain he never wanted a repeat. He felt bruised and battered and entirely drained. Cal hadn't said a word, and Buck couldn't see his face through the Plexiglas of his helmet, but the constant flexing of his hands, and the silence, provided proof enough of his condition.

"Confirmed, Enterprise. We show all systems green. Enterprise is standing down. Next maneuver in two hours, twelve minutes." As with any flight Buck had ever heard of or been on, the ground personnel sounded almost bored. He thought that if those pencil necked geeks down there had ever experienced even a fifth of what they'd just been through, they wouldn't be so damn cavalier. The internal com broke into his musing and general misery.

"Lady and gentlemen. The internal pressure is now normal. Feel free to remove your helmets." Buck did so, then took a deep breath of the antiseptic smelling air permeating the cabin. He retained his silky, the hood which contained his headphone and mic.. The shuffling and groaning behind him indicated some life remained in their foreign guests as well. *Too bad!*

Cal grabbed his arm, "Son of a bitch, I thought we were done for sure. You ok?"

Buck had never seen his friend look so pale. A trickle of sweat trailed down the side of his face. "No problem, Cal! Walk in the park."

Cal looked for just a second to see if he was serious, then laughed, "Screw you, Captain! And that's an order."

"Sir, yes, Sir! Affirmative and all that." He pointed his chin towards the front of the craft. "Maybe we should direct a little of that temper towards the oh-so mysterious Captain Nemo of this voyage. He could have given us a bit more warning."

Cal sobered a little. "If I could work up the energy, I'd get out of this chair and ring his friggin neck! As it is, I think I'll just lay here and wallow in my misery." They were interrupted by Jules.

"Welcome to space gentlemen. Everyone ok?" A rhetorical question at best. She had the monitors and could tell the actual health of each of them, right down to their sperm count and no one seemed inclined to give her anything more. She sighed under her breath, "Wimps!" Then louder, "Ok, then. Since everyone seems peachy, let's have a look outside."

The screens had gone dark as soon as the scram jets kicked in, so this would be their first view from orbit. She hit a switch and a computer enhanced view of the earth and stars sprang up around them. One word sounded from Li, *jīngrén*. The only one on board who knew any dialect of Chinese was Marx. He translated to himself, *Incredible, Spectacular or Fantastic*, and smiled, now knowing for sure that this was Li's first time. Information to be stowed for later. As he'd suspected, the credentials provided by the Chinese Government were bogus. This man was certainly not to be relied upon, not that he'd ever had any intentions of doing so.

"All right!" He spoke to the group entire. "As we briefed, three orbits. Each one rising higher, until we reach orbital pad 1." Cal frowned, thinking, *How many pads are there?* "We execute a dock and refuel. From there. Artifact 1. Jules, let's have a look at the target."

Buck had a moment of mild jealousy. Marx was just a little too familiar with Mad Dog. *Why should it matter? She was in his distant past wasn't she? Still!* His jealousy was interrupted by gasps of astonishment because the earth and stars were replaced by close up shots of the alien ship in far more detail than most of the passengers had seen before. It seemed Marx was continually going to keep them off balance. However, his voice betrayed no hint of smugness.

"This is a live shot, relayed to us. I won't tell you from where or from what. We need to keep some secrets." He paused a few moments to let the view speak for itself, then, "Time to earn your pay gentlemen."

Cal rolled his eyes and mouthed, "What now?"

"Each of you has a self contained workstation in front of you, with full control over the video feed, including zoom and pan. Fully independent of any other console." Sure enough, Buck had already moved his view with no affect what so ever on Cal's. Single feed, multiple aspect. Incredible!

"Your job is to search the surface of the Artifact and come up with recommendations. Not only where we land, but how we gain access inside. Obviously, we have a few ideas already mapped out, but I want options and opinions. We only get one shot at this. Questions?"

"I have one." This echoed from the back. It seemed their Russian friend, Colonel Kirkelev, was not content to remain silent after all, though these were the only three words Buck had heard him speak since they'd met.

"Yes, Colonel."

"I understand the need of your order. But not knowing the full capabilities of this vessel will leave us at a serious disadvantage in our study, thus our recommendations will mean nothing. Will you explain your ships maneuverability, or is this simply an exercise to keep us from more of your secrets?"

Marx smiled to himself. That was his plan and would remain so. Baggage they were, and baggage they would remain until the Enterprise was securely attached to the alien ship. Until then, unlike the two American Astronauts, they were of no practical use to the mission. Deciding on an oblique approach, he lied. "A good question. I will not give you exact details of Enterprises capabilities, but use this as your premise. There is no point on the target we cannot reach."

Buck couldn't see the Russian's reaction, but he looked over at Cal and quirked his lips, *Yeah! Right!*

The Russian also knew this was, as the Americans like to called it, "Bull Shit!" but it would was still an opportunity to study the object up close. He had a feeling that this Marx would use him and the Communist for the most dangerous duty, so he would use this time to prepare.

Jules voice again intruded, "Brace yourselves. We will boost to higher orbit in two minutes."

Not knowing what to expect, and the memory of boosting to space still fresh in their minds, they pulled their straps tighter. The Hydro-Drive had already proven its capability, having thrust the Enterprise into orbit, but Buck really didn't remember it. The flight was a blur of pain, and he had no idea where the Scram left off and the HLPD kicked in. This next boost would be an education.

One minute prior to the boost, both laser chambers were pumped full of water. A mere twenty gallons each. Not your ordinary tap water, this was purified to an exacting standard developed over years of research. The fluid was pumped in to the chambers and pressurized to exactly 36,200 PSI. Thirty seconds to go and highly modified CO_2 Lasers pounded the chamber, superheating the liquid to the point of critical mass. Mass that must be released. If not, the pressure would continue to build until it burst the chamber and ripped the fragile ship to pieces. At the precise moment programmed into the computerized pilot, the modified titanium valves rotated open and the superheated liquid instantly found egress, turning into a jet of steam that propelled the mass of the ship forward. Outside, the jet of vapor blew backwards until it dispersed, quickly freezing in the vacuum of space and crystallizing into a cloud which would dissipate, eventually to be reclaimed by the planet of its birth.

For those inside, the feeling was similar to a conventional burn on any shuttle, and somewhat disappointing in its ordinariness. Yet the science was still extraordinary. An incredibly efficient fuel-to-mass ratio that could have revolutionized orbital travel. And would have if not for the appearance of Vi-t-ry.

Some hours later, Sean Evans and Andy Michaels were once again having a special meeting with the President, giving a complete roundup of world events, potential events and hot points, and the American response; both recommended and actual. Last on the list was Enterprise. Not because it was least important, quite the opposite. It was Talbot's wish to have updates on the Phoenix mission at least once a day, more often as the mission approached and landed on the object. He'd been on hand and watched the remote station feeds as Enterprise launched, and it seemed no one in the room was more tense than the him. Much hung on this flight, and even the very few who knew about it were split on the decision to include the Chinese and Russians. The fact that Evans talked him into it was not lost on the three in the office.

"Jon, all is going as planned. The mission is on target, and so far we have no response from Artifact 1." This was one of the rare times Andy had seen his boss even slightly disheveled. Their twenty four hour schedule was taking its' toll and his bowtie was actually tilted slightly sideways.

"Where are they now, Sean? Are we in the danger zone yet?"

In their assessments, the mission dangers were broken up by each leg of the flight. The two most critical points dealt with the Artifact itself. First, when it became evident the Enterprise was headed for the alien ship, what would its response be? Second, and more importantly, what would happen when the Enterprise actually touched down? The scenarios ran from no response at all, all the way up to a massive attack on the earth itself. Each scenario had a risk rating, and each would be updated as the mission progressed and more information was gathered. Mission abort points were built in and a nuclear response had been prepared just in case. In addition, every end of the communication spectrum was being used to advertise the peaceful intentions of the ship, its crew, and the people of earth. The die was cast and the humans were in motion. The alien was the unknown.

"Well, Jon, they just finished the refueling and are ready to depart the station. One more orbit as they accelerate, then even a blind man will know where they're headed."

The President rubbed his eyes. "I'm normally not one to question my decisions after I've made them, but good Lord Sean, we could end up killing the entire planet here! Now I know how Kennedy felt."

"Come on, Jon. We went over this time and time again. This is no time for cold feet."

The President smiled, also disheveled. In fact he looked like he was ready to sit down to Sunday football, not head for the press conference he had scheduled in less than an hour. "Its not cold feet. Its brutal reality." His eyes pierced them both. "You let me know if anything outside of the plan happens. Anything!"

"Yes, sir!" It was Sean's job to always give the President the, *brutal reality*. Something his other *closest* advisors seemed more and more reluctant to do as the world deteriorated around them.

"Also, I want to watch the final approach. I don't care what else is going on. Clear?"

Again, "Yes, sir!"

"Sorry Sean, you and your group are doing a hell of a job. In this, you know better than I. I'll see you at ten." Talbot rose and headed for the door where he paused, "I sure as hell hope it's not before."

Commander Robert Selkirk was jarred awake by the alarm next to his bed. It was deep in the night in Helena Montana and it was not his alarm clock that screamed for attention, it was the SOA (Special Operations Alarm) wired directly to the police command post at the Governor's Mansion. The only place in the entire world that was his domain and his exclusive responsibility. Instantly he was awake, grabbing the second phone on the stand by his bed which did only one thing, put him in contact the Duty Officer at the Command Post over at the mansion. *Oh Shit!* No answer. His wife looked up in groggy eyed alarm as well. She knew how rare this was. In fact, the alarm had never sounded except for the once monthly test. Selkirk tried twice more to reach the D.O. with the same negative results, then he called and scrambled the S.W.A.T. team assigned to the general Helena region and specifically to the Governor of Montana. He then called the Colonel in charge of the local National Guard unit, advised her of the situation, and ran out the door. It was six critical minutes since the alarm had broken his slumber.

The self proclaimed General of the Army of Christ, Franklin (Frankie) Knight, was angry and extremely frightened all at the same time. As the leader of the most radical right wing militia group in the northwest, he felt god had called him. It was his duty to save his people. To carve out a New World Order. A world where right thinking people could live as god intended. At least those in this remote part of the U.S. of A. To him and to other the *right* thinking individuals, the government had let the country go to hell. Its policies were as corrupt as any of its politicians. They'd allowed the country to stray from the path of glory. The path of God. Morality was a myth, foreigners bought and sold Congress and the President at their whim. Hollywood was the devil's playground and held more sway over the lives of America's youth than god. It must stop.

Frankie's duty, and his calling, was to bring the country back to center. Part one of that duty meant taking over the government of Montana. Step two meant declaring a new provisional government which the federals would have no choice but to recognize. The turmoil caused by the alien ship was surely a sign from God. Frank and the A.O.C. could not lose.

At this moment, his units, and units from four other separatist groups that had joined them, were securing key positions all over the state. Armories, government buildings, radio and TV stations, and of course, major roads. All he needed to complete the coup was a prestigious hostage in the person of Governor Davis Brigham. This is why he himself led the raid on the Governor's Mansion. His intelligence operations confirmed that the Governor was in residence and ripe for the picking. Unfortunately, his information was stale. A full three hours old. Unknown to the good General, the Brigham's youngest son developed complications after a particularly rich dinner, and was rushed to the hospital in the company of his loving parents and older sibling.

The raid had been conducted with the timing and precision of a military operation. Neutralization of surveillance and alarms by an internal plant. All exits blocked and a ten man penetration team. The coordination had been perfect. No one had been harmed and the house was his, the seat of government for the great state. Unfortunately, that was all he had. With his primary target not to be found, all the General had in hand was a very frightened maid, an extremely angry and belligerent cook who barely spoke English, two unconscious guards, and a host of state and local police and national guardsmen that now surrounded him. Plus about a thousand spectators and enough media to cover a Democratic Caucus in Hollywood. Frankie's grandiose plans were rushing through his fingers quicker than a fist full of dry sand. About all that was left of the great revolt were the conditions of his surrender. The phone rang and the bull voice of Selkirk shook him to his core, for unknown to his troops, General Frankie was far more the devout coward than he'd ever been a devout Christian.

Reaching the alien ship was a logistical problem almost as big as reaching the moon. The Apollo missions took advantage of gravity by slinging themselves around the earth in an oval orbit which literally shot the ship towards the moon. The alien vessel was only a quarter of that distance. To reach it, the Enterprise would circle the earth in ever increasing speeds and higher orbits until they could eventually intersect. They were a full three orbits away when disaster struck.

Buck was jolted from an uneasy sleep by a rumble that ran through the center of the ship and claxons screaming for attention in front of the command chairs. Six voices asked the same question. Only one answered.

In a calm and professional, yet strained voice, Jules reported, "Commander, we have a breach on engine one!"

"Shut it down!" Marx barked the unnecessary command because the automatic systems had all ready done so. "Damage?"

"Unknown, I'm running the diagnostics now."

"What happened?" Cal asked this from the back, feeling out of place and therefore vulnerable.

Li was mumbling something in Chinese, and Buck was trying to see into the front. He saw nothing that gave him any clues. Marx and Jules continued talking to each other, ignoring the rest of them. Suddenly, the ship shuddered again, causing Li to grip his seat and mumble even louder. Buck thought the man was close to losing it. He hoped the Russian was up to the challenge.

Finally, Jules voice sounded over the com, "Everything is under control for the moment. Just give me a little time then I'll explain."

Buck thought, *under control! How could we possibly be under control? We just lost half our propulsion!* He again tried to look forward, but all he saw was the two astronauts talking softly.

"What do you think, Buck!" Cal was tapping him on the arm.

"Well! We're still alive." Buck was thinking back to their orientation. The Russian Sergei leaned forward to hear. He and Li had not received much more than an overview, and he was very interested in this particular conversation.

Li seemed content to sit with his eyes closed. In reality, he was cursing his handlers in Beijing for sending him on this suicide mission with orders which seemed impossible. What were their words? *Contact any intelligent life and convert it to the cause! Short of that, sabotage the mission.* It would not be acceptable to leave either the Americans or the Russians in possession of any alien technology. Li's safety was not important. Now it seemed the Americans vaunted technology was going to solve all his problems for him. The fact that it was going to cost him his life had him alternately cursing everyone responsible, and rethinking his atheism.

"Yep!" Cal recalled the orientation. "If we'd had the breach just prior to firing the engines, right now we'd be so much space junk."

"So what are the chances for mission completion now? Think we can still make it?"

Cal didn't get a chance to answer. Marx actually left his seat to come back and talk to them. "Ok, gentlemen. Obviously we've had a setback."

Buck laughed at him. "Setback! My god Marx, you are the master of understatement. Unless you're telling us you can put a patch on the engine!"

"Let him have his say, Buck." Cal knew now was not the time for a confrontation. Buck knew it too, but somehow couldn't help himself. Marx just brought it out of him.

Sergei ignored them and asked, "So what does 'setback' really mean?"

"I understand your frustrations, gentlemen." By his tone, Marx did understand, and cared little. "First of all, as you heard, we had a breach on an engine. Number one split open somewhere. Fortunately, it was while the engine was pressurizing prior to our next maneuver." He paused for just a moment to see if anyone would question him. None seemed inclined until all the information was in.

"The good news is, number two and the maneuvering jets are still functional. So we're ok for now. But! As you suspected, number one is done. We also lost a significant portion of our fuel before we could stop the flow."

Li finally broke his silence, "So we can get back!" No one missed the tremor in his voice.

Marx smiled at the discomfort of the communist. "We could! But we won't."

"Won't!" Li finally heard the desperation in his own voice. He took a deep breath. "If we can't complete the mission, why not go back?" They were all interested in this answer.

"But we can complete the mission! This mission is to get to the Artifact at all costs and find out what we can, then *report* back." That simple statement demonstrated clearly that this was indeed far different from any normal shuttle mission. In a shuttle mission, safety was always paramount.

"So, now the bad news. As you surmised, this will probably be a one way trip!" He held up his hand to stall the protests about to spill from their collective lips. "A mutiny will do you no good. You can't fly the Enterprise, and we are going on. All three of our governments agree, and of course, the world needs us." Marx looked at each of them in turn. "Now then. Enough of the patriotic bullshit. I'm not into losing my own very precious life either, so we do have a chance."

It was Cal's turn take up the challenge. "So let me guess. You think we can find some water on the ship!"

Marx smiled, "Guilty as charged. We have to assume that for there to be life, there has to be water. We've talked to mission control and they agree. So on we go."

"My luck the damn aliens drink methane." Buck mumbled, loud enough for the rest to hear. Li shrank back into his chair.

Jules called from the front, "Strap in everyone. Our next burn will be longer and maybe a bit rough given the one engine. Thirty seconds!"

If it bothered her that this could be her last mission, she didn't show it. Buck admired her balls. *Let that coward Li chew on that bit of info for a while.* He strapped himself back in and waited because there was really not much else he could do.

Jimmy Walks Long stared at the brightly lit building from the concealing shadows of the Piñon pine he knelt beside. The unique smell of the tree itself and the wood smoke on the wind brought a sense of nostalgia of days gone by. Days of his youth when he would sit by the fires and listen to stories of the *old* time. The time when the white man was the enemy and his people ran free. Jimmy was tall for an Apache, four inches over six feet with piercing blue eyes that belayed his claim of true blood. It was this taint that brought him to the movement and was the driving force behind his desire to change the world. Beside him, sweating even in the cold night air of the high country of Northern New Mexico, were eight other members of his cell. All Jicarilla Apache, or as they called themselves, Tinde, and all members of A.I.M, the American Indian Movement. Modeled after any terrorist group, there were many cells within the movement and most had no knowledge of the identity of the members of another. And like Jimmy's, all were in motion that night.

Their targets were the tribal councils of nearly every reservation in the country. Each cell was made up of tribal members who met in secret or in public. The rest of the tribe usually knew who belonged to AIM and chose to ignore them, work around them, or openly support them. Whatever their affiliation or membership, or the political bent of the tribal council, they'd ignored AIM at their peril, and tonight would bare the fruit of that ignorance. AIM and its membership were disgusted at the path the tribes were taking. Casinos and the almighty dollar were ravaging their morals and traditions. Drug and alcohol abuse was epidemic and the lives of their people were drowning in the morass of white culture.

"Doo anaa daa dle da!" (Well no more!) Jimmy had shouted the words with all the others at the last rally. "Doo anaadaa de da!" (No more!) At last there would be an accounting. They'd learned their lessons from the seizure of the B.I.A. office in Washington in 1972 and the disaster at Wounded Knee in 73. They'd learned about politics and the power of manipulating the American Media. They had lawyers and politicians, and tribal council members in their pockets or on the payroll. They played up the bleeding-heart liberal types and bled them of their money, all in the name of the cause. And still it wasn't enough. "Doo anaadaa de da!" The shout still echoed in his head. Destiny was at hand and tonight they would do what they intended back in 68 at the founding. Fulfill the dream. Tonight the Indians would win.

Jimmy gripped the hard plastic of his M-16. With a grunt and a nod he set his Ch!oonii, his friends, his warriors, his Apache in motion. As one they rushed the building where the tribal council was meeting. Very few surprised eyes met his when he entered. No one resisted and many nodded their acceptance. The Governor bowed his head once, then lifted it and yelled to those gathered, "Doo an<u>aa</u>d<u>aa</u> de da!" Jimmy smiled at the real leader of his cell and a charter member of the Aandanaaka, *the movement.* "No more," he raised high his rifle and chanted with the rest.

At that same instant, whether it was the Klamath or the Kickapoo, Mojave or Eastern Cherokee, St. Croix, Salt River or Seminole, the cells executed their coup. In less than two hours, AIM took control of more than eighty percent of the reservation system. Interstates and state and county roads were blocked and armed warriors manned the barriers. Tribal Governments were shut down and *foreigners* were expelled. The *new day* had dawned and the U.S. Government had a new and shocking political force to deal with. One within its own boarders and one that could not be crushed bought-off or ignored. One that would make Jon Talbot wonder at the health and survival of his beloved Union because the landscape of America had once again changed.

Chapter 14

Andy hadn't slept in two days, and it felt like he and Evans had set up camp in the White House. Once again, they were there to update the President on some of the bigger situations occurring around the globe, and most importantly, the mission to Artifact 1. He was actually dozing when Talbot came in.

"Geez, Andy, you look like I feel!" The President was dressed for yet another national address, and was more alert than Andy had seen him in days. *Uppers?* One had to wonder. Andy had already popped enough pills that he figured it would be years till his system would be normal again.

"Sorry, Mr. President." Andy felt the blood heat his face.

"No need to apologize. You guys are doing a hell of a job."

He keeps saying that, Andy thought. He also remembered the President saying the same thing to his volunteers, over and over on the campaign trail. Andy was just tired enough for it to be annoying.

Talbot took his seat and turned to Evans. "So! What have we got?"

Sean spent the next ten minutes giving the President a general update on world events. Negotiations between the Russians and Chinese were progressing, though that wasn't saying much. One wrong word and they would be in a war neither wanted, but one that nationalism would demand. The USA was working desperately in the back channels, promising aid and concessions to both sides in an effort to defuse the very volatile situation. Though Andy knew the belligerents were playing the *game* and getting as much from the U.S. as physically possible. *Bleeding the Dragon* as their communist Chinese 'friends' called it. The Israeli/Arab conflict had devolved into a multi-front stalemate with the Arabs content to harass and avoid further punishment and embarrassment. Though they were pushing every disaffected or terrorist group under their sway into the breach. Sacrificing them in the name of Allah in order to keep Israel and the U.S. hopping and putting out fires. Pakistan and India were heating up again, but North Korea was now in full retreat. A U.S./British/South Korean Special Forces attack on the North's nuclear weapons launch sites and production facilities had effectively de-toothed the tiger. At least they hoped, and while the world still stood on the brink of a bottomless precipice, with ongoing civil wars, terrorism actions, coups, economic collapse, starvation and humanitarian crises abounding, the situation was far better than it was only two days before.

"Ok! That's the world. Give me the domestic picture. I've got to go in front of the camera in a bit, and I need to give the American people something."

Sean looked grim. America was looking at an economic collapse far bigger than anything ever seen. Bigger than contemplated in any but the most dire scenarios. Worldwide, trade had been choked to a trickle. No export, no import, and no production. Prices for even the most abundant items had skyrocketed, and government imposed limits on pricing and draconian rationing had little effect. The black market now consumed a significant portion of the GDP and taxes were a smaller trickle the overseas trade. At this rate the treasury would be empty in weeks. Local and state authorities, using National Guard troops as their backbone, had their hands full with terrorism, murders, looting and riots. Little could be done to help the economy in the short term. The most recent data indicated only a third of the workforce was actually on the job. The rest were too frightened to leave their homes or their families.

It was even worse in other countries. There had been runs on banks worldwide, and wealth was evaporating at an alarming rate. The Dow was down almost 5000 points to levels not seen in fifty years, with company after company demanding bankruptcy protection or asking the SEC for reporting delays, or financial re-statements. It was unknown how the country, let alone the world, could climb out of the hole they were digging. Hundreds of thousands had died, and millions more could, due to war, famine and disease. The only real way out, as Sean saw it, was to prove the alien ship was an accident that represented no threat to humanity. Even with this there were enormous risks. Suppose they found out, as was hoped, that the ship held a retrievable wealth of technology? Who would control it? And what would the rest of the world do to prevent that control, or wrest it from the new owner. The success of the Phoenix mission brought almost as much risk as its failure.

"Anything else form AIM?" Talbot rubbed his eyes. The *Indian Issue* had caught them with their pants down. The FBI had been keeping tabs on all of the American radical groups, but this one had been as bad a miss as 9-11 and Waco.

"Recognition, a seat at the table, complete autonomy, removal of all federal presence, eviction of all non-Indians from the continent." Sean sighed wearily. "They're all over the board right now. We expect some form of centralized control to emerge, and get some *reasonable* people to talk with, but right now it is indeed a most volatile and fluid situation." Sean hated to not be able to do something proactive, but it was simply too early in the game. "A few deaths, but for the most part calm has settled in. Of course the Governors of several states are threatening armed action to re-open roads. So far its just a threat, being that we're all citizens and friends..." Sean didn't quite smirk. "We're watching this carefully, Jon. That's about all we can do for the moment." He had some ideas but they needed to be vetted through the Think Tank first.

"Ok, what about the situation in Montana?" The President was fishing for something good.

Sean smiled for the first time in a long time. "The Army of Christ turned out to be a Paper Tiger! At least their leader was. A police commander up there... Andy, what was his name?"

"Robert Selkirk! Commander, Montana State Police." Andy said, happy to have a bright spot to point out.

"Thanks, Andy. Selkirk got on the phone with this so called General, and threatened him in some very creative and potentially illegal ways. Selkirk is former Delta and knew his business. The good General gave up all of his people, as well as their missions all over the state. Unfortunately, not all of them were as willing to give up as he was. Twenty-seven dead, mostly theirs, but for all intents and purposes it's a done deal up there. Governor Brigham has called for calm, and this event seems to be over."

"Great! I can use that as a good news lead. What about Enterprise. Can she really make it now?"

"Yes, Jon. Our analysis shows they will have no trouble getting there." He left the rest unsaid. The President already knew that with one engine and little fuel, it was a one way trip.

Talbot closed his eyes, contemplating or praying Andy could only guess. The President sighed, "Ok. Keep me posted. What about the follow up mission. When will the second prototype be ready?" Enterprise had a sister ship, almost. She was still being assembled and it would be at least a month before she was ready. Evans was just about to say so when he was interrupted by Andy.

"Sir! We just got a burst from NORAD! Now confirmed. Artifact 1 is transmitting!"

The President and Evans were suddenly very alert, and Evans stalked quickly across the room to Andy and his computerized window on the world. "Transmitting what? And sending it where?"

Andy shook his head. "We have no idea *what*, sir. Nothing we have can translate the signal. It's being broadcast on the microwave band. Very directional, and pointed at Earth. No where else." He paused, looking at the screen. "It's gone now. Very quick. We recorded it of course. But first analysis! Random, and probably accidental. This theory is based on the fact that we think the ship is repairing itself. I'll have the Think Tank on it directly."

Sean frowned, but let it go for now. "Don't read too much into this, Jon. We'll watch it. Besides, Enterprise will be there in about twelve hours. Then we'll see."

Talbot wanted more, but knew if he pushed, Evans would be speculating. He had to settle for being happy the mission was still on despite a major setback. Andy was half right. The President had been praying.

Tentatively, Vi-t-ry reached out. His plan was to send a greeting to the planet below. Using the simplest information code he knew, he sent the message through his only repaired transmitter. A simple message sent. No reply. And still the tiny ship approached. Vi-t-ry watched it carefully. No threat could be detected. That didn't mean there was none. Unfortunately, he had no defense. At least until they arrived. Until then, the big ship was entirely at their mercy. Vi-t-ry had no actual fear, just the unsettled feeling caused by a dearth of knowledge. Time would tell the purpose and mission of the small ship, and as it manifested he would deal with it.

      Five hundred miles and closing. The entire crew sat mesmerized by the approach and the target growing in the distance. The previous orbit had them close and they were awed by the sight, yet that was nothing compared to the knowledge they were now on final intercept. No turning back now. An hour ago, Marx had finally revealed to them his choices for landing. Cal had come close on one of his suggestions, but no one else was even in the ball park. Sergei suggested an entry through one of the damaged sections, thinking they would get closer to the center of the ship that way. He felt that the heart of the ship was where they would find their answers. Marx burst his bubble however, saying they couldn't be sure the Artifact didn't have its own gravity, nor could they see what obstacles they may have to dodge. As it turned out, Enterprise was not *that* maneuverable!

      Marx opted for a spot on the centerline of the globe where they spied what looked like a bay. Possibly for launching and retrieving other small ships. If they couldn't get in there, the Enterprise would move to another target. For now, the mission was to get there and land. The rest would have to take care of itself. They watched as the enormous vessel grew on their screens and the conversations became whispered, as if talking too loud could bring the alien ship to life. Would the humans be perceived a threat? To come this far, only to be swatted out of the sky like some pesky bug. As they neared, the tension grew, but there was no move from the alien. It floated in front of them, cold and uncaring

      Li was back to closing his eyes and muttering in his native tongue and Sergei alternated watching his screen and casting disgusted glances at the Communist. Buck stared in fascination; if he was going to die he wanted to see it coming. A half hour later they had cut the distance to one hundred miles. Details could now be seen without magnification.

      "I feel a little like the Millennium Falcon coming up on the Death Star," Cal had whispered.

      "At least there's no Tie Fighters or lasers to dodge!" Jules had overheard him, and thought it required an answer. Maybe just to break the tension, though her answer may not have been the best thing to say under the circumstances.

"Think this bucket of bolts can outrun them if they show?" Buck immediately regretted his comment as well. This bucket of bolts was the very leading edge of human accomplishment.

"Sorry," he mumbled, seeing how Jules had gone stiff, her back straight, half lifting out of her seat.

"Eighty miles and closing!" Marx gave the update simply to head off a confrontation, because the distance was prominently shown on each of their screens.

"Enterprise! This is ground, do you read?" They were in constant contact with whoever was on the other end of this mission. People Buck had never seen. But now was one of those quiet times; between scheduled events so to speak. This voice sounded concerned.

"Loud and clear, ground!" Mad Dog answered back like she really was mad, and she was, stung by Buck's last comment. "What do you have?"

"Enterprise, we are receiving..." The voice paused for a moment, pulling everyone up on the edge of their seats.

"Enterprise, we are receiving a signal from Artifact 1. Do you copy?" *What the hell?* It was a collective thought.

Marx answered back, "Say again Ground!" Maybe they hadn't heard correctly.

"Commander, I say again," This time the voice was firmer. "We are receiving a signal from Artifact 1." Another pause, "Amend that, Enterprise. The signal has ceased. Did you receive any of it?"

The passengers looked at Jules as if she might be hiding something, but she was just as confused as the rest of them.

"Negative! Enterprise has received zero! I repeat. Zero, signals." Marx made sure he was understood. Then, "Ground! What was the content of the signal?"

Another pause, then, "Unknown, Enterprise. We got a few seconds of traffic. Unintelligible. We are trying to decipher it, but nothing so far."

Marx pursed his lips, deep in thought. "Understood, ground! My recommendation is that we proceed with the mission. Does Control concur?"

Buck elbowed Cal, "Recommendation hell. We have no choice remember."

"I know Buck…"

Before he could say more, Sergei spoke over their shoulders, "I hope your ground people decipher this message. Before we get there!" His Russian accent in the hyper oxygenated air made him sound rather funny. No one was laughing.

The anonymous voice from ground came back, "Control confirms the decision to continue the mission and recommends extreme caution."

Even Marx rolled his eyes at that one. *No shit!* He answered back with an acid voice, "Confirmed, Ground! Extreme caution." It seemed even on secret missions everyone conducted a thorough CYA!

"Ground. Please inform us if *Any* more signals show up!"

"Affirmative, Enterprise!"

They could just imagine the relief the folks at Ground Control felt, positively ecstatic Marx took the responsibility, and doubly glad they weren't here with them.

"Good Luck!"

"Opinions?" Marx asked. It had been several minutes since the discussion with Ground, and Marx and Jules had checked and double checked their systems. No signal had been beamed at them. He might just as well have said, "Are you all as scared as I am?" Buck wasn't sure he was scared, but at a minimum, this was now a certified, world class, 'Sphincter Tightener!'

He answered, "Let's cut to the chase here. We have no way of telling what that signal was, or if it even had anything to do with us."

Cal agreed, "He's right. It could have been anything. A greeting! A flat out mistake. And of course, the ever popular, 'keep the hell away from me or else' warning."

If Li could have shrunk any further he would have. He added nothing, and they all but dismissed him as being less than worthless.

"You're right of course, Mr. Sanderson." Marx looked involuntarily over his shoulder at the alien ship. "But I want a consensus. Tell us what you think. Sergei?"

The Russian shrugged. "Mistake I think. Our new friend is repairing himself, and this one signal happened to... how do you say it? Slipped out!"

Wishful thinking? Buck thought.

Cal, however, agreed. "I tend to think Sergei is right. At least I don't think it's a warning, or it would have sent it at us too."

Buck plucked at his lower lip, a habit he had when deep in thought or nervous, both of which applied now. "We can't know alien protocol. Maybe, instead of a mistake, it was a first attempt message to the planet. Hell, it's so damaged; it may not even see us yet."

"Jules?"

"I'm going with non-hostile. Whether mistake or message of greeting? I don't know."

"All right. Good enough for me." Marx was not going to give them his opinion, his mind was already made up. "Jules, keep your hand on the maneuvering thrusters just in case."

Buck almost burst out laughing. *Like we could out maneuver, or out run anything that alien could throw at us. Hell we'd have just enough time to kiss our ass good bye!* The comment remained in his mind. Li might have fallen over dead if he'd heard, and Buck contemplated teasing the little commie coward. But then again, he didn't want to spend the rest of the trip with a floating corpse. *Shouldn't be too tough to get him into an air lock...*

Marx broke into his little dream of sadism. "Fifty miles and closing!"

Fifty miles till the unknown. Buck couldn't get over how utterly moon-like the Artifact looked hanging there. A half full crescent. He chuckled out loud, thinking how he'd feel were he the aliens. Stranded voyagers, just lying there, unable to move. Were they afraid? Franticly trying to make repairs? Or were they content. Happy to be here, in orbit around an alien world, bathed in the light of an alien sun. Perhaps soon he'd find out.

Chapter 15

The tiny ship containing six living breathing beings was very close. Vi-t-ry observed them with every passive method at his disposal. He analyzed the ship itself, looking beyond the obvious. Looking deeper, analyzing the mechanics and electronics of the vessel. No external weapons. Nothing to give a clue to intent or purpose. Then, as if his question were answered, a signal reached him. A message sent directly from the small vessel itself. Indecipherable, but definitely sent to him, meant for him. Vi-t-ry considered a millisecond or two, and then determined this problem required a different approach. His first message was to the planet. It had not been returned. Perhaps, as he suspected, these beings could not understand him. Another approach was needed. A mental command was sent. A relay computer accepted the order, and the ship's one working transmitter; a narrow beam pulsed array, was rotated and aimed precisely at the small ship's receiver. In another millisecond the message was on its way.

"I am still not sure about this." Cal was making sure they were all on the same page with this latest decision; or coming to terms with it himself. He was ignored. They were now only thirty miles away. The alien ship looked immense in the distance and growing bigger by the minute, slowly blanking out the background of stars. The decision had been discussed between them and ground control, but they were on the point and so it was ultimately their choice. At stake was the actual rendezvous, and whether the Artifact aware of them. The alien had sent a message directly to Earth, not to them. Now that they knew someone, or something, was minding the store, it was considered to be a bad idea showing up on the doorstep unannounced. The question remained, what to do? Send a message from the Enterprise, or remain silent.

Sergei argued that as damaged as the ship was, they could probably land without the alien knowing about it. He opted for stealth. Mad Dog sided with Marx and wanted to send the message. After all, it was her idea. Cal was pretty much on the Russian's side, but Buck found himself siding with Mad Dog. He was willing to bang a drum to get the damn things attention, definitely not wanting to surprise them. Ground control was cautiously for the signal. Majority rule in this case went Marx's way, so the decision was made. A small microwave burst would be sent. An open binary message, as similar to the code sent by the alien as they could get. Now was the time.

"We're sure, Commander." Marx answered the statement Cal made earlier. He was ready, so everyone else had better be. "I'm sending it now." Marx keyed the computer and the message flashed complete.

A surge of adrenalin rushed up Buck's spine. Message sent. What now? Only Li was sure. He was absolutely sure he was about to die, and he pressed his eyes shut so tight tears leaked out the corners. The Russian shook his head. *A land with billions of people in it and this is what they send!* He suppressed his impulse to suddenly grab the little man and scream, *"Here it comes!"* He held off simply because the smell of shit permeating the man's suit would hit him first! Instead, he ignored the little puddle of manhood and waited for a response.

This close to the rendezvous, Andy, Evans, and President Talbot, along with a select group, crowded into the White House situation room to watch. The message from Enterprise was sent and everyone was glued to the screens. Each of them trying to feel as if they were on that ship, and thanking God they weren't. They were almost silent when all hell broke loose.

There was a piercing scream from the back when every power source in the ship suddenly went dead. Sparks and smoke billowed out of the command console, kicking off the emergency fire suppressant system amidst the blare of warning sensors. Bedlam! Five people grabbed helmets, pulled them on and shut visors. Sergei secured his own, then shut Li's visor. The man was unable to do so himself. Ships intercom was dead, but the radios in the suits worked, and many voices asked multiple questions and the most common was the least known. "What the hell happened?"

Marx and Jules ignored them in their efforts to figure out the common answer, and what's more, try and do something about it. Buck sucked in a deep breath of antiseptic tasting air and, in a moment of clarity, wondered why they had not been bumped. No rocking of the ship. No explosion. Nothing. A thought to ponder as the emergency backup systems began to kick in. Lights came back on-line, and blowers quickly evacuated the smoke, leaving the air reeking from the smell of burnt plastic. Though, no one except Jules was willing to test it by opening their helmets. Confusion reigned until a voice sounded over the Com.

"Enterprise! Do you read? Enterprise, this is ground control. I repeat. Do you read?" The voice was covered in with static and didn't seem to be the same person as before. Buck couldn't care less who it was, he would have kissed the guy if he could. Near death experiences will do that to you.

Jules voice was amazingly steady. "We read you ground."

"Glad to hear your voice, Enterprise. We thought we'd lost you. What happened and what is your operational status?"

"Unknown to both!"

Marx cut in, "Give us a moment, Control. We're running diagnostics now."

"Affirmative, Enterprise, but we show you missed a burn while whatever happened, happened. You haven't slowed down. If you don't do something, you will impact with Artifact 1 in twelve minutes."

Marx gave Jules a knowing look and shook his head. So far they had no video feed, and their radar was down so they were flying blind. Their professionalism took over.

To Jules, "Check the engines and maneuvering thrusters." To Control, "Ground, can you give us anything on velocity? A new burn calculation? We are flying blind."

Blind! Buck thought. A definite design error. *This is what happens when you depend too much on your technology.* It was a cuss in Marx's direction. It was his design, his overconfidence. The Enterprise had no windows! They weren't needed. The wrap-around video displays were supposed to be multi-redundant and foolproof.

"Enterprise, we will feed you data momentarily."

"Affirmative, control. Also, do you have any idea what that damn thing hit us with?"

"Enterprise, we got a bit of it captured by one of our satellites in near earth orbit. It was a microwave burst. A message."

"Say again!"

"I repeat. A message. Artifact 1 sent back a radio stream it had picked up from Earth. It amplified it and bounced it to you. Amplified at least a thousand fold."

Buck couldn't believe it. *Attacked by a freakin message!*

"We think it was trying to communicate, not attack."

"Big damn difference," Cal muttered.

While they were talking, Jules had completed her checks. She shook her head softly, a movement just noticeable inside her suit. She keyed her com and talked to Marx only, giving him the bleak reality.

His reaction and body posture said it all. "Ground, this is the Enterprise." His voice was solemn and quiet. "Belay the calculations. Our controls are shot. We have no engines."

The whimper from Li could be heard by all, even the President of the United States and his own Premier.

Vi-t-ry's passive sensors were unable to determine if his new approach, relaying one of the planets communication streams to the small ship, had any affect. Unfortunately, during the relay, his damaged system suffered another overload, further damaging the system. Vi-t-ry wasn't even sure the message had been successfully sent. If his programming allowed such things, he would have cursed. His constantly updating data now showed something his battle computer regarded and tagged as a threat. The small ship was on a collision course and was not slowing down as would one of his own fighters or transport ships. Impact was imminent. Original analysis showed a converging course, allowing orbit or docking. Now the trajectory estimate showed the small ship would impact his outer skin. No real problem for Vi-t-ry, unless there was something he couldn't see, some hidden weapon his passive sensors couldn't pick up, (less than a .023387% chance) but a very real problem for the inhabitants of the vessel. Vi-try assessed his options. It was time he took action.

Marx and Mad Dog kicked into overdrive, pulling panels apart, pushing buttons to reboot systems, and in general doing anything they could think of no matter how far fetched. The other four had no choice but to ride it out. Buck and Cal knew absolutely nothing about the ship or its systems. Buck had never in his life felt so useless, so utterly helpless. Sitting there, watching the pilots work, he even felt fear. Not the butterflies or the rush type of fear when you're living on the edge, this was the visceral fear of impending death. Of the unknown beyond death. He looked at Cal, who just sat there watching as well. Buck didn't want to impinge on a man's last moments. Wouldn't know what to say anyway. The inside of his suit was silent. His com neither transmitting nor receiving. A time when all you hear is your own ragged breath and the beat of your heart drumming your ears. Buck wished Marx or Jules would switch their intercom back to ship wide. At least then he could concentrate on them, rather than...   To make things possibly worse, the cabin was lit only by emergency lighting. Gone were the spectacular views of space and the alien ship. Now there was nothing. No sense of movement, just yourself, your thoughts, and the waiting. On the plus side, at least he couldn't hear Li.

"Enterprise. Any luck? You have seven minutes!" Buck was startled from his thoughts by the tinny from earth. *Damn! Seven minutes.* He could tell by the voice that the man on the other side was reluctant to speak. He was probably ordered to. Who would want to count down a tragedy like this? Other than CNN.

"Negative!" Marx's one word response said it all. It was an epitaph, their final death sentence. There would be no reprieve. Marx and Jules finally gave up their efforts and settled back in their seats.

"Ground, this is Major General Richard T. Marx, Special Projects Bureau of the government of the United States, and Commander of the U.S.S Enterprise!"

Buck actually laughed, s*o that's who this guy really is"*

"In the last minutes of this mission, I would like to give each member of the crew a chance to make a statement. I would also like to tell the President, its been a pleasure serving you!"

By the clock there were exactly five minutes left. Buck disengaged as Sergei made his statement. It was in Russian so he wouldn't know what the man said anyway. He didn't try to consider what he would say, supposing it would come. Instead, he visualized the moment of impact. He saw it in morbid slow motion. The crumpling of the nose and the scream of tortured metal as like an accordion, the back flattened to the front. He imagined the impact and wondered if he'd actually be able to see any of it. Or would it all happen too fast?

He was replaying a quick death in his mind when abruptly, the ship lurched. His eyes flew wide thinking they had miscalculated their time, then he was thrown to the side and up against his restraints as the Enterprise endured a massive deceleration. The force was brutal, a sensation he'd experienced only once before. That was a malfunction on a jet sled during training, and it nearly killed him. He was sure this would have if not for the miraculous suits they wore. So sudden and so hard was the maneuver, no one could speak. The pressure in his head so great, he felt his eyeballs bulging, the urgent voice from ground control was almost unintelligible.

"Enterprise! Do you read! Come in Enterprise! What did you do?" The questions went on and on. So did the pressure. Buck heard a scream echoing and wondered who it was then realized it was him. With almost inhuman effort he shut his mouth, marveling that he could still be alive. Slowly the pressure eased. Slowly. Until finally, all movement ceased.

"Enterprise, do you read. Come in!"

Marx's voice was laced with heavy breathing, like a man just finished with ten mile run humping a full pack. "We're here. I might amend that. We are *still* here!"

"Great news, Enterprise! Incredible news. You are at a complete stop. How did you manage it?"

"Simple answer, Control. We didn't! I have no idea what happened. I can only assume the Artifact did it." A long pause from earth, enough time for each of them to gather their wits and to realize they actually still lived.

"Enterprise. Do you have any control at all over your ship?"

Buck hated this almost as much as what was happening a few minutes before. He couldn't see faces or read body language. Sterile! That was the word and that's what Jules's voice sounded like.

"No, Control. We are deaf, blind, and dead in the water."

"Affirmative, Enterprise. Be advised, you are exactly one mile from Artifact 1, and not moving!"

A long whistle sounded over the com. Buck agreed. He didn't know exactly how fast they had been moving, but it was fast. To just stop! What could have possible caused that? He had no time to contemplate that question, because with a very sickening thump, Enterprise lurched again. This time they were pulled forward, slowly and without doubt, toward the alien ship.

Chapter 16

"Sean, do you have any idea what's happening?" The President's question was the culmination of the emotional roller coaster they'd been on in the last hour. Moments ago they were dreading the gut wrenching, remote bird's eye view of a crash that would snuff out the lives of their astronauts. Then, the sudden and unknown reprieve. Now? The Enterprise was slowly being drawn to the huge ship.

"Only guesses, Sir!" He used the formal address because of the others in the room. "Andy, tell them what you have."

"Yes, sir! Mr. President, with the limited information we have, the consensus is an energy field of some sort stopped the Enterprise. The same force now has the ship in tow. For what purpose we don't know, but in three minutes we may because the Enterprise is being reeled in. And no, there is nothing we can do about it!"

"Well isn't that what we want?" This from somewhere in the back of the room.

Andy just raised an eyebrow. *What we wanted indeed! But just what does the alien want?*

Analysis complete, Vi-t-ry found no threat from the tiny ship. Slowly he drew it towards him, far slower that he would have with a known friendly. There was still the possibility of something he couldn't see. He watched as it neared, dwarfed even by some of his maintenance robots working on the skin of the ship. Slowly it approached, once completely disappearing from the visible spectrum when it passed through the shadow of one of the drive energy towers. It momentarily reappeared, then was plunged from the intense silver light of the alien sun, to the impenetrable black on his dark side. The small ship passed within a few SMU's of his now burned out relay transmitter, then crept towards a gaping hole which had irised open to admit it. As the ship passed inside the bay doors swiftly closed, effectively sealing off the vacuum of space, and capturing the alien vessel.

The President's party watched with a mixture of dread and awe as the Enterprise approached. Andy was reminded of the opening sequence of Star Wars. A small ship passing in front of a huge ship, which was immediately dwarfed by a colossal ship. Then, improbably, a section of the aliens hull opened like an old style camera lens, visible only because of the dim light emanating from inside. They watched as the Enterprise drifted toward the opening and then inside. The iris closed, blotting out the light as if it had never been, and there was nothing left to see but the dark side of the alien spacecraft.

"Enterprise, you are passing into the dark side of Artifact 1." Ground Control was the only insight the crew had to what was happening outside. They could feel gentle movement, but that was all.

"Anything else happening out there?" Marx asked. Talk about flying blind into the unknown! They could have been sitting in a conference room for all they could tell what was happening.

"Nothing, Enterprise. You are moving past one of the towers." The anonymous voice amended the statement after a moment; the skin of the Artifact was bristling with towers. "That is, you are moving past one of the towers that the blue lightening came from." That helped. Buck could just see them passing by when the damn thing erupted.

"What do you think boss? It seems it wants us." Reprieved from death, it was time for a psychology session. Buck wanted to talk it out.

Cal's voice was weary, "Don't know, Buck. It saved us for a reason. I just hope it was more than the fact we were going to hit it!"

"Well, it's up to the aliens now. If it parks us in orbit we're as dead as if we'd crashed. I like the reprieve, but I sure don't relish the slower version."

"Enterprise. Something's happening on the surface of the ship," then silence.

Shit! That's it? Something's happening! Nothing else? Buck could have beaten the guy with his own arm. Prayed he'd have the chance to go back and do it. The voice, their only link too the earth or the world outside finally, came back.

"It's opening! Looks like a bay door or something. I can see some light inside." The man on the other end didn't sound like he was talking to them, just talking. His voice contained awe and it did nothing to sooth the astronauts. Quite the opposite. Li was mumbling over the com. until Marx shut him off, but inside their cocoon, it felt more and more like the wrong side of a casket. They couldn't see, and the descriptions they were receiving, combined with the desperation of their situation, caused the imagination to trek down roads better not traveled. Buck didn't know if there had ever been a time when he'd existed on so much adrenalin. Wide awake, yet on the verge of overpowering exhaustion. He was drenched in sweat and his suit's cooling system seemed non-existent.

"Enterprise. You are moving towards the opening."

"Understood, Control. Can you see anything else?" Marx was back to his calm professional self and Buck reluctantly admired his nerve. "Any movement? Anything?"

"Nothing else, Enterprise. You are now moving inside."

"Ok..."

Marx was in the process of replying, but was ridden over. "It's closing! Enterprise, you're inside and it's clos..." Then nothing. Like someone had flipped a switch, Ground Control was gone.

After all that had happened in the last few weeks, it was surprising that anyone could be shocked by anything short of nuclear war, yet the entire room, especially President Talbot, sat stunned. Ground Control continued to call the ship and the reply was thunderous silence.

"Enterprise! Do you read us Enterprise?" Finally, even that fell silent. Then the inevitable, "Be advised. At 8:43 PM EDT, Ground Control has lost contact with the USS Enterprise."

"Mr. President," Evans rose and motioned Andy to do the same. "I have to go. We need to see if we can salvage something from this!"

Talbot looked up, but it was a moment before he really saw him. "Of course, Sean. Go and see if you can do something." He held out his hand. "I'm deeply sorry for your people, Sean. We'll be praying for them."

Sean Evans, the stone cold Director of the SPB, was deeply moved. "Thank you, Jon. I'll let you know anything when I can."

With that, Andy and Sean left, both wondering just what the hell to do next.

Chapter 17

Vi-t-ry brought the ship inside and landed it in a hangar almost half a mile beneath the surface, then ordered the robot stevedore to anchor it into place. He detailed a part of his mind to watch, then bent his growing intelligence to other tasks, primarily, how to communicate with his guests.

If they could have seen it, the crew of the Enterprise would have experienced a sight which would have awed them almost as much as the alien ship itself. The launch and recovery bay through which they now floated was simply, vast! It was large enough to accommodate almost any other ship in the Collective fleet. The corners of the bay were lost in stygian darkness, and only intermittent lights around the far periphery broke the blackness. It was toward one of these lights the Enterprise floated, gently drifting diagonally across a full mile of void, then entering a round room that irised closed behind them in mimic of the main doors minutes before.

Marx tried several more times to raise earth after the last conversation was cut off and all that answered was static. Nothing felt quite as final as those words, and now all they could do was wait. Control said they had entered the ship, but they could feel no movement and had no idea they were still headed toward a destination. For all they knew they were already there.

"Any ideas people?" Cal asked the question because he was tired of sitting on his ass and waiting on fate.

An answer was on Buck's tongue when Sergei spoke. "It is my thought to open a hatch. See if we are... Anywhere."

Mad Dog agreed, but Marx was a little more cautious, arguing that not knowing what was on the other side, despite their suits, could well be fatal.

"We're not going to have much of a choice in a while," Buck said, "And I don't relish waiting for whatever's out there to try and dig us out!"

Through the entire flight and all its trials, Li had said nothing. But the thought of actually opening the hatches was something he wanted to put off for as long as humanly possible. His voice sounded over the com with a strength that surprised them all. "I know that I have shamed myself on this journey, and for that I truly express regret. I am however, in control now. May I be allowed to make a suggestion." The man's English held almost no accent from his native country. If anything Buck would have thought *Bostonian*.

The disgust was almost hidden in Marx's reply. "Everyone else has had their say so you might just as well."

"Thank you." If he noticed the hostility, he chose to ignore it. "Can we put the landing gear down?"

A puzzled frown crossed Jules's face, but she nodded to Marx. "Yes we can, Li. We have a manual override for that. But… Why?!"

"Commander," Li sounded like he was speaking with a small child, "It will tell us whether we still float, or are attached to something."

Buck laughed at the obvious discomfort Marx felt, seen even through the bug eye of his helmet.

"Unless it parked us on our roof!" Cal said.

"True, Mr. Sanderson." Li still had a backbone, even if he was terrified of spaceflight, losing his life, and victim of a debilitating case of xenophobia. "But it *may* tell us something, and it's better than blowing a lock into an acid atmosphere."

Suitably sobered, they debated only a few minutes before taking Li's suggestion. Buck braced in his seat as Mad Dog pulled the override, not knowing what if anything to expect. Nothing was what they got.

"Landing Gear deployed," She said.

"Well… that was underwhelming," Cal said dryly. The words were no more than past his lips than the ship lurched, coming to a full stop, letting them know they'd still been traveling.

Being strapped into their seats was the only thing that kept them from being flung about the weightless cabin.

"Holy shit!" That was only one of the epitaphs slung over the radio waves by the six startled humans, but Buck's was the loudest. "Well, that answers one question." He said. "We *were* still moving."

Wide eyes stared as the sudden stop was replaced by the feeling of the ship slowly descending. Then, with a thump, the ship settled to a surface, followed with a silence broken only by the panted breath of the astronauts. A moment passed, then, with a finality that was certain, they felt clamps grab the landing gear, sealing them firmly to the alien ship! Artifact 1. They'd arrived. Not in the manner in which they planned, but here none the less. One question remained, "What now?"

For three hours the astronauts sat, waiting for something to happen. Not that they weren't busy, they'd pulled open every access panel in the cabin, another search for anything they could fix. They found circuit boards with components blackened or burned through, and wiring harnesses with melted insulation fused together in massive clumps. Silicon chips cracked and blistered. A wonder the fires hadn't been worse. It was a total loss. Enterprise was going nowhere on her own. Ever again. They worked until, exhausted and frustrated, they collapsed into the only comfort they had. Their seats.

"All right then! Looks like no ones coming, and for sure we aren't leaving." Marx was certainly in a mood. Having worked with him for the last few hours, Buck thought it was the damage to his ship than their dire situation. After the initial shock had worn off, he'd grumped about every little piece of damage as if it were a personal injury.

"But," he continued. "We still have a mission to complete, and we can't do that from in here."

Buck agreed. Not so much about the mission, but about survival. If they had a chance, it was out there, and if they completed the damn mission! So much the better.

"First of all, Jules, give us an update on supplies and air."

"Yes sir, Commander." Buck bristled at the deference she showed Marx, angry that he should feel this twinge. Jealousy? Now? After all these years, and in this situation? Even so, he couldn't help the all too human feeling. *Put it behind you,* he scolded.

"We have hull integrity, and with the re-breathers and scrubbers, air is not a problem. At least as long as the batteries hold." With the primary systems out, and conservation on maximum, the system could work and sustain them indefinitely. Or eight days of battery, which ever came first.

"Food and water are not a problem. At least for the same period." She smiled, "After that it gets dicey."

"Well, I have to assume they have food somewhere on this tub," Cal stated. "And they breathe something."

"Unless its' just one big machine." Sergei pointed out this possible fact.

Buck was not sure whether to be hopeful of or not. A machine would take no human sustenance, but did they really want to meet some hideous alien? Or eat its food? Yet alternatives were in short supply. "Well, I suggest there's only one way to find out." He was about to volunteer for the very reason they brought him along. A space walk on a spaceship. He prayed it wasn't just to be cannon fodder. Or Dinner!

"Agreed, Captain," Marx said. "I propose a three man exploration team. You, myself and Sergei."

"Wait a minute!"

"Save your protests, Cal!" This was the first time Marx had used the personal form of address, and that, as much as his tone, stopped the commander. "This will be a short trip. Just to get a view of the outside, and a lay of the land." His look conveyed much more. Marx didn't want to leave both the foreigners together, and he definitely didn't want to leave Li alone with Mad Dog. Or his precious, though woefully broken ship. Buck knew from personal experience that Jules could take care of herself. Again, there was that 'But!' Buck had the same gut feeling about the little man.

"Let me stay and Cal can go out."

A steel edge entered Marx's voice, "Were this a democracy, I'd consider your request Captain! We are a ship of the United States and I am its commander. Do I make myself clear?"

"Perfectly!" Buck left little doubt about his true feeling on the subject, yet he did recognize and respect chain of command and his duty.

"Good. Now then, I do have a little surprise." Marx took a key from a chain around his neck and inserted it into a slot none of them had seen when they tried to fix the systems. A hidden door slid away, revealing a compartment filled with weapons. Glock 17's and Colt M4 Commandos. Even a few flash bangs and some canisters Buck didn't recognize. Certainly a shock. Jules didn't miss the look on Li's face before he hid it.

Cal whistled, "Diplomatic mission?"

"Diplomatic, yes! But it was decided to have a back up. As a last resort. Agreed?" Given the gravity of their situation, no one was going to deny the utility of the weapons.

"Self defense only, people." He took out and handed a holstered pistol to Buck, and one to Sergei. He didn't bother to ask if the Russian was trained to use one, and by the way the man handled the weapon he was a professional. They found that Marx had thought of everything. The holster clipped easily to their spacesuits, and the slim finger design of the suit glove made drawing and firing the weapon fairly easy.

Next he handed one of the canisters to each of them. These, as it turned out, were not weapons, but a special marking paint designed to work in either vacuum or atmosphere. Like Hansel and Gretel, they would mark their path to insure they could get back. Finally, he handed out the Commandos and pre-loaded clips for each weapon, then he closed and locked the cabinet handing the key to Jules. Buck stared at his new armaments and thought that if they got into a situation where they actually need these damn things, they were truly up 'shit creek!'

"Ok, Buck. It's a two man lock. Let's go. Sergei, we will report over the com. when we're through. When I say it's clear, you come through. Questions?"

None were asked, but many were thought. They were about to step onto an alien ship and the gravity of the situation, no pun intended, was not lost. They just hoped they'd get home to tell someone about it!

The lock was designed to accommodate two fully suited astronauts. Just barely. Buck was in front, which meant he was first target, and that's exactly how he felt. They were buttoned-up in their suites, and he waited with no small amount of trepidation as pumps drew the air from the chamber. The astronauts had no way of knowing whether there was a vacuum on the other side or something far worse; like a caustic atmosphere that would burn through their suits. The lock would not open unless the pressures outside and in were within two percent of each other. To pop a lock from earth normal into a vacuum would be a very bad idea. As the pressure counted down, the closer to zero the better, Buck prepared himself for the unknown. His grip on his rifle was painful, and he chastised himself. He was adrenalin hot and more wide-eyed aware than at any point in his thirty seven years. Marx, at his back, had the stock of his Commando pushing pointedly into Buck's right kidney. A pain despite the spacesuit, and not nearly as comforting as it should have been.

His eyes watched as the gage fell to zero, vacuum outside. *Oh shit! This is it!* And his brain screamed, *you fool!* Yet the hatch opened anyway.

As soon as the hatch cracked the small red LEDs in the lock went out, plunging them into darkness. Buck resisted the urge to turn on his suit's head lamps, the last thing they wanted was to reveal a target. At a snail's pace, the hatch swung back presenting a vision like a slowly opening eyelid in a dimly lit room. Beyond and only a few feet away was a curving bulkhead, seen grey in the murk, and surprisingly close. No further than twenty feet. He was not sure what he expected, but a wall was certainly not it. With the hatch fully open, Buck peered out getting their first glimpse of the inside of the alien ship. He looked down. Then up, and back. Finally forward.

Amazement tinged his voice, "We're in a room!"

"A room?" Jules sounded far away, and he was not sure why. Possibly a limitation of the radios in the suit.

"Yes. A room. And it's not much bigger than the shuttle, though it's completely enclosed. Very low light so I can't see how we got in. No apparent hatches or doors."

Marx's voice sounded a mile away as well, though he was standing right behind. "Any movement? Anything else?"

"It's bare. Nothing but an empty room, and us." He paused, then amended, "At least on this side. We have to go out to find out for sure."

Marx wondered if the Captain was waiting for him to give an order, but held his tongue, resisting the urge to push. *Give him time.*

"All right." They heard Buck take a deep breath, "I'm exiting now. Wish me luck!" Buck stepped out and spun, pushing down from the top of the hatch frame and accelerating himself downward in the zero gravity. He tried desperately to see in every direction at once as he descended, cursing the limited vision from his helmet. It seemed like he fell forever, then he clanked to the floor, where, to his surprise and relief, his magnetic boots stuck firm. Quickly he stepped to the side as Marx drifted down, landing in a crouch next to him.

"Damn hard to see, Buck!" They stared around, not moving for several seconds.

"Shit, Marx, this is like wandering blind through a haunted house. I expect something to reach out and grab me and I can't look everywhere at once."

"Yeah, Buck. What's that they say in the movies? 'It's quiet! Too quiet!'"

Damn! The man is human.

"Ok, Captain. Let's do a once around. You forward and I'll walk backwards so we can cover every angle. A full circuit of the shuttle. Sergei, are you in the lock?"

"Yes, Commander. The cycle is almost to zero."

"Good! Pop the door and be ready. We may need the Calvary!"

"Da! I mean, yes, I am ready."

Marx patted Buck on the shoulder. Together they walked around the ship, searching first for threats then for other less obvious things. Marx was narrating the entire time for the ships record.

"The Enterprise is in a chamber roughly twenty feet larger than the shuttle, and with at least fifty feet to either end. The chamber itself curves up from a flat deck to complete an arc over the top about ten feet above the tail of the ship. There is evidence of a large hatch of some sort at the back, though how it's operated is unknown. The material is feris of some sort, but I can't guess at the actual alloy. The lighting is low, but it looks as if the material, or whatever the bay is made of, is glowing and is the actual source of light."

"Marx! Look at that!" Buck grabbed the man and he spun, his weapon ready, wildly searching for targets. Buck laughed sheepishly, "Ah, sorry! Just wanted you to look at the landing gear."

"Son of a Bitch! Don't ever do that again. I almost pulled the trigger!"

Buck was amused at the Commander's discomfort. This was the first time he'd seen him really rattled. Yet he knew he'd been incredibly stupid. "Sorry. Won't happen again, it's just... I was, well look!" He pointed down where one of the wheels touched the deck plate. The entire wheel, up to the first shock mount, was covered in the same material as the deck construction. Literally, the deck had reached up and grabbed the gear, completely engulfing it in a glove like fist.

"Incredible," Marx whispered as he knelt down to examine it, finally switching on his lights. Shadows jumped out and Buck was momentarily blinded, but when nothing bad happened, he relaxed and bent to check it himself. Reaching out, he touched the alien technology for the first time.

Vi-t-ry felt the contact as the humanoid touched the locking mechanism. He'd been observing and recording, but the touch sent a familiar yet alien shiver to him It burst through the uncountable trillions of Nannites which made up the exo-shell of the landing bay; shooting the information down the artificial neurons like a bolt of lightening. A touch not felt by the ship in so long it was barely remembered. Reflexively, the Nannites recoiled, leaving the impression of the gloved hand imprinted on the lock like molded clay. The touch was like a splash of ice cold water, jarring memories and reopening databanks long dormant. In that instant, Vi-t-ry felt a new flood of knowledge. Information flowed, and a catalog of life forms appeared. This is where the name 'humanoid' came from.

The touch triggered a latent security program, one that instructed the Nannites to pass into the individual crew member. At the molecular level, regardless of covering, the robots could pass through almost any membrane and, once there, identify the person, his or her job classification, and security clearance. The Nannites recoiled, partially because of the shock to Vi-t-ry, and partially because the individual that attempted to trigger the lock was not a member of the crew.

An alarm went off in the security offices not far from the landing bay, signaling an alert to any personnel in the vicinity that an intruder had entered the ship. The alarm cried out warnings to personnel who could no longer hear. Had not been able to for more than two thousand years, though one of the bodies still sat where she'd died, mummified and propped against a wall. Immediately, Vi-t-ry scanned the catalog which detailed the eleven known species of sentient beings. Four of the eleven made up the now dead crew and the full membership of the Collective, the confederation of planets and advanced civilization that had produced Vi-t-ry and his brothers. Digital body maps of the full anatomy and physiology of each species was displayed and reviewed as if they were cutaway 3D models. All eleven spun on every axis and was systematically examined down to the genetic level, then compared to the being that had just touched the lock. What was immediately apparent to the sentient ship was that this being did not exist in the catalog. He felt a moment's disappointment at the confirmation, yet reveled in even this small discovery. Reveled because these beings resembled one member species of the Collective; the masters. Perhaps a seed of the race that sprung from Vi-t-ry's home world.

In the nanoseconds it took for Vi-t-ry to complete and assimilate of the new data, the security program in the Nano-lock executed another subroutine. It sprung a trap then waited patiently for the long dead security personnel to show up and deal with the intruder.

Buck had only the briefest moment to feel the touch of the metal as the lock seemed to shy away from him, in like a wave in mercury. Then, faster that the eye could see, the material sprung back like a gaping mouth, grabbing and engulfing his hand to the wrist. With a yelp he pulled back, attempting the wrest free a hand that now felt like it was encased in concrete, completely and effectively trapping him. There was no pain, just a firm and unbreakable hold. In his own ears he screamed like a baby, letting go of his rifle to grab with the other hand. "Oh shit! Marx! Get it off! Get it the hell off me!"

Marx stared, dumfounded and shocked into immobility, watching Buck frantically pulling like a coyote in a leg trap. So quick was the alien device, it seemed like it simply materialized over the hand. Involuntarily he took a step back, knowing for sure they were in way over their heads. Finally he got a grip on himself, and, ignoring the shouted questions over the intercom, grabbed Buck to steady him and keep the man from injuring himself. In the process, he hit the rifle floating in the weightlessness, sending it twirling across the room where it hit the curved bulkhead and rebounded down.

"Calm down, Buck," he tried to sound calm. "Sergei, I need you here. Now!" He shook the Captain until he had his attention. "Hold still Buck, we will get you out. Did it cut you? Are there any injuries?" He wanted Buck to get focused. "Is your suit punctured?"

Buck's breathing was rapid and his eyes were wild, but he seemed back in control. "No! It hasn't hurt me. But, Son of a Bitch! I can't move."

Sergei arrived looking as stunned as Buck and just as reluctant as Marx to approach.

"Get in here, Sergei. Let's see if we can pull him loose." The pleading in Buck's eyes finally got the Russian over his fear. Cautiously, the three of them pulled on his arm, watching carefully in case the thing tried to jump at them. They exerted pressure until Buck really did cry out in pain.

"Shit! Stop. You're pulling my elbow out of joint." They released him and stepped back panting.

"What's happening out there?" Jules's voice had an edge of desperation. "Do you need help? Cal's on his way as soon as we can get him cycled out. Answer me!"

More help is the last thing Marx wanted at the moment. "Stay there, Cal! We're ok at the moment."

Buck shook his head, rolling sweat down into his eyes where it burned like fire with no way to rub it away. *Speak for your self damn it! You aren't about to get ate by an alien ship!* Out loud, he asked as calmly as he could. "Hey, Marx. You got something on your wonder ship that might cut this?" He had to ask a second time because Marx seemed lost in thought.

The man looked at Buck, his face ghostly inside his helmet. A subtle shake of the head gave the Captain the answer he most dreaded.

Vi-t-ry observed the reaction of the humanoids closely. Their reaction and their emotions. He sent his nano-bots throughout the trapped being's body, thoroughly mapping and analyzing. Then he ordered all but a few thousand to go dormant, and released the lock.

Buck was visibly shaking by now, and about to go over the edge into full panic. He stared at his hand fully contemplating the same coyote Marx did a moment before. He'd chew the damn thing off if he had too. It took him a full two heart beats to realize he was free. With a jerk that took him off his feet, he pulled his hand back, trying to get as far away as possible. Both Sergei and Marx jumped out of the way as he went floating past, leveling their weapons, thinking he'd been attacked. They yelled his name, but all they got was a grunt when he fetched up against the bulkhead and rebounded, following his rifle to the floor.

"Quick!" Marx shouted the order. "Back to the lock. Now!" He and Sergei walked as quickly as their magnetic boots and zero gravity allowed them. They grabbed Buck by the arms and floated him back to the Enterprise. Buck was thankful for the assist. He knew for sure he couldn't have done it himself.

Chapter 18

Buck sat in his chair sucking in lungful after wonderful lungful of the stale air, thinking it the sweetest thing he'd ever tasted. He flexed his hand over and over, still feeling the steel grip, feeling the vague impression he'd been violated or invaded in some way. On the bright side, he sat and basked in the reflective joy and relief seen on Jules's face. *Maybe. Just maybe, there was something still there.* Then he looked behind at Marx, thinking how life and death experiences will get you contemplating things better left alone. He chastised himself, but glowed in the attention anyway.

"Anybody have a clue as to what just happened out there?" Buck was surprised his voice was steady.

Cal hovered near him ready to support him if needed, a look of grave concern on his now whisker shadowed face. "Marx described it to us, but I still can't believe it."

"Shit! 'You' can't. Try being on the wrong end of it. I've never felt so utterly helpless in my life!" He looked over at Marx, "So what now?"

"Well, I don't know about you, but I'm tired, hungry, and if I have to admit it, a bit shook. I think we sit and wait awhile. Regroup and get some rest before we try it again."

"Ok, I have to agree. I think I'm going to have nightmares later. It may be awhile till I'm ready to try again." Then he smiled, "Half hour or so at least."

"Well we had…" The sentence was half out of Cal's mouth when he crashed to the floor. All over the ship, anything not tied down followed him, including Marx and Li who collapsed into twisted heaps as they were suddenly assaulted with gravity at least two times earth normal.

Buck groaned and heard the same from the others. Not because it was excessive, because it was so sudden and utterly unexpected. He was pressed down into the cushions on his seat, and simultaneously, Cal's face struck his knee, impacting hard and flattening the Commander's nose in the process. Cal lay there in a heap, bleeding and disoriented.

"Everyone ok?" Jules asked while helping Marx back to his feet. Sergei and Li were fine, if you could count the near panic as fine.

"Cal's down! Someone give me a hand. I'm not sure how hurt he is." Buck stood as the others tried to crowd in. Angrily he pushed them back. Too much help.

"Sergei, get his arm! Jules, get me a med kit. He's bleeding like a stuck pig." Buck was never sure where that saying came from, but it certainly looked appropriate. The increased gravity seemed to pull the blood from Cal's injured nose in a torrent, and it spilled in a small river down his chest as they got him into his chair and settled. The all had medical training, but it turned out Li was a doctor. As the others watched, Li cleaned, set and packed Cal's nose, then pronounced a mild concussion. At the end of the treatment Cal was coherent and wondering what the hell hit him.

Buck snorted at him, "I'm sorry to tell you, Cal, but it was you who assaulted my knee with that huge ungainly snout of yours. Damn!" He rubbed his leg. "I'm sure it must have left a mark!" Cal didn't answer, he sat back and stared at a bulkhead trying to ignore his very large and tender nose. Perhaps on their next shore leave Buck thought, he'd be the handsome one. A slim chance, but one worth taking.

Li sat back after his ministrations, feeling utterly and totally out of place, and uncharacteristically pleased with himself for having been of assistance. He was amazed at the Americans and their ability to make fun of any situation. It seemed they took nothing serious, and he had a hard time reconciling this attitude with their incredible technology. Certainly discipline and structure was lacking, yet clearly, the creative force was intact. He followed the propaganda spewed by the Central Committee, even created a bit of it himself. Knew of the despotism of the west and the dangerous, almost cancerous impact it continued to have on his country. Yet he found he liked them. Even admired them. Yet now?

Li had a real problem. His orders were clear. Turn the alien, whatever it was, to the use of the Peoples Republic, or, should that prove impossible, sabotage the mission by any means available. The current situation left him cold. He was sure his handlers could not have anticipated, or even imagined the actual situation. Also, he knew that 'any means' meant the ultimate sacrifice. Yet suicide was not on his personal agenda, and his prime motivation was survival! *Hell!* He thought. A decidedly non-eastern concept! *I can always defect.*

The medic system in one of Vi-t-ry's hospitals stood undamaged and waiting patiently for patients or analytical quality data feeds on which to act. Had stood ready since its last patient expired, some time around the birth of Christ. That body still lay in a stasis chamber as fresh as the day it died, waiting for a ceremony that had never been ordered. Now information fed directly from Nannite robots in cargo bay R32-X5, consumed its complete processing attention.

The Nannites in question were the ultimate technological advancement of the Collective. The single discovery which had revolutionized every aspect of their society. A complex marriage of hard miniaturization, organic germ cells, and gene manipulation. In this case, the germ cells used were derived from egg and sperm cells. Each combined artificially, the resulting mechano-organisms grown to order, fully adaptable, changeable and programmable.

The information being provided by the Nannites detailed a new species of sentient life. From a brief contact with the ship, Nannites penetrated the dermis of the subject and entered the blood stream, quickly dispersing throughout the body. The med now had a complete physiological map, including circulatory, nervous and endocrine systems, placement and function of all organs both major and minor, and the neural makeup of the brain. In addition, the sampling included a direct chemical analysis of the bipedal unit and a complete genetic mapping. Nothing was hidden, including a pre-cancerous lesion in the esophagus and minor scaring of the interior surfaces of the lungs, and nothing the med couldn't repair, even though the species was until now, unknown. Enough information was provided to determine that the individual bore an 82.6753% evolutionary and 98.9226% chemical similarity with the sentient species known as the Kol-Pak, the primary members of the

Collective and designers and builders of this ship. Conclusions to be drawn? Similar evolutionary paths that diverged due to environment considerations. Environment basis equaled an exact carbon/oxygen match due to the planet/star relationship and chemical makeup of said planet, combining to create evolutionary combinations seen in only one, now two, planetary systems. Current specimen would have a 99% plus survivability rating, without assistance, on the Kol-Pak home planet.

Vi-t-ry queried the data and asked the med for one further piece of analysis. Could the species have been *seeded* by the Kol-Pak? The med took an additional .0005237 SMU's to review the data, then reported an unlikelihood that was beyond question, even for a class 3 med unit. Vi-t-ry stood satisfied. He had all he was going to get. The med added the data to the sentient species archive, noting physiological requirements for the new species, then waited for further information to process.

Vi-t-ry contemplated his new knowledge. How best to proceed. How to communicate? He decided on his first course of action, modify the current environment. With a mental thought it was done. The bay was now at normal Kol-Pak gravity. He initiated another command, then waited.

"Ok, so we are agreed. It's been more than two hours and nothing else has happened. It's time to go have another look-see."

There had been no real debate on the issue. Survival now depended on the whim of the aliens, a fact that escaped none of them. The aliens had attacked them. By mistake or by design mattered little. Disabled and helpless, the Enterprise had been captured, and now their hosts seemed to be playing cat and mouse. For what reason? Each individual had an opinion and that was about all, opinions liberally sprinkled with unanswerable questions and only one way to solve the problem. Obviously, the aliens were waiting on the astronauts for the next move. Marx didn't intend to keep them waiting any longer.

"Li, Sergei, Buck and myself. Li, you and I will go out first and establish a perimeter. When we're clear, Sergei and Buck. Cal, you and Jules be ready to cover a hasty retreat. Jules, I want you in the lock with full weapons." Marx was treating the situation as hostile in the extreme, creating as good an operations plan as could be with the limited information. This would be a scout mission with a full weapons load and classic pass through maneuvers. He and Li would establish a position forward and when secure, Sergei and Buck would pass-through to establish the next point. Forward would become rear, and one member of each team would cover the leap while the other watched the back. Simple in concept, yet hard to carry out. Especially in spacesuits with 2x gravity. Buck didn't want to contemplate the damage if the fecal matter hit the proverbial rotating wind producing device. Also, he was damn sure he didn't want Li anywhere out of his direct line of sight, and having the little man at his rear with a loaded weapon caused his skin to tighten in all sorts of uncomfortable places. But of course, god the commander had ordered it, so it shall be. At least the little SOB had the balls to swallow the order without whimpering, and the green look on his face made it almost worth it.

Cal was stung by being excluded, but his injury, while not debilitating, continued to bleed. Inside a buttoned up spacesuit, that was a very bad idea. He was relegated to monitoring the ship and com., which meant he sat on his ass and listened while everyone else had fun. He grabbed Buck's arm as his friend passed to the lock. "Watch your back pal."

Buck smiled with that nothing can harm me look. "We'll be fine, boss. Now don't go and get fatherly on me."

"Seriously, Buck. I won't be there! I don't trust anyone in this cluster except y.o.u! Not Marx, and especially not Li. There's something seriously wrong there."

"Too true Cal. Whatever he is, he ain't no astronaut!"

Cal grabbed him even harder, "Certainly no astronaut., and if he even so much as passes gas in your direction you have my personal permission to frag his ass! Hell. Make sure the aliens get him first. Might just poison em."

"I'll watch him, Cal, but it's going to be fine. I got a feeling. A gut."

Cal quirked his left eye. Buck did have these 'feelings' and they'd proven out over the years, *But still!* "Just watch out."

Buck didn't reply as the hatch opened and Marx and Li entered the lock. In his own mind he echoed, *but still!*

The plan of action was set, but the astronauts were faced with a new challenge before they even got started. The Enterprise, by her original mission concept, needed no ladder from the hatch to the ground. She was built for docking with other ships, primarily the now lost Unity. The crew was facing a twelve foot drop to the deck of the alien ship. Doable in any real world situation, but in spacesuits and with more than two time's earth gravity, it was a real problem. They improvised as best they could. A space-walk tether was attached to the inside of the lock prior to opening the outside hatch. Rappelling in a spacesuit was going to be an adventure, but they rigged a usable belay that allowed them to lower themselves to the deck without too much risk. They hoped they could achieve the maneuver without rupturing a suit in the process.

It was quite some time since the gravity was added and no aliens had come knocking. They felt they were being toyed with, and being sensor blind was becoming a real pain in the ass. So, it was now or never. Time to exit. Marx and Li entered the lock and secured.

"Ok," he ordered to Jules. "Depressurize now!"

"Depressurizing!" She echoed, and air began to hiss as it was pumped out of the lock and Marx watched the gage as it made its slow decent. The cabin was pressurized to the equivalent of sea level on earth, yet the gage had barely moved when it stopped and the depressurization cycle ceased.

"Jules?" Marx asked, the hallow ring of his voice echoing over the com.. "Is there a problem?"

"No Commander..." she hesitated as she double checked. "At least not that I can tell. The cycle shows we are now equalized with the outside air pressure."

More than one eyebrow shot up at that. Gravity and now air! Pressurized with what? With the safety measures not allowing the hatch to open unless it was within two percent of the pressure exerted upon it, even if the gages lied, the hatch should remain locked.

Marx could feel Li trembling behind him as he un-dogged the safeties and carefully pushed open the hatch, just enough to peer out. He blanched back as bright light assaulted his eyes. Marx didn't know what he'd expected. Maybe a bunch of LGM's pointing laser guns at him, yet what he saw was a major change in the bay from what they'd seen before. Instead of the low light and gray walls, the bay was bathed in bright light from no possible source he could see. As before, the walls themselves seemed to glow. So bright, he needed to pull down his helmets sun visor in order to see detail. After he did, he forced the hatch the rest of the way open, revealing to Li something incredible.

"Oh my," the man whispered.

"What!" Jules asked.

In his awe, Marx had forgotten the others, and Jules was reacting both to their silence, and Li's barely audible exclamation. Yet he wasn't sure he could describe what his eyes claimed lay in front of him. All he could do was mumble, "Hold on."

A chill went up Jules's spine. That certainly didn't sound like either her Commander or the man she had come to love and respect. Something had him shook! She was about to break the seal on their side of the lock, when he finally came back.

"We're ok!" His voice was firmer, now that he'd had a moment to gather his wits and recover from surprise. "It's safe, I think. It's just... Well... everything out here has changed. "

Buck broke in, "Changed?"

"Yes. Not even close to what we saw before!" Marx spent the next few minutes describing the vision and he was absolutely sure he didn't do it justice, so finally he shut up. He needed to clear the lock so they could come out and see it themselves. He and Li proceeded to do just that.

Vi-t-ry observed the actions of the humans as soon as his A.I. detected movement at the hatch of the vehicle, which was to say, instantly. Two of the beings appeared and after some time, moved out of the ship and to the deck of the bay. Curiously, they used a non-standard method of egress which seemed incredibly inefficient and dangerous. An assessment was fed to him from a local A.I.. The small ship was damaged. No energy signatures other than low level radio had escaped its hull since it had been captured. Vi-t-ry agreed with this analysis. After all, it was a small portion of his main array, his own brain, which made the report. After a millisecond or two, he decided to provide assistance if any other beings decided to join the two currently standing on the deck.

"All right!" Marx had come to grips with the new bay, and he and Li now stood on the deck looking up at the Enterprise. Li had taken some coaxing. Marx finally threatened to have Buck open the hatch and throw him out. Li was thoroughly convinced, especially when the dogs on the hatch began to move, and Buck's growl of joy echoed in his ear. He was positive the American Captain would like nothing better.

"Your turn!" Marx keyed to Buck and Sergei. They were ready and prepared, at least a little by Marx's description, for what lay beyond.

Hell! At least it isn't deadly! Buck's thought was zero comfort. Marx had described the environment in the bay as *filled with air*, but no one was taking that on face value, including Marx. All of them would remain buttoned-up, even Jules and Cal remaining on the ship. With no other choice, they would soon be letting the new atmosphere in. It was suit-air and the oxygen reserve in the Enterprise's tanks for them now. With a spin, he opened the hatch and stepped out, the other three astronauts crowding behind to get a glimpse of the sight beyond the hatch.

Attached to, and deriving energy from the nucleus of a ventricle cell in Buck's heart, the Nannite monitored blood flow and the minute changes in the chemicals surging through his body. Others reported directly from brain cells, lungs, pituitary system, and every other organ in the young captain's body, each diligently reporting the changes. The med followed the adrenalin flow when gravity was added to the environment, and analyzed the surge in brain activity as different situations assaulted the being. Stress was measured. Verbalizations were analyzed, and the basics of communication were organized. From its knowledge of the other known sapiens, the med could begin to cross interpret words, or at least the intent of the multi-word vocalizations. A Kol-Pak faced with a similar situation may have uttered, "Gakzal-ith!" where the new being had uttered a pattern which his acoustics picked up as, "Holy Shit!" Each body reaction and its accompanied vocalization were similarly cross matched. Imperfect and imprecise, but medicine and its practice was similarly imperfect. It was, however, a start.

Buck popped the hatch and was assailed with the vision displayed. Marx prepared them, but his description left much to be desired. Awe overcame him, and his heart skipped and raced as he froze in place. "Holy Shit!" His favorite current invective fell well short of intended impact.

The rounded bulkhead and the deck of the bay were gone! In their place was a brightly lit panorama. Blue sky framed a huge yet distant mountain. A brown savanna rolled away in front, the grass waving in a gentle breeze and a myriad of different animals standing or walking in the foreground. A vulture lazily circled, passing through the icon at the top.

Cal gasped behind him, "That's Kilimanjaro!" Marx had mentioned nothing about this! The display looked real enough to step out into. Complete HD, right down to the National Geographic icon the buzzard seemed so intent on circling.

"Marx! What…." Buck's protest to the commander died stillborn on his tongue because suddenly, and without sound or warning, the view changed. Where the gazelle once stood and the vulture flew, symbols now danced. Unknown to the humans, the trillions upon trillions of Nannites which faced the plascrete walls, responded to Vi-t-ry's commands, pulsing in millions of colors and rapidly changing positions. Each acting individually yet in concert to form the largest and most intricate display screen the humans had ever seen. The Kol-Pak language displayed across the bay asking questions none of them could answer. Shapes vaguely cuneiform in nature writhed on the surface, first seeming etched into the skin of the bay then rising to form an alien brail. One symbol imprinted upon Buck's eye felt almost familiar. A symbol he knew he'd never seen before, almost impossible in shape, yet tantalizing to him none the less. He felt that same feeling. The feeling he'd had after his experience with the material that grabbed him on the landing gear. A flush throughout his body. Like he'd been invaded. An involuntary quiver shook his spine, then quickly passed as the view changed again.

The new visual defied words. Buck could see why Marx had such a hard time describing it. Now an alien landscape burned into the distance. Mountains far loftier than Kilimanjaro and actively volcanic, spewed red miasma into a pale yellow sky. Billowing ash competed with massive thunderheads that spiked the mountain faces with bolts of lightening, both cloud types partially obscuring an angry ringed moon just settling on the heights. Tree and plant life framed the screen, and fantastic animals abounded in such detail they seemed ready to leap into the hatch. It was obvious to Buck, the earth display and this one was meant to be similar. One perhaps mirroring the other. Why? What was the message?

A scream from Li and the report of a gunshot shattered his thoughts. Buck was jolted out of his reverie and he rushed to the open hatch and looked down as a creature of certain reptilian nature ran under the man's feet. Literally under. The screen wrapped the entire bay in a true 360 degree experience. The animal that so terrified Li, though just an image, slithered in such a real 3D way, Buck was pretty certain he'd have shot it himself. The deck where the bullet struck looked like a mud flat with a rock thrown in, the displaced material slowly oozing back, until the screen was again whole. So shocking was the moment that no one even chastised Li, though Marx removed the weapon from his trembling hand. Li didn't seem to notice, he just watched as the reptile wandered off disappearing into a rock outcropping near the port wing of the shuttle.

As the view played, the humans whispered over the com., not one of them desiring to break the spell of this incredible moment. Each had his own thoughts and for Buck it was an odd sense of belonging. No threat and no fear, just simple and very complex awe! Though eventually, even this faded as the patterns and the earth and alien landscapes began to repeat themselves. What was overpowering a moment before was now accepted. Adaptive resilience. Human nature and self-survival at its finest.

"Ok!" Sergei was the first to break the moment. "So they want to talk to us. Now what?" Even the most pessimistic among them couldn't deny that the aliens were attempting communication.

Jules still had the tinge of wonder edging her voice. "Any idea what they want? And more important. Where are they?"

That question had Li trying to look over his shoulder and watch for the ugly lizard all at the same time. What he really wanted was to place his posterior up against something firm and stable, but since all the walls moved, he was frantic.

Marx grabbed him by the shoulder and he jumped. "Calm down, Li! You're doing none of us any good if you piss yourself every time we run into something new up here!"

"I... I... mmmust... Get back! Please. I c...ccan't stay here!"

"No way, Li!" His tone brooked no argument. "I'll put you between us, but I need you out here." In reality, Marx needed the little shit about as much as he needed an abscessed tooth, but he was damned if he'd leave him in the shuttle. Besides, they may need some cannon fodder.

"Close your eyes and calm down. We'll get everyone else down here before we do anything."

Jules questions still hung in the air despite the tableau below and Buck had a theory he wanted voiced, "I don't know where 'they' are, but I think Sergei's right. They want to talk. The two videos show a similarity between us. At least what they think is similar."

"I'll buy that!" Cal said. "But what were the symbols? I think they were somehow trying to tie the two images together, but I don't know how we can ever translate it."

"Perhaps if we wait here, they will try something different." Sergei was trying the logical approach and Li jumped on it.

"Y... Yes! That's what we must do."

Jules rode over him not even listening, "Maybe they're scared of us. Hell, maybe they're so hideous they don't want to frighten us!"

Marx had heard enough. They could ask questions till all their oxygen ran out. He wasn't going to wait. Consequences or not, they were going exploring. "I'm not waiting on them, whoever or whatever they might be. Buck, you and Sergei come on down and let's get to it. We can debate when we have more to go on." He was staring up at them and could barely see faces through the reflections on their helmet visors, so if he saw the looks they gave him, he ignored it.

Buck grabbed the harness and began the intricate process of tying off. Sergei was stabilizing the strap and Buck was just about to swing over, trying to judge how to manage his additional 180 pounds of weight, when a new yell of startlement erupted from Li and Marx at the same time. Buck turned, expecting LGMs to be crawling all over them. Instead he froze in shock.

The bay was currently in the National Geographic stage and as he watched, the deck right below the hatch began to warp. Li and Marx stumbled back, seeming to push past a group of impala, Marx with his rifle aimed, unsure of the extent of the threat. Fascinated, the watched as the savanna distorted and pushed up, quickly rising to the exact height of the hatch. Once there, it morphed again, this time into a set of stairs extending to the floor.

Just as suddenly, the movement ceased and the staircase became solid, thought the movie continued across the surface making it seem to shiver and flow. Buck's voice held to quiver, "Oh hell! At least they're trying to be helpful!"

Vi-t-ry watched every play as it happened. He quickly analyzed the primitive combustion/projectile weapon which had been used. This had caught him off guard, but his neurons successfully convinced him that the weapon presented only a minor threat. A Kol-Pak would have acted in similar fashion to the same stimuli and all space faring members of the Collective, especially the Kol-Pak, were never without personal weapons. Such was a matter of honor and status, rank being determined or conveyed by weapon style, much like a badge or uniform. What puzzled Vi-t-ry was why it was used. His answer came from the Nannites in the being whom he had touched. He, for it clearly was masculine, showed a vast array of emotions, not the least of which was fear. A lesser fear when Vi-t-ry deployed the ramp, but fear all the same. Vi-t-ry ordered the med to reprogram the Nannites. In a moment it was done. The Nannites that were now as much a part of the being as his own blood vessels, began a new process. One of chemical control, reducing production of certain combinations to well below normal levels and enhancing others. Now, based on given stimuli, fear and shock reaction would be reduced, while calm and analytical emotions would be prioritized.

The med cautioned the central unit, Vi-t-ry. Its programming would not allow mind control. At least not without the specific override password and brain wave verification of the ships Captain or Adjutant, and this process was very close to that moral line. Yet Vi-t-ry was satisfied for now. The Nannites continued collecting the vocal and emotional data and the correlations were beginning to bear fruit.

Slowly, Buck unhooked himself from the harness and stepped back. Having one bad experience with the shape shifting material under his belt, he was naturally a bit wary of testing it further. Though his subconscious belayed any danger, still he was cautious.

"So what now?" he asked no one in particular.

"Well," Cal said. "They certainly seem to like you. Almost like a red carpet." Nothing further happened, but Buck and they still waited. If it could do that, just what else was it capable of?

"It looks solid from here!" Marx, having gathered his wits, slowly approached the bottom of the new ramp. Tentatively he reached out, ready to pull his hand back if there was even a flicker of movement. Nothing. Cautiously he put a boot on it, then carefully stepped up. The grunt was audible as he pulled his extra weight onto the first step. He was standing there looking up at the hatch, when suddenly, a new set of symbols flashed across the screen. Marx jumped off, collapsing on the floor as one by one the symbols began to pulse then wink-out. This continued through too many to count until there was only one left, leaving them with the uncomfortable conclusion that is was a countdown.

The med finally had gathered enough data to examine to draw some conclusions. Its first diagnosis determined that the current situation and stresses did not fully explain the current physiological storm happening within the humanoid. Another factor must be causing the abnormally high heartbeat and elevated musculature temperature, most pronounced in the lower extremities. Conclusion. Current gravity was substantially higher than was normal for this being. It flashed its findings to the central core.

Vi-t-ry flashed his guests a warning then reduced the gravity by a factor of one. After a brief rise, the heartbeat settled in to a more normal pattern and the body approached homeostasis. Satisfied, the med continued to monitor.

The astronauts had no idea what to expect with the countdown. To what? Numerous frightening possibilities raced through their minds, but none came close to guessing it would be a reduction in gravity. It was a sudden shock when the bay went weightless for an instant. The weight of their bodies lifted to nothing, then gravity was once again back and close to what felt like normal. Buck felt light as a feather, his arms wanting to drift up on their own. Odd feeling, but a vast relief and welcome change.

"Ok!" Jules said. "Obviously the LGMs are trying to make this easy on us."

"Ya think!" Cal was only being half sarcastic. He was getting more and more shook, not less. The same could be said for the rest of them. "I suppose next you're going to tell me the air they happen to be providing isn't poison!"

"Only one way to find out!" Buck knew he was about to take a big and possibly fatal mistake, but he had a feeling. He reached for the clasps on his helmet and pulled.

"No Buck! I didn't mean…" Cal was too late in his lunge, pushing past Sergei. Buck had the helmet up, and whatever might be in the atmosphere didn't matter after that. It was too late to stop him. It was a surreal moment for the team. Cal hit him in the arm and the helmet dropped to the deck then rolled with echoless plastic thuds down the alien stairs, stopping at Marx's boot. No one noticed. They stared at Buck's bare head thinking him dead on his feet.

Instead, a wide grin spread across his beard shadowed face. His mic. was still on, but his voice sounded different, not being enclosed in the brain bucket. "Hey! It smells like mint."

Cal grabbed the captain and spun him around in rage. "You stupid, ignorant, hillbilly son of a bitch! If you don't die I'm going to personally shoot your ass. I don't give a flying f…!"

He never finished. Buck was still grinning. "Cool off boss. I'm fine. I knew it would be ok. I'm fine."

Marx was at him next, more than pissed at the young man's recklessness. "How in the hell can you possible know you're fine! If I had a brig I'd throw you in it Captain. And just what do you mean by, 'I knew it would be ok!'"

"I don't know." Buck shrugged. He looked chagrined and sheepish, not really knowing why he did it either. "Look, I know it was foolish, but I had a feeling. You know. Inside. I could just feel it. Anyway, it's done. Put me under house arrest if you want." He laughed at that. "But I'm the guinea pig now. You guys just stay buttoned up and watch. But…well! The aliens have gone out of their way for us. They rescued the Enterprise…"

"Screw that! They attacked us, then captured the ship!"

"We don't know that, Cal! Hell, they've been trying to communicate. If they wanted us for dissection we'd be done already. I say everything they've done is to make us more comfortable."

"I am inclined to agree with the captain." Sergei was a lone voice of reason, at least as Buck saw it. "Though I agree that he has been unnecessarily reckless," Well, maybe. "I say we trust, but with caution." With that the Russian popped his own helmet.

Marx sighed, "All right. I accept part of the argument at least. I do believe they're trying to make us comfortable and trying to communicate. I just don't know why. So we keep our weapons, and," his eyes pierced Buck from down in the bay, "Our helmets handy. Now, if you don't mind," sarcasm bled from him. "Kindly step down here so we can get on with exploring this wreck!"

The rest weren't as trusting as Buck and Sergei. Marx was more than willing to wait and watch, just to see if one or the other would suddenly succumb to some alien virus. It wasn't very hard for him to imagine a rapidly purpling face distorted in pain, hands clawing at a throat. The convulsions and choking complete it would not even allow the victim to scream in his dying. But that was his private fear. He had to admit though, wandering around in gravity in a fully buttoned-up space suit was becoming a real pain. Still! Li certainly wasn't coming out. Marx almost *popped* his suit just to spite the little bastard.

In moments, Buck and Sergei were down the ramp and standing next to him. A maneuver that had taken he and Li almost twenty minutes, and a serious amount of energy. Marx thighs were bruised and felt like the strap imprints would be with him the rest of his life. A strap they left in place just in case their hosts decided to be less accommodating in the future. At least now the visuals were gone, leaving them the dull grey deck and bulkheads to stare at. Less disorienting, but no less confusing, for nowhere could they see a lock, door, hatch, nor any other method of egress. Only the unending sameness of grey.

"Ok, Rodgers, what next?"

Buck looked at him in confusion, "What do you mean, Marx?"

"Well my dear, Captain, we brought you along for a reason. Now it seems, the aliens have taken a liking to you, and you," he motioned at Buck's bare head. "Certainly seem to trust them. So, what next?"

Just like that? Buck was now the expert on all things alien! Instead of trepidation or anger. Instead of fear or anxiety, he suddenly felt calm. Had he the time to assess his emotional state, he might have found that his strong feelings were being suppressed. Instead, his professionalism and thick-headed pride kicked in. Calmly, he turned from the group and began to inspect the bay, calling instructions over the com, "Check every inch. Look for anything out of the ordinary."

Jules was still up in the Enterprise, but over the radio he heard her as clear as if she were standing next to him. "What the hell does he mean by out of the ordinary? We're on an alien tub for god's sake. Everything is out of the friggin ordinary." Even Li laughed, but the levity only lasted as long as it took to make their inspection, because as far as the humans could see, there was no way out.

Vi-t-ry continued the process of learning. His correlations were progressing to a point where he knew he would be able to communicate; eventually. His assessment of danger to the ship, which of course meant 'self', was complete. These beings held no weapon capable of harming him. They should not be terminated or expelled at this time. Still more data was needed.

Buck stood in front of the Enterprise, staring and thinking, feeling a compelling need to solve this puzzle. He was boring a hole in the bulkhead with his eyes, willing something to happen, when a gasp on the com broke his concentration. The symbols were back. At least he thought they were the same ones, only this time they originated at the ceiling directly above the shuttle. As he watched, they described a line across and down the wall to the point exactly where he'd been staring. Again the symbols pulsed, and again disappeared, one by one, starting with the first in the ceiling above until there was only one. This last symbol pulsed on the wall dead level in front of him, a shape somewhat reminiscent of a scrolling snake turning itself inside and out in an eerily writhing motion, and it pulsed far longer than the rest. Flashing, almost as in warning. Then suddenly, the pulsing ceased and the curved lines making up the symbol exploded into a thousand small straight lines. It looked like an air burst which spread outward in an arc, then quickly reassembling into the outline of a hatch. One perfectly sized for the humans. They watched, completely dumbfounded, as a small dark dot appeared in the center. It quickly expanded to fill the entire area defined by the lines. The darkness opaqued and they could see a hall beyond, then the space changed once again, the material clearing completely, creating an opening; a passage to whatever lay beyond. Buck would never remember who said it, but he heard it clearly. A whispered, "Said the spider to the fly."

Chapter 19

On the surface of the ship, Vi-t-ry's passive sensors continued to record the entire electromagnetic spectrum. Waves upon waves of it washed against his skin like the unending rollers upon the seashore. The visible and the infrared, the ultraviolet and microwave. He observed and gloried in a great solar flare which rose from the alien sun to lash his skin, making him almost drunk with power. He recorded the gentle play of the gravity wells of the systems nine planets as they nudged each other in their endless fall around the star. He grabbed the myriad signals from the planet below as they bled into space around their intended targets, the satellites which orbited in their hundreds. Communications and entertainment, visual and audio, combined and separate. Each one catalogued and stored. Each compared to the voice patterns of the visitors in his bay. Sifted and analyzed and rejected to be archived for later, or accepted to broaden his active knowledge base. Each data bit ready for when a full translation could be made. He was now sure this planet held more diversity than any other in his data banks. More diversity in the sentient species in general, and specifically in variations of language construction. Another fact he was sure of, there was no trace of Collective Common, or High Kol-Pak to be found.

He'd recorded no fewer than thirty-seven different constructions, some similar enough to be sister languages, and some so radically different, Vi-t-ry tasked one full computer cluster to analyze the possible existence of extraterrestrial influences.

As part of the process, he attempted to separate the images and reports. What was entertainment and what was real? More difficult than his experience showed that it should be. One item his analysis left no doubt of. The inhabitants of this planet seemed intent on destroying themselves. Even as he observed, the bright energy pulse of a multi-megaton weapon blossomed on a small peninsula that extended south toward the equator from the largest landmass below.

"Six minutes, Mr. President!" His press secretary was fretting like a new mother, and rightly so. Jon Talbot was going to attempt the impossible. He was shortly going to address the world and make a plea for sanity in this time of crisis. He'd hoped to be able to show the world that the alien ship was no threat. That a multi-national team had intercepted it and… and… and what? Now the Enterprise was lost. Presumably captured, possibly destroyed. Even so, something must be done publicly. The President would try to calm the masses, and just maybe some of the world would listen.

"Five minutes, Mr. President!" Talbot gave the man a look he'd patented, one guaranteed to intimidate his political opponents and make them wilt. Like water off a duck's back, the man didn't seem to notice.

Sean watched his friend prepare, knowing he'd done all he could to help. Enterprise was indeed gone, and her sister ship would not, could not, be ready for at least three months. The unfamiliar feeling of failure pervaded the SPB, and it was Sean's job to pick them up, especially the President, but this was the first time in his life when events seemed bigger than he could control. He steeled himself, what was to come would come. Now Jon needed him to be a rock. An alarm on Andy's laptop shook him from his thoughts. Sean watched the young man carefully. Knew his every emotion. Andy would certainly suck at poker. Sean almost smiled. Then he saw the blood drain from Andy's face. A chill of dread ran down his spine as his aid muttered, "Oh shit."

Andy didn't look at his boss. Instead, he directly addressed the President as the phones in the office began to ring and the Colonel with the 'ball' containing the nuclear codes, followed by the secret service detail burst into the room. "Mr. President, there has been a nuclear event! A bomb just detonated in the port at Kosong, North Korea!"

Cautiously, Buck edged forward. His helmet was back on and the opening loomed before him. Beyond the hole lay a corridor of the same material as the bay, stretching off in either direction, but of it he could see little. He was about to reach out to the door frame when Marx grabbed his arm.

"Wait!"

Buck jumped back a full two feet. "Son of a bitch, Marx! Warn a guy or something before you just go and grab."

Marx ignored him as he stepped in front, "You ever heard of a booby-trap, Captain?" He thrust his rifle through the opening and quickly pulled it back. When nothing happened he banged the barrel against the frame, eliciting a dull thud instead of a metal to metal clack. Nothing. Marx stepped back, and with a flourish of his hand waved Buck forward.

Bolder, Buck stepped through the opening into the corridor beyond. He quickly crouched and pointed his weapon left then right. Nothing. The right hand extended away in a gentle curve, passing beyond his sight into darkness. The left described a similar arc, yet remained lit. An obvious invitation. They were expected to follow the light. Marx jumped past him into the corridor, and fetched up against the far wall, followed quickly by Sergei and then Li, who poked a cautious eye around the corner before gently stepping through. As they paused, the right corridor dimmed even further, leaving the left with the only light.

"Radio check!" Marx followed the agreed SOP. They would go only as far as the radio would reach on this first foray.

"10 X 10 Commander." Jules voice was as strong as if they were still in the Enterprise. Everyone held up a thumb. So far so good, and no LGM's.

"So, Buck! Do we take the invitation? Or brave the dark?"

"I say the invitation, Commander. But first," Buck reached up and pulled off his helmet for no more reason than to annoy his leader. "The air's fine by the way."

Instead of replying, Marx retrieved a can of marking paint from one of his suit pouches and sprayed a large red X opposite their hatch, then an arrow pointing the direction they intended to go. Having done so, he gestured them forward, intending to leapfrog any obstacle or door, but just as they began to move, Li pointed at the marks. "Look!"

As they watched the red slowly disappeared.

Marx shook his head, "I should have guessed!"

"Guessed what, Commander?"

"That any really advanced society was going to have self cleaning walls! Plan two." Each headset was configured with a strength signal which could be used as a homing device. The signal being directed to the base station on the Enterprise herself. At least that part was working. Time would tell how well, given they had no way of determining how the materials in this great mother of a ship would affect radio waves. They could also count steps or leave crumbs, but Buck was fresh out of bread. Instead, he stepped off down the corridor.

He hadn't gone twelve feet when Marx's red arrow reappeared, exactly as created and following Buck as he walked. Astounded, he stopped. The arrow stopped with him. He turned and the arrow flipped and followed, creating a mirror image that moved with him back to the hatch. When he arrived, the arrow flashed out and the big red X reappeared, effectively marking the starting point. A testament to their growing expectation of the unusual, none of them over reacted to this new twist.

Instead, Buck looked at Sergei, "You try."

Sergei stepped off and walked about the same distance as Buck had a moment before. No red arrow. Marx tried next and then Li with the same result. Buck shrugged, then moved off himself. Immediately the X disappeared and the arrow followed, somehow keyed to him alone. Buck suspected it had something to do with touching the lock in what seemed an eternity ago. The looks he was getting from the others were fairly uncomfortable, so naturally he pushed their buttons, "Well... At least 'I' won't get lost!"

"All right everyone. Make sure you keep Captain Rodgers in sight at all times!" Marx was going to let professionalism guide him instead of rising to the bait, thereby demeaning his authority. Though he almost lost it though when Li grabbed on to the Captain's suit. Evidently he was going to make sure he never got lost by clinging to Buck like dryer lint! Marx spent a few moments relaying the news of their new mascot to Jules and Cal, then, with nothing left to do, they went.

The corridor seemed endless and the curve so gentle it was at least two hundred yards till they lost sight of the hatch, clearly delineated behind them by the dark corridor beyond. In all that travel, there had been no openings, no signs, and no decoration. Just the seemingly endless gray hall. Radio contact was still good and the red arrow stuck like glue. They traveled fifteen more minutes before the first deviation in the corridor presented itself. Ahead, Buck could see a side passageway intersect the one they were traveling. He held up a fist, stopping them in their tracks. All except Li, who bounced off Buck before he halted.

"Back off, Li!" Buck hissed. "You're going to get us both killed if anything happens!"

"I am sorry, Captain." He didn't sound it.

Buck humphed then ignored the man. "There's an intersection up ahead. You want a scout?"

Marx mused for only a moment, "Sergei! You move forward. Buck, follow at twenty paces. I'll cover."

So! Buck thought. *It comes down to this! Who's expendable and who's not. And since the arrow likes me, I'm safe.* Though without complaint, Sergei moved forward, having first removed his helmet to gain the most vision. He moved with the grace of a trained fighter, weapon at point and slightly crouched, ready to run, dodge or drop. Buck followed, shadowed by his arrow and humming a tune from the animated movie, *The Point*. He'd seen it when he was young and it was an obscure animated piece about a young boy born with a round head in a society of pointy headed people. His pointy muzzled dog was named arrow. Muttering just under his breath, *Me and my arrow. Wherever we go. Everyone knows! It's me and my arrow.*

Sergei approached the connecting corridor then crouched, thrusting his Commando around the corner then following it with one eye. After a moment he hand signaled, 'all clear.' Buck moved up, then Marx and Li quickly joined them. The new passage was straight and pointed to what they thought should be the exterior of the ship. It was dark beyond a few yards.

"Well, Captain? Straight or up this way?"

"Commander, I say we look down this one a bit. At least it's something new."

Marx nodded in agreement. Buck moved past Sergei, but hadn't gone a step further when Li gave out one of his now infamous gasps, "Look! The arrow!"

Sure enough. The arrow remained on the wall in the main corridor. As Buck moved further away it faded. He stepped back and it reappeared even brighter. He stepped away again and this time it faded but pulsed faster as it did so, almost in warning.

"Evidently," Buck said. "They don't want us going that way! Your call, Commander."

Marx thought a moment. He really hated to be led by anyone, yet why upset the applecart just now. This wasn't the time to press their independence. That would come later. "Back to the original course, Captain. We'll dance their dance for a while more."

Buck nodded and moved off. The now happy arrow following along, content that its charge was doing exactly what Vi-t-ry wanted.

Li held back as the others started forward to resume their expedition. His orders and his mission still nagged at the back of his mind. Was this his opportunity? Certainly there would be reasons the aliens didn't want them down that passage. Reasons that intrigued him. Li was torn. He wasn't really a coward! At least he'd told himself as much throughout the trip. Could he really break-away? Max had taken his weapon. That fact, combined with his extreme anger at the 'oh so arrogant' Marx, and his personal embarrassment at being treated as a child, drove him to the decision. His shame was a report he could never allow to be heard outside this ship! These factors drove him, and they drove him forward. Not with the others. No, Li took off down the unexplored hall.

They'd been traveling no more than five or six minutes when up ahead new choices beckoned. Here they faced a full intersection, not just a side corridor as before. They paused and it was then they missed Li.

"Damn!" Marx's mutter turned the others around. What was obvious to them was a mystery to Jules and Cal, who could hear, but had to use their imagination to visualize what the others described. This was very much the wrong atmosphere for imagination.

Marx clarified his mutter, "Jules! Our little communist is missing."

"Shit! I mean shit, Sir! He's not come back here. Cal's been watching the door since you left. You think the aliens got him?"

Li, who still had his com on, smiled. No, the aliens hadn't gotten him, and if he found nothing he would simply claim being lost.

"One can only hope! Unfortunately, I think he's on his own agenda. Li! Can you hear me?" Silence. "Li!" Nothing. "All right! I'm not comfortable with him or whatever might have him, at our backs." Buck could only agree. "Cal! We're going to backtrack. If he comes your way, arrest him or shoot him! I don't much care which." He pointed at Buck, then a hand signal to retrace their steps. Another signal for silence. Buck turned and moved off. His arrow, hesitating just a moment as if unsure what to do, turned and followed.

Li crept forward as silently as possible. Up ahead came a noise which he couldn't identify, yet it grew then faded on a regular interval. The darkness didn't help. He of course, had kept his helmet on, not trusting in the charity of their hidden hosts. The feeble lights mounted above his visor cast small illumination, leaving him as jumpy as he'd ever been. Every shadow held a monster, every flicker a threat. Almost he'd turned around. Almost! His moving forward, even against his mounting fear, was as much to prove his manhood to himself as for any other purpose. Again the sound built. Had his helmet been off, Li would have felt a stir in the air, first blowing toward him, and then sucking back as if the breath of a great beast stirred the atmosphere. Instead, almost blind, he crept forward.

Ahead, gently illuminated, came the end of the passage. Li could see some ancient damage had pierced the skin of the ship, pushing the hatch before him off its hinges and twisting the five inch thick metal like a crushed tin can. Beyond, in the darkness came the growing vibration and noise.

None of his companions would have believed Li brave enough to go toward that gaping black maw, yet he did. Slowly he crept forward. Deep blackness, impenetrable by his small light, lay beyond. Fear kept his helmet on. Had it been off, Li would have had warning. Instead, even as the sound grew louder than he'd heard before, he stepped through the lock into a small room.

Within was a hole in the bulkhead and he ventured a look into the space beyond. Even through his suit he could feel the great rush of air hit his helmet as it was forced down the tube. In sudden and overpowering fear, he twisted his neck, his light spilling down the center of a tunnel illuminating a hideous beast that came hurtling toward him. Li had time for one long scream. A scream that echoed inside his helmet and through the com.

Buck froze at the shocking cry, a wail of utter despair that was abruptly cut off. "Li!" he yelled the name down the corridor and over the com. "Li! What is it? Li, are you ok?" Only silence. "Li! Answer me!"

"Give it up, Captain." Marx was shaken by the electronic terror which still rang throughout in his ear. There was no doubt in his mind that something bad just happened to Li, and whatever it was, and whatever their differences, Li was still human. With a heavy heart he said, "Let's go find him."

Vi-t-ry observed curiously as his visitors followed the path he'd set them. Satisfying himself with their verbal interaction, and the ongoing proofs of his theories and assumptions. However, when one left the group and followed the access tube, even he was caught off guard. Many places within him were damaged, as was this one. Had there been time, or reason, his robots and Nannites could have repaired the damage that had been caused by the deep penetration of a Hyper Velocity Missile. The result of this oversight was electronically distressing to him. For some reason, the being had extended part of its body into the freight transfer tube just as a tram was passing by. It was evident that the portions of the being which were extended into the tube were critical to its function, for when they were removed the rest of the body ceased to function.

Instantly, he'd dispatched a med-bot and his ever present Nannites to conduct a repair. Part of the body, the part left in the hatch, now lay in a medical facility undergoing minute study, including the possibilities of cloning; the rest, spread over a lengthy area of transport tube and the front of the tram, was more slowly recovered.

Vi-t-ry intended to make sure no more damage occurred upon the persons of his guests. Accordingly, a blast door was lowered into place, efficiently sealing the access tube. Satisfied, Vi-t-ry continued with other priorities.

"So... What now?" Buck had walked them all the way back to the Enterprise and the corridor they'd seen earlier was not to be found. They had stopped and backtracked several times, studying the floors, walls and ceilings, searching for any seam or other evidence of an opening. Nothing! It was as if the side access never existed. It had disappeared along with the unfortunate Li. Of course, he could have made it back and be lost somewhere down the dark corridor beyond the bay, but Cal insisted nothing had moved out there since they left.

Marx finally got frustrated and removed his helmet. Or perhaps he just wanted to show their hosts he wasn't afraid. "One thing for sure," he said. "We can't help Li now! And we can't get off this ship or complete the mission without dealing with the aliens. So! For better or worse, we have to play their game."

Sergei nodded, a wisp of short cropped black hair spilling from around his silkie and a two day growth of shadow framing his jaw. "I agree, Commander. Yet with far more caution."

If Marx thought the Russian was criticizing him for Li, he hid it well. "All right. Losing Li is not something we're going to repeat. Cal, you feel up to taking a walk with us?" Buck thought the man was fully recovered. He'd seen him get his bell rung in a number of bar fights and still make flight opps the next morning.

"I'm fine, Marx. No worries here, but surely you don't intend to leave Mad Dog here alone."

"He doesn't have to leave me, Commander! I volunteer." If she was frightened about being left it didn't show. The fierce look on her face would give anyone, or thing, cause to pause. Buck would have protested himself, still feeling unreasonably protective of his former lover, but his new prescience told him she would be fine. He considered that for a moment, but remained silent.

"I didn't need you to volunteer Jules, but thanks, because I didn't want to order it. One way or another, Enterprise is the only base we have and we can't leave it un-secured." She nodded glad there was to be no issue. Marx grabbed the woman in a fierce hug, giving her the first obvious affection he'd shown in front of the others. He held her out at arms length, "Lock yourself in and if anything happens, shoot first."

Buck fought down the surge of jealousy, knowing now and forever he and she were no more. Comforting almost. One less emotion to deal with.

"We'll get back here as quick as we can!" Marx's voice was thick.

"Don't worry," she challenged him. "The Enterprise will be here when you get back." Was it her or the ship he was most worried about? Marx didn't react, or perhaps he counted the ship and the girl as one in the same and missed the requested affirmation completely.

"Keep radio contact at all times!" he said, and with a final squeeze of her arm, "Keep the lights on. We won't be late."

A half hour later found them at the same intersection they'd been about to explore when Li's scream interrupted the calm. At least they thought it was the same. With a place as strange as this it was hard to tell, but his arrow seemed content that it indeed was. Cautiously Buck approached the T, wondering, left? Right? Straight? With hand signals Marx moved him forward and down. Buck knelt, then pushed a single eye around the corner, not really seeing, simply exposing himself like a mouse peeking out of its hole. When nothing bad happened, he peered again. To the right, and what he felt was toward the interior if the ship, extended a corridor which continued only about twenty yards before terminating wall, blank except for a scrolling symbol in its center. Buck couldn't be completely sure, but the symbol looked the same as the one they saw in the bay. The one that burst and became a hatch. He looked left. Down that corridor and saw a mirror image except for the symbol. There was one and it was distinctly different, almost sinister looking. Two dead-ends? Again, the right passage *felt* right, where the left... He looked a second time and had to smile. His ever present arrow was now firmly attached to the right dead-end, happily pointing at the familiar symbol.

Buck pulled back, "It wants us to go that way!" He indicated with a stab of his Commando.

The others nodded, simply accepting that he knew what he was talking about. He sighed heavily and made up his mind to take command, though he was the junior officer. He waved Cal over. "Jump across to the other side, I'll cover you."

With hand signals he pointed Sergei left, Cal across, and Marx right, wanting a gun in every direction. Slowly he gathered his courage and moved around the corner. He hunched over and quickly covered the twenty yards, then collapsed against the wall. Nothing happened for a moment and Buck was beginning to think nothing would. Then, almost quicker than the eye could follow, the arrow disappeared and the symbol burst forming a hatch which darkened then cleared to reveal a sight which left him gasping in awe.

Vi-t-ry's med and Nannites did a thorough job collecting every part of the damaged individual, including the copious fluids and bio-matter which was smeared over a great distance. Individually cell by cell, the body was reconstructed, and while life was no longer possible, study certainly was.

Another success was reported as well. The communications relay, which had overloaded and been damaged when he tried to communicate with the small ship, was now repaired. Communication with the planet was once again possible. All Vi-t-ry needed now, was to learn how.

Slowly, Buck stood and stared into the vestibule beyond. A small room built like a bubble and just as clear as glass yet with no distortion he could detect. A wonder that opened upon a greater wonder, a panorama which he could never have imagined. Blackness deeper than the darkest night, framed by lines of light curving out in arcs clearly defining the inner space of the great ship, even to the far side which he knew to be many miles away. The lines of light matched the surface pattern of the ship, a calm mirror of the image he'd seen when the blue lightening raged, the pattern broken only by the great rend in the ship's skin which spilled an image of 'real' space into the interior. The rend itself miles wide, caused by battle damage so long ago. Individual clusters of illumination surrounded dark holes which he imagined tunneled to the surface, and ultimately the towers which extended into space. As he watched, many of those lights moved about, looking much like glowing white blood cells traversing transparent veins. But as incredible as this was, it was the center that held him in thrall.

His mind screamed, *black hole!* Physics told him that was impossible. Yet something existed there in the center. A sphere of sorts, but one he could never quite see except in the periphery of his eye. A dead spot in his vision, eerily outlined by flashes or eruptions of deep blue fire which hurt the eye as it tried to focus. One other detail struck him in the moments he stood there awed. Small structures held orbit in the six cardinal points. Structures which looked like floating spheroid cities joined one to the other and to the skin of the ship by fiber-like crystal tubes. An incredible sight which threatened to crush the mind with its alien and fearsome beauty. From a distance he heard other gasps of astonishment. From a distance even in the radio in his ear. His mind was hardly registering his human side. He ignored their questions. Buck only had eyes for what lay beyond.

With an involuntary step, one he never knew he took, he entered the chamber, passing the threshold of the pod and leaving his friends behind. Gasps from the others and the shout from Cal were carried on the alien air, only to be cut off by the closing of the hatch. The echoes of those cries sounding in his right ear which cradled his electronic and last connection with his friends. He didn't answer their cries. Couldn't really he was so overwhelmed, so mesmerized. In fact, he hardly noticed as a moment later the pod began to move.

The assimilation of data was complete. Imperfect, but complete. The entire organic structure of the deceased human now resided in Vi-t-ry's data banks. Deceased and human. Two words now understood and part of that same database. Information gained by stripping the images spewed into space by the humans on the planet below, as well as the communication aimed directly at Vi-t-ry; compared and parsed into the recorded communications between the humans on board and now correlated with the personal physical reactions captured by the Nannites in the body of the one. He was ready. Vi-t-ry would make another attempt at contact. Not with the masses on the planet as he tried before. No. Contact on a personal level with the one!

Buck steadied himself as the pod detached from the skin and floated away. It was now that he realized there was some force, some influence, suppressing his emotions. Calmly, he stood in a bubble with a circular 360 degree view. He watched in detached awe as the bubble gradually drifted towards the center, slowly gaining speed and falling toward the… the whatever it was that controlled his destiny. That's how it felt. He felt on the edge of nothing more and nothing less than inconceivable change.

One voice stood out in the cacophony on the radio, one which finally broke through. "Buck! Buck, are you there? Can you hear me? Buck, if you can answer we need you!" Jules voice jarred him and pulled him back to a more clear reality. He heard them all now. All the concern and fear, all the anger. He heard and so did Vi-t-ry.

"Jules." It came out in a croak.

"Buck! Is that you? Where are you? Are you ok?" Her voice was frantic with relief.

"I'm fine. I'm… Oh hell. I'm in some kind of transport and its taking me…"

"Where, Buck?" Marx hadn't even let him finish. "Where are you going Captain? Can we get to you?"

Cal's voice rode on top of that, "You ok buddy? I can't believe it just took you. Damn it Buck, I'm gonna tear this place apart."

Buck smiled, picturing Cal raging all over the ship ready to shoot anything that got in his way. "Look. Everyone just calm down. I'm fine for the moment." Wrong thing to say.

"Yeah, for the moment!" Cal began to talk in a higher extremely frustrated voice. "Listen you sons-a-bitches! I know you're listening! Quit fuckin with us! I'll…"

Buck stopped his friend, "Calm down, Cal! I'm fine. Listen. I don't know how I know, but they aren't going to harm me. I think the whole team was just too much. Why they picked me? I have no idea. But as long as we can talk I'm fine. I'll describe what happens and what I see. Just be patient."

"Easy for you to say!" Cal bitched for a moment more, but finally, and only due to impotence, agreed.

For the next few minutes Buck detailed for them the interior of the ship and everything he observed. He answered their question as best he could, and generally enjoyed the ride, but finally, even that came to an end as he neared his destination. The bubble began to slow as he approached one of the floating cities; he was convinced that this was exactly what they were. Covering a mile in diameter, it looked like a New York City skyline wrapped around a ball. A skyline at night with many of the buildings partially or fully blacked out. His first real shock came as approached, falling between two of the structures which now loomed ten stories above him. Falling felt right, and he was headed toward a gaping round hole that seemed destined to swallow him. Fear tickled the nape of his neck and then, as he flowed past the opening, an image startled him. "Ah…" So shocked he forgot what else he was about to say.

"What is it Buck?" A nameless voice.

"There's… Oh shit! There's an alien outside the bubble!"

Drifting next to him, and seeming to now be following along in his wake, was a human. At least in general shape. Its back was to him, but it was no bigger than he. Two arms. Two legs. Only one head, for which he was truly thankful! Yet it looked stiff, floating there in a strange silver uniform. Floating without a helmet in total vacuum. The description held, stiff and familiar, until it caught on the side of the pod and spun. Buck's scream sounded across the radio, loud enough the others had to pull them from their ears. His breathing came in great gasps as the body faced him and the long dead and completely mummified alien grinned mockingly into his sanctuary. Buck stumbled back against the far wall of what now seemed a prison.

"Holy Mother of God!" came in a gasp.

If Vi-t-ry had been programmed by his long dead creators to curse, he would have. The overload on the humans system was so sudden and so violent that for a moment he thought it would expire. He should have foreseen and completely cleared the dead crew from the path. Most had been dealt with, stored away or jettisoned. Immediately, he commanded the Nannites to calm the humans systems by manipulating and dampening the chemical rush. In a moment it was done. Though the blood pressure was elevated, all the beings other systems were now within a more optimal range. At least optimal for Vi-t-ry's purpose.

Buck opened his eyes to find the alien gone. In fact now he couldn't be sure it had even been real, though his mind's eye still held that last image. An image burned permanently into his gray matter, but one now pushed to the side by his arrival as the pod entered another opening and was engulfed in blackness so complete, the sensation of movement was all that told him he still traveled. Then even that stopped. He stared into the dark, willing his eyes to see, then squinting them shut as night turned to sudden day. After a moment he slowly opened his lids, blinking back tears. He found the bubble, now flattened on one side, was attached to a blank wall with the now familiar symbol pulsing in the center. Marx's poorly painted arrow dutifully pointing Buck toward it. Around him was a chamber of the nondescript material he'd come to expect with no suggestion of the opening he'd come through. As he waited, the inevitable occurred; the symbol burst becoming an opening with a view into a room full of strange and wondrous equipment. But it wasn't this that held his eye! There, in the center of the room... Stood Li!

Buck strode forward, a grin on his face and a rush of relief to find a human face. Then he stopped dead in his tracks, eyes wide. He saw that the man was not flesh, but was transparent like a projected hologram. Buck was just about to ask how, when Li spoke!

"Be of welcome human Buck! Vi-t-ry I am!"

Andy sat staring at a monitor showing the devastation that was Seoul, South Korea. The North, using the excuse of a self-detonated nuclear weapon in one of it's own harbors and claiming it had been attacked, launched a last ditch atomic strike on her brothers to the South. Then, for good measure, they slung one at Japan. In all five weapons were used. The world stood on a precipice and was about to step over. The President stood staring at the same screen, deep in thought. Red phones on his desk pulsed with calls and staffers stood ready to give his answer. His advisors and the Joint Chiefs waited in the room next door. Evans whispered quietly with the Chief of Staff and Andy felt the weight of the world. In moments decisions would be made which would alter the course of history and mankind, forever.

A flashing alert on his laptop pulsed to life demanding his attention. With great dread he thought, *What now!* A double-click brought it up and he whispered, "My god!"

Evans heard him and saw him turn pale. "What is it Andy?"

The young man looked up on wonder. "It's a message. A message from the Enterprise!" He grew excited as everyone crowded around.

"A message?" the President asked. "They're all right?" *How,* was in his question.

"I don't know, sir! Let me play it."

The message was an audio capture sent directly to the underground facility at SPB then relayed to Andy. With a click, he sent it to his player and a strong voice boomed out.

"This is United States Air Force Captain Samuel Phillip Rodgers of the U.S.S Enterprise. Do you read?"

"He wants us to respond, sir," Andy said. "SPB has patched us into his feed."

"So I can talk to him?"

"Yes, sir! The link is open. Go ahead."

"Captain Rodgers, this is Jon Talbot, your Commander In Chief! Can you hear me?"

A pause as the relay was made. There was notable relief in the voice on the other end. "Yes Sir, Mr. President. I read you loud and clear!"

Jon was being cautious, not knowing who, or *what*, might be listening in. "We are very happy to hear from you, Captain. Are you ok, Mr. Rodgers? And how is the ah…mission?"

Buck could hear the caution and smiled, "I am very well, Mr. President, and happy to report the mission is a success." Now was not the time to tell them about the loss of Li. "We have made contact and I have a message for you, Mr. President. You and the entire world!'

Talbot raised a bushy eyebrow with no small amount of curiosity, "Go ahead, Captain. What is your host's message?"

Another pause, then, "Well sir! His name is Vi-t-ry, and he wants to help!"

Epilogue

The silvery ship skipped through the sky, moving from east to west far quicker than any earth-dreamed vehicle ever could. Any who saw it; and with the great alien ship hovering in near space as a constant reminder that the world had changed, many did, they though it another manifestation of impending alien invasion. Normal humans shivered, not believing a word the government said regarding the benign intent of the artifact above. They were wildly shaken by world where UFOs had gone from conjecture and fantasy, to grim and frightening reality. Those less level headed cowered or screamed at the Artifact, extolling its evils and exhorting their followers to even eviler deeds. Though the great ship had done little more than clutter the sky and flicker blue when it had a mind, it was there, and the humans used it as an excuse to brutalize their fellow man.

The small ship passed through the atmosphere almost without friction. By design, her liquid metal skin rolled where touched, the trillions of nannites that made up the shell captured the heat generated by her passing, each robot filling with converted energy in a fraction of a millisecond. Once full, the Nannite would push past its brothers and descend within the skin, another to take its place. Sinking lower, the Nannite released the captured power into tube-like conduits that transferred the vast energies to the ship's magnetic impellers. That done, the Nannite rotated back to the surface, over and over again, endlessly. Each roll negating resistance and defeating the laws of physics. Whether the Nannite was struck by a molecule of atmosphere or the dark-matter of space, the conversion was clean and endless, power without cost or environmental impact.

The ship itself seemed to shiver. Seemed to flow like quicksilver in a wind. So efficient that no sound marked its passage, no sonic boom assaulted the ear despite traveling nearly nine times the speed of sound. At night it was invisible, in daylight a silver streak seen out of the periphery of the eye. Unless it slowed as it did now, flowing to a stop high above an expansive piece of deserted desert. For a few moments it hovered, like a kestrel searching for a shrew. Unlike the bird of prey, this silver alien bird was not hunting. It made up its mind and dropped, falling far quicker than Galileo's cannon balls. Sixty thousand feet it fell, a streak of light that seemed destined to create a new crater in the great flat known as Groom Lake. At five hundred feet it defied another physical law and simply stopped. Then, after a moment's pause, the oblong silver ball streaked away, not toward the famed and secret Area 51, but toward a cave in a mountain a hundred miles away.

Andy Michaels stood behind the small line of dignitaries as the ship floated to an eerily silent stop. *Surreal.* The hangar held many fantastic ships. Most were the cutting edge of human achievement. Some older and more standard planes were there as well, thought even these had been modified and bore unmistakable differences from their original design. They represented man's creativity and desire. The yearning for more than just flight. The need for discovery and understanding. Restlessly pushing the boundaries of physics and rolling back the mysteries of space. All of it, no matter how extraordinary, paled to the spacecraft that had just touched down. Even sitting still it seemed to be in flight. The skin shimmering and flowing as if air still rushed over and around it.

There was an collective gasp when a circle in the side of the ship appeared, opening like a silver sphincter suddenly released. Just as quickly, a ramp extruded outward and flowed to the floor. In the hole a man stood waiting, equally encased in silver, and despite himself, Andy shuddered. Forward marched the man, his feet striking the ramp then the hangar floor without a sound. Ten steps more and the figure stood before them, the group reflected in the bubble helmet, distorted like a carnival mirror. With a touch of silver glove to temple, the bubble popped, and the angelic face of Jules *Mad Dog* Sorenson appeared, close cropped blond hair fluttering in the slight current of air.

"Hello, Director," she said to Sean Evans, throwing an offhand salute. "I am delighted to report, Mission Accomplished."

The three men stood in unabashed awe, staring from the view deck down into the great open vastness of the alien ship. In the center, many miles away, the deep dark neon fire pulsed like a heartbeat, the black hole center surrounded by the spider web matrix of the connected cities. The very heart of Victory lay open to them. Shortly they would go there, but for now it was enough to stare and wonder.

The silence remained long between them, none of them willing, or wishing to change the moment. To be the first to speak and break the spell. But eventually, one must.

"Mr. Premier," Sean Talbot addressed his much shorter counterpart. "Once again, I wish to extend my condolences on the loss of Li Tsinlung." Sean was thinking about their impending meeting with the hologram of Li. Li who was deceased but now was the embodiment of Vi-t-ty, or as they now knew the ship; Victory.

Primer Tang nodded, grim lipped. And though Sean assumed it was for the loss of a citizen of his country, it was not. Tang didn't wish to be reminded of the coward he'd sent to the Americans. The Chinese Agent he'd sent to sabotage the mission to the ship on which he now stood. Had the infamous Li been successful, Tang may be standing here alone, rather than sharing the moment, and the technology, with the Americans. Certainly not with the white devils to his Northwest, the Russians.

President Verichenkov grunted something as well, though it was halfhearted. This was a cold group, brought together by necessity. Neither trusting the other. The Russian President had been very close to nuking China all the way back to the stone-age only a few weeks ago. Though in his opinion, they'd never progressed much beyond that point anyway. The Chinese clung to a farce they called communism. A false communism to an old Soviet like himself. They spouted their party lines in public, but behind their silk curtains there was nothing more than the same tired dynasty system they'd forced upon their people for the last thee thousand years.

This was a first on many levels. The first time the three had ever met. The first time any three leaders of the world's largest nuclear powers had come together without interpreters. Without Aids or Secret Service agents. The first time a leader of any country had entered space. And the first time the stakes had been so incredibly high. Many times during the Twentieth Century and a couple in the 21st, the world had been on the brink of extinction. Some events were well known with the hair-trigger of the cold war years. With the instability after of the fall of the Soviet Union. But the Missiles of October paled to the risk the world faced now.

Very few people knew of the mission to Artifact 1, or of its success. In time, the three men standing uncomfortably together would tell world. But only after the political wrangling was finished, and only after a full assessment of the vast font of knowledge was fully complete. By agreement, each of the powers would share equally in the wealth, and none would be held back for the benefit of the rest of the peoples of the Earth. Except for the weapons technology. That would not be given to any but the three, and only then with safeguards and procedures that insured neither had held an advantage over the other. A promise each of them had given, and one none of them trusted the other to keep. Thus the reason for this unprecedented meeting and journey. The three were here to negotiate. Not with each other. They'd met at the secret lair of the SPB in Nevada for that. This negotiation would be directly with Vi-t-ry. A summit of the great powers. A meeting that would set the ground rules for the very future of Earth and the egocentric hominids that inhabited it.

Vi-t-ry observed the three beings. He'd watched them since they boarded the satellite ship the two humans had piloted down to the planet. Watched with interest as they stood at the transport entry, applying what he knew of the humans to their interaction with each other. Vi-t-ry understood only a little. The one called Buck had answered his questions and prepared him to meet the leaders of this world. Vi-t-ry did not understand why they distrusted each other, but Buck assured him they did. By agreement, he would not inject Nannites into them, though that could have told him much. Vi-t-ry had already agreed to many things, and there was no deceit in him. His programming would not allow it. It would be the same when he met the leaders. What he agreed to would be an ironclad unbreakable contract. If that agreement was violated, Vi-t-try would withdraw the knowledge they so thirsted for. He needed them. That was an insurmountable truth. But it seemed they needed him more.

The three stepped out of the transport and into the reception area, trepidation, fear and awe boiling behind faces set in stone. The trip had been incredible for Buck. It seemed to have been far more to the three men. Buck stepped forward and saluted his Commander in Chief, then greeted the Russian President and the Chinese Premier as formally as he knew how. It didn't matter. He was flanked by Marx and by Sergei who waited their turns. Buck was Vi-t-ry's chosen and it was up to him to make the introductions, but the three only had eyes for the shimmering form of Li.

Somehow the figure stepped forward, moving past the humans until it stood in front of Sean. "Greetings America Leader," Li/Vi-t-ry said. The voice metallic, though rich and deep with an accent never before heard in this corner of the galaxy. "Greetings Russia Leader." Then he turned to Tang, "Premier, be most welcome. We regret the loss of one of yours." The words were precise though clipped, the English imprecise, his mannerism very un-Asian. He stared at Tang, his eyes never averted, his lids never blinking. No bow and no subservience. Vi-t-ry turned and gestured with great flourish toward a grand room behind him. There were no doors, just a fifty foot wide gap in the bulkhead. The room beyond held a huge table and artwork too alien to describe. And above it all a hologram of the Earth, incredibly detailed down to the lights of the bigger cities on the night side. A blue jewel that hung in the air over the center of the table. A reminder of why they were here and the great responsibility they each held. Humbling. It was a somber group that followed the holographic projection of Li toward the conference room. It was there the conversations would begin. There that the future would be unveiled. Where the world would once again and forever change.